John Paxton Sheriff was born in Liverpool and spent much of his childhood in Wales. He served in the army for fifteen years, married his childhood sweetheart and had three children before moving to Australia. Returning to live in Wales, he became a full-time author and has written extensively for local newspapers, and magazines published in the UK, Australia and the USA.

DYING TO KNOW YOU

When freelance photographer Penny Lane discovers a dead body on Hoylake beach she makes a terrible error of judgement. Now she must put matters right. Her overnight transformation from photographer to amateur private eye is easy, but the body count increases frighteningly, and tracking down the killer is difficult. Encouraged by her crime writer husband Josh, she finds herself at odds with the police, and rubs shoulders with villains in seedy Liverpool nightclubs. As Penny follows a trail that rakes up the past and shows her a menacing future, she's led to an unexpected and shockingly brutal success.

Books by John Paxton Sheriff
Published by The House of Ulverscroft:

A CONFUSION OF MURDERS
THE CLUTCHES OF DEATH
DEATHLY SUSPENSE

JOHN PAXTON SHERIFF

DYING TO KNOW YOU

Complete and Unabridged

ULVERSCROFT
Leicester

First published in Great Britain in 2008 by
Robert Hale Limited
London

First Large Print Edition
published 2008
by arrangement with
Robert Hale Limited
London

British Library CIP Data

Sheriff, John Paxton, *1936* –
   Dying to know you.—Large print ed.—
   Ulverscroft large print series: crime
   1. Murder—Investigation—England—Liverpool—
   Fiction 2. Women private investigators—England—
   Liverpool—Fiction 3. Detective and mystery stories
   4. Large type books
   I. Title
   823.9'2 [F]

   ISBN 978–1–84782–405–9

Published by
F. A. Thorpe (Publishing)
Anstey, Leicestershire

Set by Words & Graphics Ltd.
Anstey, Leicestershire
Printed and bound in Great Britain by
T. J. International Ltd., Padstow, Cornwall

This book is printed on acid-free paper

For
Jacqueline, Deborah and John

Author's Note

In the writing of this novel I have again taken the liberty of tinkering with the local geography. Hoylake Police Station *is* located in Queens Road, but the police officers I have placed in there are figments of my imagination. The station's opening hours have been adjusted.

Although I have not delved deeply into police matters, for the information I have used or kept in the background I am indebted to Detective Inspector Martin Leahy of Merseyside Police, whose help has been invaluable.

Prologue

Heavy droplets from overhanging branches were like bullets punching into the car's roof as he parked against the kerb midway between street lights, watched and waited for a few minutes, then climbed out into the rain. His leather gloves squeaked on wet metal as he carefully closed the door. The central locking beeped. Amber light flashed on wet stone walls.

It was a narrow road lined with architect-designed houses with fancy names set back beyond long walled gardens with lawns bounded by tall trees. When he hurried across the pavement his feet encountered deep puddles, the splashing changing to the crunch of gravel as he hunched his shoulders and walked through wrought-iron gates and up the deeply shaded edge of Dunacre's wide drive and quickly used a key to let himself into the house.

In a dim hallway cloyingly scented with potpourri, he leaned back against the front door and listened. A fridge-freezer hummed, a clock ticked, tiny sounds struggling to reach him through thick silence that deadened the ears. Beneath that muffling blanket he could hear his pulse hissing, the soft whisper of his breathing, the rustle of his clothing as he moved.

He stepped away from the door and touched his pocket. His fingers felt for the hard outline of the knife. He took a deep breath and cautiously but swiftly climbed the carpeted stairs to the landing.

Faint light filtered through the open vertical blinds hanging in a small window. Heavy brass handles glittered on white doors. He followed his long shadow past the bathroom where water plinked, past the open door of a home office where a computer monitor gleamed eerily, past two more closed doors. At the next door he stopped. He pressed his ear to the smooth panel. Held his breath. And again he heard nothing to suggest that she was awake.

Satisfied, he reached into his pocket and pulled out the knife. It had a curved wooden handle with ends of dull brass. He slipped off a glove for an instant and used a thumbnail to open the sharp blade. It locked with a metallic snick. Steeling himself, his bottom lip caught between his teeth, he grasped the door handle with his left hand and stepped into the room.

Human warmth. A familiar, delicate

perfume. Flimsy white underwear with the sheen of silk strewn across the crumpled duvet at the foot of the king-size bed. Radio alarms glowing on two bedside tables, their red numerals casting a faint lurid glow over the room and telling him the same time: half an hour after midnight.

In the bed, a sleeping woman.

Suddenly his heart was thundering, his chest tight.

He could feel a tremor in the muscles of his legs as he approached the head of the bed, a numbing weakness in his arms, in the hand holding the open knife. His eyes were drawn to the thick blonde hair draped with abandon across the crimson pillow, the soft skin of a naked arm flung wide, a hand's curled fingers, the full unpainted mouth moistly parted in sleep. The top of the duvet had been pushed down. Beneath the silk nightgown that was exposed, the woman's breasts rose and fell with her slow, even breathing.

His knees pushed against the soft edge of the mattress. For a moment he hesitated. Then, carefully, he bent almost close enough to feel her moist breath on his face and placed his left forearm flat across her breasts, his wrist limp. It was the lightest of touches. He could feel the tingling pressure of warm mounds rising and falling beneath his sleeve

— but that was all. She did not stir. Her eyes remained closed.

He stood like that, awkwardly bent, his weight unsupported, all his attention directed towards the hand holding the knife. Then his lips pulled back from his teeth. His eyes closed, quivered, flickered open. He moved his hand and placed the knife's needle-sharp point just under the woman's left breast and, without hesitation, he put the full weight of his shoulder behind hand and wrist and forearm and drove the blade cleanly into the woman's body until the brass hilt was cruelly dimpling the warm, smooth silk.

In that warm depression dark blood pooled to crawl in thin, spidery tendrils.

The woman stiffened. Her body jerked once, spasmodically, against his restraining forearm. She gasped; sighed. The relaxed fingers clenched, then slowly uncurled. In the same instant she became still. It was a final, fateful settling that seemed to push the weight of her body down into the softness of the bed. The warm breasts no longer rose and fell. Between parted lips her teeth, glossy in death, had become as ugly as those seen clenched in a naked skull. Light from the radio alarms and the uncurtained window glinted on the whites of sightless eyes visible between slitted eyelids that had almost, but not quite, flickered open.

Suddenly he was sweating.

He forced his hand open, lifted it from the knife's protruding handle and stood up. Working awkwardly with his gloved hand he fumbled for his wallet and from it took out a credit card. He looked at the name embossed on the front, for a moment anticipating the simple act he was about to perform, the consequent terrifying chain of events.

Then he leaned forward and slipped the rectangle of coloured plastic between the dead woman's breasts.

It was done. Finished. Without another glance at the dead woman or his surroundings, he left the room, hurried down the stairs and out of the house. Fine rain mingled with the cold sweat beading his brow. He shivered, dashed it away, then slipped into the deeper shadows under the trees and crunched down the drive, splashed through the puddles lying in pavement hollows to where the car was parked and slid into the warm interior. When he sat back he was breathing hard. He clicked open the glove compartment, rummaged for his silver hip flask and took several deep swallows of the smoky whisky.

As he screwed the cap on and put away the flask he reflected with satisfaction on the terror that would be aroused in the man whose name was embossed on the credit card; remembered — now with a pang of almost unbearable sadness — the spongy resistance as a blade slipped into a woman's warm flesh and the soft exhalation that was her final breath. He loosened his tie and pulled it down, undid the top button of his shirt, ran a finger through his hair and tried to relax. But when he looked at his reflection in the rear-view mirror he saw a man with a white face and deep-set, haunted eyes bright with unshed tears, and was shocked.

He took a deep, shuddering breath, started the car and swiftly drove away.

1

Day One — Monday 18 September

When Josh emerged from the bathroom with shaving-soap on his ear and told me not to come back from the beach until I'd found a nice juicy corpse for him, I took it with the usual pinch of salt. Crime writers are always looking for a body buried in the undergrowth, or a man to come bursting into the room with a gun; photographers for a decisive moment to be captured on film.

Maybe, I told him sweetly, I could combine the two, photograph a convenient cadaver and leave us both satisfied.

I didn't know it at the time, but it was a mildly sarcastic parting shot that managed to be both flippant and prescient.

The late summer storm raging over the Irish Sea had abated towards dawn that Monday, and it was a beautiful morning when I drove into Hoylake and parked. White clouds like mighty clipper ships were billowing across bright blue skies, the warm wind moaning under the café's door ruffled the sleeping black cat's fur and, outside The

Thirsty Goose, the pavements at the golf course end of North Parade were drying rapidly in a fresh breeze smelling strongly of sea and salt.

Inside, my chair was pulled back, coffee waiting.

'My advice,' Joanna Lamb said, 'is to stay away from the beach and that surf rolling in like thunder 'cross the bay — '

'Bit early for Kipling, isn't it?'

'Perhaps, and I know he wasn't writing about *Liverpool* Bay. But the point I'm making still stands, and it's never too early to listen to common sense. All I'm saying is steer well clear of whatever's been washed up.'

I cocked an amused eyebrow at my younger friend.

'I'm not about to snap a shapely leg because of a gentle breeze and some interesting flotsam and jetsam. Besides, this lull after the storm is too good to miss. Think of all that lovely bleached driftwood along the high-waterline. That white surf you mentioned, rolling in against a backdrop of green hills — '

'Welsh hills, and only if you look in the right direction.'

'Which I will.'

'And if you're down that end of the beach

8

it's even *more* isolated — '

'But close to the golf course, and a golf course means *people* — even this early in the day.' I shook my head firmly. 'No, it's still summer, the skies are blue and how often has that happened lately? If I want photographs, then today's the day to get 'em.'

'Well, just make sure some bright spark doesn't get *you*. I've told you before, you should use camouflage. Wrap that Nikon in dirty hessian or something, leave the flashy camera bag at home.'

Joanna was looking with genuine concern at the green-and-black Lowepro bag inside which lay one of my expensive Nikon D2Xs cameras. Then she sighed, glanced at her watch and drained her coffee.

'I've got to go.'

'I thought Gareth was defending someone in Liverpool?'

Her smile twinkled. 'He is. That means I've got the office to myself, so I'll have time for another cup of coffee *and* a choccy bicky before I start.'

'While the cat's away . . . '

'Yes, well, *I'll* be playing, but I'm deadly serious with my advice. Take care, look out for unkempt strangers with windblown hair and shifty eyes — and make sure you've got your mobile phone.'

The doorbell pinged as she swept out. I watched the slim figure lean into the wind with one hand clamped to her blonde hair, then sat back and prepared to nurse what was left of my coffee in solitary bliss.

I smiled, entirely comfortable, more than happy with my lot.

It was almost 9.30 and The Thirsty Goose was empty. Each weekday morning Joanna and I pop in for coffee before work. Joanna is secretary to Gareth Owen, an ambitious young solicitor licensed to represent his clients in the higher courts.

Josh and I work from a bungalow in which two of the three bedrooms have been converted into offices, my delicious husband laptopping his mysteries, me selling prints of landscapes on fine art paper and abstracts to private buyers and multi-national corporations through a website called Penny Lane Panoramas — Penny Lane being me, not a street in Liverpool. Yes, I know, Josh and Penny Lane, sounds like a couple of kids out playing hopscotch, but his is the name on his birth certificate whereas I was christened Penelope but prefer the shorter version.

I also dabble in freelance journalism. Illustrated articles for county magazines, some restaurant reviews and business profiles — and the press pass gained by being a member of the world's oldest organization for journalists has come in handy in weird and wonderful ways.

Anyway, like many photographers I've gone digital. My cameras are all brand new which is, I suppose, another reason to heed Joanna's advice, and a tote bag fashioned from a square of sacking would certainly blend with my clothing.

Oh yes, I get some odd looks and can understand why. Outdoor photography doesn't call for high-heeled, patent-leather shoes and costumes by Dior. When heading for the woods or the beach I dress for the task, which means an ex-army sweater over baggy cargo pants, thick green socks and Hawkshead hiking boots and my greying dark hair tucked up under a faded blue Benny. A thin cotton one in the summer. Over the sweater I usually wear one of those gilets with zip or Velcro pockets everywhere and a wide, inside flap pocket across the back.

Dressed for action, I feel confident and secure. Nevertheless, Joanna did have a point with her warning to take care. A storm-battered shore scattered with debris could be tricky underfoot for anyone, even a nimble woman in her mid-fifties, so before I left The Thirsty Goose I checked that I had my Nokia in one pocket, the battered box of waterproof pink plasters in another and the tarnished police whistle on its green cord around my neck. Under the baggy sweater, of course.

And, as I slung my camera bag over my shoulder and left the café to the musical chimes of The Thirsty Goose's bell, I was still chuckling at visions of me trying to drag the whistle out from under my top layer and blow it furiously while gabbling to the police on the Nokia.

The sun was already hot and, despite the breeze, I was regretting the heavy sweater by the time I'd covered the few hundred yards to the stretch of beach flanking the Royal Liverpool golf course. But sea breezes are notoriously chill. Sure enough, as I started across the sand, warm turned to cool and the breeze became a moderate on-shore gale that had blown all the way from Ireland and was carrying a fine, stinging salt spray. The gilet clamped itself to my body. A film of evaporating perspiration was cold on my upper lip.

But I'm nothing if not cunning. I crunched down the slope until I was below the shelf marking the high-waterline so that I could walk along it with my back half turned to the sea. That done, there was just one more choice to be made.

Hoylake is on the Wirral peninsula's short

bit of sea coast, and the golf course wraps around into the estuary of the River Dee. There's never very much shelter from the elements, and strong winds can make soft sand a challenge for the strongest of walkers — which I am — and I regularly jog five miles with Josh — but even I have my limits. It was a quick assessment of wind direction, then the decision: the stiff breeze was blowing from the north-east, so I would go with it.

With a quick glance out beyond the surf at the dazzling, unending expanse of white horses, I set off. I had the beach to myself. Or almost. Just two figures could be seen, walking together some way ahead of me. And I'd been right about the golf course meaning people, too, because on a hole quite close to the beach I could see a group putting on one of the greens, nearby another lone golfer preparing to tee off.

Although I'd suggested to Joanna that on a day such as this the shore would be littered with treasure, the reality was much different. Driftwood could range from shapeless bits of bleached, bark-less timber to splintered fragments of packing cases bearing faded, stencilled lettering. I walked slowly for fifteen minutes, bent frequently to examine half-buried objects, but found nothing attractive enough to photograph. And in such a manner

— searching, examining, rejecting — I made my way around the curve where bay turned into estuary until I found myself close to the low, rocky outcrop known as Murphy's Shelf.

The name's origin is buried in the past, but the shelf is a wonderful windbreak. Not yet far enough around the bend to benefit from the limited shelter afforded by the famous links, I gratefully crunched up the slope, carefully lowered my bag onto a flat stone and turned to rest my back against the warm rock.

The two figures I had noticed earlier had been reduced to one, and that single figure was far away. On the beach, at least, I was alone.

I closed my eyes. My heart was pumping pleasantly. The sun was hot, the incoming surf thunderous; its ebb the fierce hiss of salt water on glistening wet sand and pebbles. With my eyes closed I could visualize the scene exactly as it would appear when reviewed on the camera's LCD screen. A slow shutter speed would blur the surf, a polarizing filter would intensify the blue of the sky . . .

I smiled, breathed in deeply, feeling the wind lift my hair as I dragged off the thin Benny. I scrunched it into a ball, opened my eyes and looked down for my bag — and jumped out of my skin.

I was looking at a man lying face down, half buried in the sand.

Well, not exactly looking at all of him. He was lying sort of around the corner of the rock, his head towards me, which was why I hadn't spotted him sooner. What I was looking at was the back of his head. But when I moved to get a closer look I could see that the rest of his body was stretched out and the back of his grey shirt, wrinkled, dusted with dry sand, was stained black with blood.

And from the centre of that broad back the handle of a knife jutted.

Delayed shock hit me like a low punch. I gasped. My legs went weak. I slid down the rock until I was sitting on a narrow ledge. My palms flattened against rough stone. My heart's previous pleasant pumping increased to a rapid pounding that thudded in my ears and made my head swim.

Still slumped there, struggling to regain composure, I forced myself to look again at the man — and think logically.

This side of Murphy's Shelf was clearly visible to anybody on the beach to the east. So if anyone had been standing here as I left North Parade, I would have seen them. I had seen nothing, no sign of movement. In all probability, this man had already been lying here when I left The Thirsty Goose.

The person who had *attacked* him . . .

I remembered the figure I had seen in the distance, and felt a tiny tremor of fear.

Then I shook myself — after a hasty look around — and told myself to stop being silly. I was wasting time. A knife in the back and the deathly stillness of a body did not automatically rule out the presence of life.

Tightening my lips, I slid from the narrow ledge and dropped to my knees in the sand. I leaned forward. Steeling myself, I reached out and touched the man's neck. I shivered. His skin was still warm. I moved my hand down underneath, pressed my trembling fingertips to the hollow where I knew a strong pulse should be throbbing.

There was not the faintest flutter of movement. The man *was* dead.

I felt a faint tremor of sadness and compassion, at once chased away by another frisson of fear. Awkwardly I twisted my head and once again looked hastily about me. The outlook up the estuary towards West Kirby and Heswall was blocked by the rocky bulk of Murphy's Shelf. To the east, back the way I had come, a man was walking away from me towing a small white dog — much too far away for me to attract with a shout that would be seriously weakened by a sudden shortness of breath.

I snatched my hand away from the dead man's warm skin, climbed to my feet and deliberately took several deep, steadying breaths. Then I pushed the crumpled Benny into a pocket and pulled out my mobile phone. I clicked it on, listened to the three bleeps as I keyed 999, the fourth when I pressed send. As it began to ring I very quickly pressed the button to halt the call and clutched the phone to my chest, frowning.

For a few tense moments I waited. If the phone rang now, I knew it would be the police following up the missed call. If they did . . . well, it didn't matter because I knew I would have to phone them eventually. But just now I needed time to think, and the extra wait before the emergency services arrived would go unnoticed by the dead man.

What had disturbed me was the object I had glimpsed while dialling the emergency number.

Buried in the sand close to the dead man's jeans-clad thigh, but disturbed and revealed by my knee as I leaned forward to feel for the non-existent pulse, there was an object I recognized. It glinted a rich yellow in the bright sunlight. Dumpy, squat yet attractive, it was a small bronze copy of the Great Buddha, the Daibutsu of Kamakura, Japan.

Fine grains of sand were caught in the folds beneath his chin, sleeves and hands, and his hooded eyelids were clogged. For one chilling moment I thought of this man lying face down in the sand, imagined his dead, sightless eyes, and shuddered. Then I took another deep breath, put away the phone and stretched out an unsteady hand to pick up the miniature idol.

And again I stopped.

After a moment's pause I reached down, unzipped the camera bag, took out the Nikon and switched it on. Working swiftly, I composed the picture in the viewfinder and photographed the dead man and the bronze figure. A quick review told me I'd got what I wanted. Nevertheless, I took a second, then a third, stepped back and took a fourth. Then I switched off the camera and put it away.

I reached into one of the gilet's pockets and found a packet of tissues, pulled one out, unfolded it. Using the thin paper handkerchief in what I knew was a vain attempt to avoid smudging any existing fingerprints — and, I admitted guiltily, to avoid imprinting my own on the smooth metal — I lifted the small, glossy Buddha out of the hot sand.

The wind gusted. Grains of sand took flight from creases and folds and it was as if the tiny eyes opened. I closed my eyes, swallowed, then swiftly wrapped the bronze figurine in the tissue paper and thrust it into the gilet's deep, wide pocket.

Only then did I open my eyes.

Only then did I, at last, dial 999 and lean back against the warm rock to await the arrival of the police.

★　★　★

'I've compromised a crime scene.'

'What does that mean?'

'It's something I read in an American mystery novel. I think it's illegal.'

'And incredibly stupid. And you didn't get that out of any book. You're Inspector Jack Frost's number one fan. You know exactly what you've done.'

From the other side of the desk Joanna eyed me across the top of her coffee cup. 'I take it you're talking about the man they found on the beach?'

'Not they. Me.'

'Really!' Suddenly there was intense interest in Joanna's grey eyes. 'So there *was* something in what I said about taking care. Only you didn't, did you, and so you've been very lucky. Think what might have happened if the killer had been hanging around.'

I preferred not to. I was sipping hot coffee in my friend's first-floor office overlooking Market Street and trying to banish from my mind memories of a man lying on his face in the sand, a knife in his back and his shirt stained with blood. The police had been kind. It had been a matter of answering a few questions, telling them how I'd stumbled across the body, but all the while striving to keep the guilt out of my eyes as the bronze Buddha weighing down the pocket of my gilet suddenly seemed to be red hot.

Then the lonely trudge across the sand with the sea breeze cold on my cheeks. Walking, as one does when conscious of being watched, with two left feet and the added handicap of that damned Buddha banging awkwardly against my hip.

'What did you do?' Joanna said. 'Trample all over the killer's footprints? Wipe finger-prints off the murder weapon?'

'It was a knife,' I said, 'and I didn't touch it.'

'Ah, yes. The grapevine says his shirt was soaked with blood.'

'Dark, sticky ... horrible,' I said, and shuddered. I squeezed my eyes shut for a moment, then opened them. 'I saw something in the sand by the body. I didn't want anybody else to see it so — '

'You took it.'

'Yes.'

'And it's in your pocket. It was there all the time you were talking to the police.'

'Yes.'

Joanna was pulling funny faces, twisting her lips this way and that way as she thought hard.

'If you've gone to great lengths to hide this object from the eyes of the law,' she said, 'it must be incriminating. It points the finger. It would lead the police to the killer.'

'Not necessarily. It's something I recognized. It belongs to someone I know. So actually I was doing the police a favour. If I'd left it there it could have been misleading.'

Joanna sighed. 'A red herring rather than a red-hot clue.'

'How the hell do I know?'

'Mm.' Joanna looked thoughtful. 'You do realize your actions, reactions and unusually pink cheeks won't have gone unnoticed?'

'They did.'

'How d'you know?'

'I'm here, aren't I?'

'That's what the police do. Give suspects enough rope.'

'Very funny.'

'How long had this man been dead?'

'They weren't going to tell me that, were

they?' I shrugged. 'His skin was still warm. But it was hot in the sun, he was lying on warm sand, conditions have to be taken into account . . . '

'But if he had been dead for just a short while,' Joanna said, 'the killer could have been watching you.'

That thought turned my mouth dry. I finished my coffee in haste, stood up and turned to go.

'Don't forget your bag.'

Tight-lipped, I snatched my camera bag from the floor, winced at the solid thud as the heavy object in my pocket swung and hit the chair, then made a beeline for the door.

'I'll send you a card in Holloway,' Joanna called.

2

'Will this do?'

'Hmm?'

'You said you wanted a nice juicy corpse.'

I was back home in Heswall, standing in Josh's office at the front of the bungalow. He was looking up at me, his fingers poised over the Apple Mac's keyboard.

'Hah. I meant the human version, someone who's been horribly done to death, not a poor bedraggled herring gull washed up with the tide.'

'Take a look.' I handed him the Nikon.

He took it, squinted at the LCD, and his eyebrows shot up.

'Bloody hell!'

'Look closer.'

He thumbed through the pictures I'd taken.

'What's this?' He pointed.

I brought my hand from behind my back and plonked the little idol on his desk.

'That,' he said, bending forward for a closer look, 'is familiar.' Then he snapped his head up. 'God, that man with a knife stuck in his back isn't — ?'

23

'No.' I shook my head. 'The idol's his, I'm as sure of it as you are, but the dead man is not Dr Sebastian Tombs.'

'Mm. But, hang about, there must be more than *one* of those little Eastern charmers.'

'Probably. But, given the circumstances . . .'

'What circumstances?'

'Well, it's the first I've seen so they're not all that common; Sebastian Tombs is the local GP and police surgeon and I know he's got one and — '

'And?'

'It's got an inscription on the base. Like, *To Sebastian, with thanks.*'

Josh rolled his eyes. Then he put the camera down and swivelled away from the desk, frowning. 'So, what are you saying? Tombs was on duty at the crime scene, wasn't he? Are you saying he dropped this when he was examining the corpse?'

'Nope. I got there first. I can guarantee it was there before Tombs arrived.'

'You're not suggesting he's the killer?'

'What I'm suggesting is that if I'd left this where it was, that's what the police would have considered.'

Josh shook his head. 'You said it yourself: he's the police surgeon. They'd never suspect him. No, there's got to be another, reasonable explanation.'

'Of course there has. I removed this from the crime scene to stop the police from getting confused.'

'I'll point that out to them when you're banged up in Holloway.'

I grinned. 'Joanna's going to send me a card.'

'A get-well-soon one would be appropriate.' He caught my fierce glower and spread his hands placatingly. 'Seriously though, what *are* you going to do? I mean, why *did* you take it?'

'Spur of the moment. Thoughts raced through my head; such astounding possibilities I went dizzy.'

'Well, we've named one: Sebastian Tombs committed murder. What others did you come up with?'

'He dropped it some time ago, by accident, and the killer chose that spot at random to commit murder. Or the killer had it in his possession, and planted it to incriminate Tombs. Or the murdered man had it in *his* possession, and *he* dropped it. Or maybe it's of immense value; the killer murdered that poor man to rob him, but in the struggle the idol got buried in the sand.'

'Wow!'

'Call yourself a mystery writer,' I said smugly.

25

'A writer of *plausible* mysteries,' Josh said.

'Nothing is implausible,' I said, 'until proved otherwise.'

'Hold on a minute, surely that's double Dutch — '

'I'm in shock.'

'Now that,' Josh said, 'really is implausible.' He tilted his head. 'No, it's impossible: you, my dear, are unshockable.'

And when, with that parting shot, he swung back to his computer, I knew I'd get no more from him for the rest of that afternoon.

★　★　★

I'd told Josh that taking the idol from the scene of the crime had been a spur of the moment thing, and that was absolutely right. Now that I had it I was regretting my actions because I had no idea what I was going to do.

Sebastian Tombs had been our GP for donkey's years. For some time I'd been vaguely aware of the chunky idol on the edge of his desk along with various pens and tweezers and shiny pebbles and an old stethoscope with rotting tubes that had gathered a fine coating of dust.

However, as I hadn't been in need of his

professional services for a while I had no idea when the little statuette had gone missing. And as I knew nothing about the man on the beach or how long he had been dead, I had no idea if he and the idol were linked.

What I did know for certain was that the statuette had been found, by me, buried in the sand at the scene of the murder. I had removed it from the scene of a crime. By doing so it was possible I had interfered with a police investigation. Unless I could justify my actions when the police found out what I had done — and they certainly would — I was in trouble.

The obvious way forward was to confront Sebastian Tombs and ask him bluntly what was going on. That way I'd have answers when I *was* questioned by the police. The trouble was, Tombs might be very reluctant to give me any information. I was a humble photographer, a scribbler of illustrated articles for country mags and superior profiles for the national glossies. As a police surgeon he had been closely involved with dangerous criminals. His evidence had almost certainly sent murderers to prison, and many of them would have vowed to get even.

If I did question Sebastian Tombs he would either respond with a perfectly reasonable explanation, or treat the matter very seriously and ask me to accompany him to the police station.

Nevertheless, I knew that I had to talk to him. I had a hunch something was wrong and, short of throwing the idol in the bin and forgetting I'd ever seen it, there was really nothing else I could do.

⋆ ⋆ ⋆

With nothing on my camera's SanDisk memory card but pictures that could get me into deep trouble, my website up to date and no hot orders to fill, I was at a loss. Being married to a writer sounds great, except that for most of the time they're with you in body but their brilliant minds are drifting across a distant planet where nothing flourishes but ideas. Old, lovable, grey-haired, lofty, blue-eyed Josh was a dear, and would tolerate interruptions provided they were meaningful — whatever the hell that means — and didn't come too often. My quota, I feared, was all used up.

So I slipped into my office, made a few phone calls, turned down a telephone request to photograph a wedding — I don't do wedding photography — ordered ink cartridges for my Epson R2400 photo printer, scribbled reminders on Post-it notes and stuck them like sunflower petals around the computer monitor, gazed out of the window to where the willow tree trailed slender green branches over the pond that had been as dry as Death Valley since Josh dug the hole two summers ago and threw in the spade — then said sod it, made a quick detour into the kitchen to pour double measures of the Macallan into crystal glasses and toddled through to disturb the muse.

'Josh, that little idol's driving me nuts.'

'Dump it.'

'I've thought of that. I can't do it.'

He hadn't turned around. He was engrossed in his latest mystery, his eyes fixed on the laptop where Microsoft Word was displaying a full-screen view of the page he was working on.

'Don't you think,' he said absently, 'that you're bestowing importance on something not worth the bother?'

'I'll only know that when I talk to Sebastian Tombs.'

'He's a busy man.' He sighed, and swivelled his chair. 'Like me.'

'I know. I'm sorry. But I've got to do it. I'll make an appointment, pretend I'm sick.'

'Then what?' He took the glass I handed him, sipped the whisky, lifted an eyebrow. 'You going to risk accusing a man of murder with the door locked and your arm clamped in the sleeve of a sphygmomanometer?'

'Pardon?'

'Blood pressure whatsit.'

'Damn. I don't know. I don't know what to *do*! Help me, Josh.'

'Pop round there this evening. Return the idol. Give it to his receptionist. Say you found it — but don't say where.'

I hesitated, then his words registered and gave me a brainwave.

'All right, we will do it this evening but not at the surgery because I think they're closed. GPs' new contract, remember? But Tombs is a bit of a plonky, likes a game of cribbage and spends most of every Friday evening in the Golden Fleece. Let's go there, have a bar meal or maybe something more exotic and . . . see what transpires.'

Josh nodded. 'I don't mind doing that. In fact, I'll enjoy it. But promise me one thing: if Tombs is there, you hand over the idol, and that's it. No questions. No mention of bodies.'

'He'll ask me where I found it.'

'Lie.'

'Josh!'

'I do it all day and every day.' He grinned. 'I write mysteries; you're married to a *professional* liar; haven't you learnt *anything*?'

30

We got to the pub at nine o'clock when the sun was floating low in hazy blue skies, the wind had dropped to a warm breeze barely stirring the summer leaves and Sebastian Tombs — I hoped — would be mellow enough to soak up my blunt questions but not so sozzled he couldn't dig up the answers. I'd committed a misdemeanour, or a felony, or whatever they call it in the States, and I needed justification.

The Golden Fleece was set back off the main road in landscaped gardens bounded by ancient stone walls that had been given a makeover. Josh drove in, took his Range Rover in a tyre-scrubbing circuit of the floodlit fountain cascading into the central island's ornate pool and pulled into a parking bay opposite the main entrance.

I climbed out, slung my camera bag over my shoulder and looked around the car-park. Tombs, befitting his name and occupation, drove a black Audi. I couldn't see it.

'Remember,' Josh said, as he held the doors open and I walked through into the warm lighting, 'the little yellow idol belongs to the good doctor. Return it. Retreat with dignity.'

I smiled sweetly, but already my eyes were scrutinizing the people in the room looking for the blocky figure of the general practitioner and police surgeon. Florid, with crinkly grey hair, his location was usually given away by his booming laugh. Tonight the only merriment was coming in nervous giggles from a blonde-haired young woman perched at the bar who appeared to have forgotten her skirt.

It was a small bar with just a few tall stools and a carpeted space where an old loose-covered settee and a couple of comfortable chairs were placed for the convenience of drinkers whose balance was impaired. A well-pierced young man was sitting close to the giggly girl, absently touching her long fair hair with one hand, his tongue clicking against his glass as he drank. An elderly man with whiskers but no collar or socks appeared to be asleep on the settee. Conversation away from the bar, in the rest of the largish room, was a comfortable murmur. I wandered away to find a table while Josh veered off and ordered drinks. The barman was understandably hot and harassed. I had time to look around, and when Josh came over carefully carrying two brimming glasses in which ice jingled beneath slices of lemon I knew Sebastian Tombs wasn't in the Golden Fleece.

That, for a Friday night, was probably

unprecedented, and suddenly I was uneasy.

Josh picked up my concern at once.

'Doctors get sick, too,' he said, sitting down with his back to the bar. 'They have wives and families. Emergencies happen.'

I put the camera bag by my feet, clutched the ice-cold glass of gin and tonic and frowned.

'Thanks a lot, soldier. You were helping until you threw in the emergency word.'

'How about tricky situation? Something his wife can't handle.'

'No,' I said, 'let's stick with emergency. A certain DI Billy Dancer's just come in and walked over to the bar. He looks . . . bleak.'

Josh didn't look round. I knew he was already gleefully expanding the situation in his mind and shifting characters around a mental set to create a scene suitable for inclusion in his book. They say soldiers have the thousand yard stare when they return from combat. So do writers; my husband was born with it. I sat half watching his brain ticking over, fiddled with my slippery slice of lemon and put my full attention into peeping over his shoulder.

Dancer had collared the barman and was asking questions. The barman shook his head. Dancer nodded, turned to survey the room — and spotted me.

'DI Dancer,' I said, 'is heading this way.'

'Great,' Josh said, and I could see he meant it.

The tall, gaunt detective with a liking for alpaca suits that hung on him like a becalmed schooner's sails came towards us carrying his pint. I wondered if that was a good sign. Do policemen on duty drink? Had he been prodding the barman for the name of the girl with no skirt? Was I clutching at straws blowing in a fickle breeze?

'Evening, Inspector,' I said. 'Can I ask you to join us?'

'As if you had a choice.'

'Always nice to know where we stand,' I said, as he plonked himself down. 'Josh, this is Detective Inspector Dancer. He spoke to me on the beach this morning. I think he's on the prowl, hunting villains.'

'Making enquiries about a missing person,' he said. He had the sepulchral voice of a grave digger, and my heart sank.

'Anyone we know?' The question was idiotic. I heard Josh chuckle into his drink.

'So far you've been doing all the digging,' Dancer said. 'I'll ask just the one question: is there anything you want to add to the statement you made this morning?'

The idol was heavy in my bag; I'd gone

cold at the casual mention of digging. Now I gulped.

'Goodness, did I make a statement?'

'Verbal. And incomplete.'

Josh had told me to lie, but that was when we'd been looking forward to the meeting with Sebastian Tombs. Instead I was face to face with a suspicious policeman giving me the cold-eyed stare. I decided to sidestep.

'I might be able to help if I knew what this was about.'

Dancer said, 'You found a dead man. Now another man has gone missing. Not seriously missing, not yet; he might be on his way home even now. But if something has happened to him, it's possible it could have been prevented.'

'You can't possibly know — '

'Please!'

Dancer had cut in sharply. His gaze was withering. And suddenly the room was humming with silence.

'*You* can't possibly know,' Dancer said, more softly, 'but when you get to know me better you'll realize I know *everything*. Eventually. And I don't like liars. I don't like those who lie by omission, and I especially don't like elderly ladies with fancy cameras who tell porkies and think they're being cute.'

'Ageism, sexism, and downright rude,' Josh

said to no one in particular, and Dancer stopped him with a glance.

'Three months ago,' Dancer said, 'a businessman's wife was murdered. Ffion Lynch. Formerly Ffion Sharkey, a pretty Welsh girl who came over the border and got in with the wrong crowd. She was stabbed. Husband Terry Lynch walked in, found her dead in bed.'

Suddenly Josh was nodding. 'I remember it. Lynch is a well-known Liverpool villain.'

'Shut up,' Dancer said softly.

His eyes bored relentlessly into Josh's. He tested the silence for its lasting quality, slowly sat back, took a drink of beer, put the glass down. He turned his gaze on me.

'The murder was front-page news, but one important detail was hushed up. Before the murderer walked out, he slipped a credit card between the dead woman's breasts. Naturally, the credit card had a name on it.' He paused. 'See where this is going?'

'It's pointless asking more questions,' I said primly, 'when you've as good as told both of us to shut up.'

'Then let me answer for you. By three this afternoon we'd identified the dead man you found on the beach. His name was Ronnie Humphreys. Ronnie was an associate of the murdered woman's husband — and some

36

three months ago, Ronnie Humphreys is recorded as contacting his bank to report a missing credit card.'

'Jesus,' Josh said softly.

'The way we saw it at the time,' Dancer said, 'is the bloke who murdered the woman was very kindly leaving us the name of his next victim using a stolen card. So officers talked to that bloke, Ronnie Humphreys, but got nowhere. We couldn't dig up a connection' — he grinned nastily at me — 'and Ronnie wouldn't accept police protection. Well, today he was murdered, you found him on the beach, so it seems we were right all along — and he should've listened.'

'But surely that could be the end of it,' Josh said. 'The killer named his next victim, murdered him — and that's it, job done.'

'Be lovely, wouldn't it? Except that Sebastian Tombs is also connected to Humphreys and the Lynchs through forensic work done on an earlier murder — '

'Committed by Jamie Lynch, Terry's brother,' Josh said.

'Bloody hell!' Dancer said. 'Will you give it a rest?'

He glowered, drank some more beer, shrugged. 'Anyway, if I'm right then a pattern's taking shape. We know Humphreys was named by the killer. But what about

Tombs? He's connected, and he's missing — but there was nothing on Humphreys to warn us who was next to die; nothing to lead us to suspect Tombs would be the next to get popped.'

He looked at me — and waited.

My lips felt stiff. My heart felt cold and dead.

'Mind you,' Dancer went on musingly, 'I say there was nothing on Humphreys, but it was pretty obvious from the crime scene something had been removed. Sand shifts naturally in certain ways, gets pushed into patterns by wind and sea . . . '

I sighed.

'You'd better look at this,' I said.

I reached down for my camera case, unzipped it and handed my Nikon to Dancer. As he switched on the camera and squinted at the display I turned to my handbag and took out the little yellow idol bearing Sebastian Tombs's name.

★   ★   ★

Josh had soap on his ear again when he came out of the *en suite*, and his uncontrollable grey hair was all over the place. He had always grumbled about it, then modern youth had discovered gel and thrown away their combs and suddenly Josh was an elderly fashion icon without even trying.

I was lying on my back under the duvet, snug in pyjamas. His bedside light was on, mine off. My eyes were wet. He came and sat by me. The bed sank as he leaned forward and gently kissed my eyelids.

'Do you think he's dead?'

'Sebastian Tombs?' He considered, then nodded. 'Mm. Yes, I think he is.'

'I'll get him, you know. If Sebastian's dead, I'll get the man who's killed him. And if he's still alive then I'll get the man who murdered that other man before he can get to Sebastian — what was his name, Ronnie Humphreys?'

'You're a photographer, not a private eye.'

'The start of a new career . . . '

'*We'll* get him,' Josh said.

I chuckled. It broke, and became a sort of half sob.

'My writer,' I said. 'The professional liar. You invent murderers, chase them through a book then catch them on the last page. This is real life . . . and I'm scared.'

He squeezed my hand. I reached up and touched the soapy lobe of his ear with my finger.

'But real life is tomorrow,' I said, 'and now it's late so I want you to do something for me. I want you to get into bed. Switch off

39

your light. Then do exactly what Dancer told you to do.'

'Oh yes, I remember that: he told me to shut up.'

I pushed his warm, solid hip. He walked around the bed and got in. Switched off the light.

'Two out of three,' he said, snuggling close. 'That's the best I can do.'

'It's enough. Always has been, always will be.'

I turned to him and mumbled something against his chest but the mumble became a hot sob and this time the sobs wouldn't stop and I knew I was making a warm damp patch on his pyjama jacket and I didn't care. All I cared about was me, and Sebastian Tombs, and my terrible, terrible mistake.

I'm fifty-five years old. That night, my hand curled in Josh's big, comfortable paw, I cried myself to sleep.

3

Day Two — Tuesday 19 September

'What's that old saying?' I said. 'Something about today being the first day of the rest of my life — is that it?'

'Close enough,' Josh said, 'but it's daft anyway. Just some motivation guru stating the obvious.'

'So I'll try a different one: today is the day Penny Lane changes horses in midstream.' Then I grimaced. 'Sorry. That sounds pathetic, doesn't it? I know what I mean, but it came out all wrong. How about I wear a different hat?'

He flicked what looked like an amused but sceptical glance in my direction then went back to slicing organic bananas onto two yellow bowls heaped with crunchy muesli which I always think looks like that nasty stuff littering the bottom of bird cages. The percolator was bubbling away, Josh was busy at the pine table with his back to the kitchen window, and the sunlight flooding across the garden and bone-dry pond was turning steam from the percolator into wisps of morning mist and casting his long shadow all the way to the breakfast bar from where I was watching. I was in my dressing-gown; my eyelids were red and swollen and I had the sniffles, yet my fervour was undimmed. But being fervent about changing horses — or hats — in midstream didn't mean I had a clue how to go about it, the *it* being investigating a murder I couldn't be certain had happened but which might and if it did it would be one I'd caused. Through my own stupidity.

I was joined at the breakfast bar by Josh, lean, tanned and athletic looking in a white shorty bath-robe. He was fresh from his usual morning twenty lengths at the local fitness centre's pool — ex-army, he naturally called it the gym — and, bathed in shafts of summer sunshine through which motes drifted like gold dust, we crunched and lapped our way through muesli and full-cream milk, sipped hot Kenyan coffee laced with Bailey's, exchanged furtive glances and thought private thoughts that I knew were in violent opposition.

Josh finished eating first. I watched him take his empty bowl to the sink then cross to the pine Welsh dresser and switch on the radio. It's one of those Bush retro models in beige plastic with a big round dial, lovely mellow tone, but it was tuned to local radio and someone was chirpily reading the news.

Suddenly I was unable to swallow. I pushed my bowl away.

'If you can't stomach news bulletins,' Josh said with his back to me, 'you're no Sam Spade.'

'How about Kinsey Millhone,' I said, naming Josh's favourite fictional sleuth.

'I prefer Penny Lane, ace photographer.'

'You know, I *am* determined to go ahead with this, Josh.'

'More fool you. You've not started and your face is showing the strain. You'll be treading on sensitive police toes. *And* it's too bloody dangerous.'

'Not necessarily. When Dancer mentioned that woman's murder — '

'Ffion Lynch. Body discovered by her husband, Terry Lynch.'

' — you said there were underworld connections. That suggests mobsters settling differences. I'm a woman and an outsider, they won't even *notice* me.' I pouted. 'Anyway, last night you said you'd help me.'

The news reader was cut off in mid-sentence as Josh snapped off the radio. He picked up the percolator, returned to his stool, poured more coffee, slid my mug towards me and pinned me with blue eyes that now showed concern bordering on anger.

He has this mannerism that makes me love him to bits. Like a contemplative cleric he rests his elbows somewhere handy — his ribs, if there's nowhere else — then steeples his fingers. The tips touch his chin. Sometimes he nods very slowly, sometimes he closes his eyes, but it's his mouth I watch most of all. If he's pensive, he'll purse his lips. If he's disturbed, those lips will become a firm line, while anger will tighten them into a thin droopy line — I call it his moody mouth — and cause the big muscles at the angle of his jaw to bulge.

His hands steepled now. He was nodding. The lips were somewhere between pursed and thin.

'If circumstances were normal,' he said, 'I'd agree. About you going unnoticed. But look at your intentions. You're setting out to locate a killer buried in the ranks of Merseyside criminals. They'll *close* ranks, Penny, and you'll either come up against a grubby brick wall of silence, or get squashed like an annoying fly, end up as a blob of strawberry jam.'

'What about helping me? You didn't answer.'

'Things always look different in daylight.'

'Usually better. All right, then if you won't provide the muscle, prepare me. Forewarned is forearmed. Be a perceptive crime writer and tell me what you know — then what you deduce — before I go and talk to DI Dancer.'

He frowned. 'Before you *what*?'

'I'm going to be squeaky clean from the start, Josh, make sure the detective inspector is *aware* of my intentions — '

'Hoping his men will rush hotfoot to save you when you run into trouble — as you certainly will? Forget it. He won't stand for interference, and he's already about to lock you up for nicking an idol and obstructing a police investigation.'

'So give me some intriguing information to help while away the lonely hours of my incarceration.'

That brought a crooked grin. Then he went thoughtful and began tracing a pattern on the top of the bar with a forefinger as I collected mugs and percolator and carried everything to the sink. When I turned and stood with my back to the sunlight flooding through the window he'd turned on his stool and we were facing each other like adversaries across the width of the room.

'Dancer said a pattern could be taking shape,' Josh said. 'It began with the credit card left on Ffion Lynch's body. That card pointed to

Humphreys. The idol you took from Humphreys' body suggests Dancer's right: we know it belongs to Sebastian Tombs, it bears his name, and he's missing. The killer is playing a deadly game of catch me if you can, warning his intended victims and the police.' He pursed his lips. 'Indirectly, he's also warning you, and you should take it seriously.'

Despite the warm sunshine, I shivered.

'I know. But go on. What about that earlier murder, the one before Ffion? Did the killer leave a message on that body?'

'I don't know, nor do I remember the man's name. But that one *was* a gang killing, a drive-by shooting. Two main mobs are engaged in the same dirty deeds, one headed by Liverpool villain Terry Lynch, the other by a man called Ernie Gallagher. He lives in Chester. One of Gallagher's men was shot dead at the entrance to an alley near Liverpool city centre. Jamie Lynch, Terry Lynch's younger brother, was convicted of the murder and sentenced to life.'

I was amazed. I said, 'You were doing this last night, Josh. In front of Dancer. Sticking in your two pennyworth. How on earth d'you *know* so much?'

'You know the answer to that. I'm a crime writer. It pays me to delve into the seamier side of life.'

I reached over and touched his hand and smiled absently, my mind already elsewhere. 'All right. And Sebastian Tombs, as police surgeon, testified at Jamie Lynch's trial?'

Josh nodded.

'So this is what we've got. A Gallagher mobster is murdered in a drive-by shooting by Jamie Lynch. The young Lynch is put away for life. Then Terry Lynch's wife is murdered by an unknown killer — surely a crime with no link to that earlier murder — '

'Gallagher's lot exacting revenge?'

'Mm, that's possible, isn't it? Or probable?' I thought for a moment, then went on, 'So we've got one drive-by shooting, and two more murders — Ffion and Humphreys — which *might* be linked to the first but are *definitely* linked to each other by a credit card. And if that nasty little yellow idol was telling the truth, there is going to be — or has already been — a fourth killing. That fourth will be the missing Sebastian Tombs.'

'Yes, but so far that fourth hasn't happened,' Josh said. 'If Sebastian Tombs is safe and well and even now recovering from a monumental binge in some dingy net-curtained B & B — you said yourself he's a plonky, and I know he's unmarried — then all this complicated analysis is a waste of time. Tombs alive means your lifting that idol from the crime scene did no harm. Your conscience will be clear. The crime you discovered out there by the golf course will be investigated, as it should be, by the police.'

'Maybe. Call me a pessimist, but I can't see even an unmarried Sebastian Tombs doing what you suggest and waking up with a hangover in a grotty bed-sit. I have this horrible feeling of dread — '

'Yes, and you're too soft-hearted.'

'What's that mean?'

'Private investigators are hard-bitten characters. Thick-skinned blokes. And villains are manipulative creatures. They'll see you coming, and when they start pouring out some outrageously imaginative sob story you'll be offering condolences, a shoulder to cry on and a clean tissue. No, make that a box.'

'Don't be daft. And anyway, going back a bit, what d'you mean *complicated* analysis?'

'How would you describe it? This sequence of murders and sinister objects — or ordinary objects made sinister by their placing — is beginning to sound like the plot of one of Jeffery Deaver's thrillers.' His smile was wry. 'Working it out would probably be a doddle for that quadriplegic genius of his, Lincoln Rhyme, but perhaps now you can understand why I don't think a female photographer of advanced years is cut out for PI work.'

Rather proud of my astute, logical reasoning, sharply resentful of Josh's amused scepticism but as stubborn as ever and even more determined, I slid off my stool.

'I'm surprised you didn't say 'mere female photographer',' I said. 'You, Josh, are a conceited, patronizing prick who writes third-rate books and lives on his wife's earnings. I, a simpleminded but successful shutter clicker, am off to the police station to cajole and bamboozle that lean detective in the loose suit.'

'He'll lead you — '

'A merry dance,' I finished for him, then grinned and rolled my eyes. 'Fine. I hope he does, because if we're snuggled that close I'll be in his face and wringing him dry with my polished interrogation techniques.'

*　★　★

I telephoned first, of course, because the shining image of me as a successful private investigator had me stalking serenely past an infuriated but helpless uniformed desk sergeant with a face like a bulldog sucking lemons. A stereotype from watching too much TV, I know, but the phone call worked. DI Dancer agreed to see me, and the time was set for ten o'clock.

Plain sailing, calm seas, passage assured — but Dancer's side of the brief telephone conversation sounded creepily like a bug-eyed spider luring a victim into its sticky lair. He was up to something, and I planted a smacker on Josh's lips and left the bungalow wondering, with a little tingle of excitement, if I'd ever return.

Ten minutes later I parked my red Ka in the car-park alongside Hoylake's 'old house' Police Station in Queens Road — known to old-timers as the Wendy House — spoke to a fair-haired constable behind the reception desk who had enough equipment around her hips to exhaust an Everest sherpa, and was directed to an office at the end of a gloomy corridor on the first floor where DI Dancer sat behind a littered desk glaring at anything that moved.

He caught me cold as I walked through the door.

'How's it going, Penny Lane? Come to confess?'

'To what?'

'How about murder? If you hadn't phoned in I was sending someone to pick you up. For questioning, first off, and if that got us nowhere — '

'Actually,' I cut in, 'I think we've got our

confessions entangled.' I sank primly onto the hard chair he indicated. 'You think I'm here to spill the beans, confess to murder, when all I want to do is make you aware of my intentions. Confess, if you must use that word, to unreasonable urges.'

'My God, what is she talking about?' he breathed.

'If I were you,' said the redheaded man in jeans and T-shirt sitting at a computer beneath a huge cork board plastered with notes and charts and photographs of what looked like Benidorm, 'I'd call for backup.'

'That's DS Hood,' Dancer said. 'Nickname Robin.' He waited for me to grin or sneer, I did neither so he pounced. 'What unreasonable urges?'

'Yesterday morning I made a mistake,' I said. 'Now I'm desperate to make amends. I can do that by helping the police with their enquiries — if you see what I mean.'

'No way,' Dancer said. 'Besides, you're a suspect.'

'Don't be ridiculous.'

'According to Tombs's receptionist, that idol — '

'Buddha.'

' — must have been taken from his surgery. I checked. It used to be in full view on his desk. There were no break-ins reported;

you're one of Tombs's patients; the idol was in your pocket.' He sneered. 'You say you picked it up. I say you could've been about to plant it but got disturbed.'

'I reported the crime.'

'A cunning ruse.'

'So now I'm the killer's accomplice?'

'That's a minor role, doesn't suit you at all,' Dancer said, his voice chilling.

'We got your fingerprints off the idol,' Hood said, swinging away from the computer as I gaped, speechless. 'Checked them against those lifted from the credit card slipped between Ffion Lynch's boobs.' He swivelled his chair to and fro, watching me. 'Guess what?'

'No match,' I said, in a plaintive voice that carried more hope than conviction.

'Nah,' Hood said. 'But that won't stop us. There were no prints on the knife used to kill her so you were probably using gloves — '

'And the knife used on Ronnie Humphreys hasn't been found.' Dancer looked at me pensively. 'The next step is a search warrant — '

'The knife,' I said, 'was stuck in that poor man's back.'

'No prints,' he said doggedly, 'so it was gloves again — '

'Look,' I said with desperation, 'I know you're joking, I know you don't believe I'm the killer and you're trying to frighten me off, but it won't work. I'm determined. I promise I won't get in your way. But I made a mistake that's put a man in danger and . . . ' A sudden thought appalled me. 'You haven't found another dead body?'

Dancer shook his head.

'Thank heavens. And, rest assured, you can forget about me. I've told you — more or less — what I'm going to do, and now I'll disappear. I'll be so invisible it'll be as if I don't exist.'

Dancer sighed. 'Many a true word. If *I* don't scare you, think about the man wielding a bloody sharp knife and planting nasty messages. Then multiply that one villain by the first number that comes into your head. If you make it a big one you might be close to understanding what your unreasonable urges have let you in for.'

'Yes, well, that was me trying to be clever with words — something I get from my husband. The truth is, my urges match yours: we're both desperate to find a killer. I think that makes them reasonable.'

'Either way, I want them suppressed,' Dancer said, handing me a card. 'But if you can't manage that, Penny' — he hesitated — 'Mrs Lane . . . '

'No. We're going to be seeing a lot of each

other, so Penny's fine. If I can call you Billy.'

He ignored that, and narrowed his eyes. 'I thought you were going to disappear?'

'Oh, I will, but if I happen to be somewhere and something interesting occurs — '

'Or information that might help solve the case accidentally falls into your lap . . . ' He shook his head. 'Dream on, Penny — but if the dream becomes a nightmare, *please* phone that number.'

We left it at that and with a frosty smile I walked out of Dancer's office and clattered down the stairs. I was planning nothing illegal, so the best the DI could do was issue that sombre unofficial warning appealing to my common sense. Josh could have told him he was wasting his time. He believed that I, like most women, had thought processes that flew off at tangents like bullets wildly ricocheting into empty space and made decisions motivated by heart not head.

My next move probably proved him right. I was crunching across to my car in bright sunshine when I realized I was being watched by a tall man wearing a white track suit, trainers to match, wraparound shades and a bleached denim baseball cap.

Five minutes later I was sitting in The Thirsty Goose drinking coffee bought for me by Liverpool villain Terry Lynch.

4

'From your website.'

I'd asked him how he recognized me, and what he wanted. He'd taken off the shades and exposed weird eyes as pale as gin with more ice than angostura. He hadn't answered the question, or explained why he wanted to talk to me, and it was curiosity and dread of the unknown that drove me to accept the invitation of a villain and walk with him in silence with my hair lifting to the cool breeze blowing in off the Irish sea.

So now I put that question to him again, and over the steaming cup his smile crinkled and softened those cold eyes without adding warmth.

'I read about you in last night's newspaper.'

My eyebrows lifted in surprise.

'I missed that; didn't even know I was mentioned — but you still haven't answered the question. Unless you want to buy some expensive prints.'

He chuckled. 'They're mind-blowin'ly impressive, they'd go down well in my clubs. Throw the overconfident gamblers off balance. Tilt the odds in the house's favour.

Send the tight-arses lingerin' over half of lager totterin' cross-eyed to the bar.' He nodded slowly with a half smile as he reflected with amusement, then said, 'Yeah, all right, so I'm curious. You found Ronnie Humphreys' body, but shouldn't that be the end of it for you?'

'I found the body, but you know that, from the paper. Anyway, I was a bit shaken up at the time so Dancer called me in for questioning. He was hoping I'd seen something. Sifted through my memories overnight and remembered vital clues.'

'Had you?'

'A man in the distance, too far away to see clearly . . . ' I shrugged.

He was watching me closely and I was treading on eggshells because I hadn't seen the newspaper article. If there'd been mention there of my removing the idol from the crime scene, of the photographs I'd taken, it would be an easy jump for him to assume I'd been led from there to reading about the previous crime and knew about his involvement — and the credit card. If he was an innocent man, that wouldn't matter. On the other hand . . .

'What about you?' I said. 'What were you doing at the police station?'

The eyes were thoughtful. 'My wife was murdered. They never found her killer. So when something comes up they update me. Keep me informed.'

I nodded. He was trying to shock me, while I was wondering what had happened to my polished interrogation technique. Chance had delivered Terry Lynch into my hands and I was telling lies and treading water.

'Keep you informed?'

Gosh. Now I was an echo. Scintillating stuff.

'Yeah, like, let me know if something's happened that'll move the investigation in the right direction.'

'And has it?'

'Ronnie Humphreys worked for me. But that's a connection that's always been there. What matters is the killer named Ronnie as his next victim and went ahead and killed him — and he's left another callin' card.'

I knew he must mean the Buddha, but how did he know about it?

'Really? Was that in the paper?'

'No.'

'Then . . . ?'

'I told you, I was talkin' to Dancer. He was forthcoming.'

'With details? A name?'

'A callin' card of some kind. That's all he said.'

'Why? If he was forthcoming, why stop there?'

57

Lynch sighed and shook his head. 'You're talkin' in ever-decreasin' circles, love. What's botherin' you?'

Until he asked the question I hadn't realized anything was. But now he'd pointed it out it dawned on me that because I was sitting across a small table from a man whose wife had been murdered, I was experiencing intense feelings of . . . I don't know . . . morbid interest? I had been watching him intently for signs of reawakened grief, of renewed anger — for freshly stirred emotion of *any* kind — and there was nothing there, not a glimmer, and that apparent absence of feeling was knocking me sideways.

Was I looking at a guilty man? And if so, guilty of what?

'We're sitting here because a man's dead,' I said softly. 'Your wife's been murdered, and I'm asking stupid, pointless questions.'

Well, that at least was the truth!

'She died some time ago, I'm over it — '

'Does one ever . . . ?'

'Six months. Almost — and I have difficulty recalling her face.'

My lips parted slightly. I knew that couldn't be true.

'And then,' I said, 'there's your brother, in prison, serving a life sentence for . . . '

I trailed off, knowing I was pushing him

58

and appalled by my insensitivity, unable to take my eyes from his lean face.

Lynch shook his head.

'No, he's not.'

'But — '

'He's dead.'

'Oh my God.'

The pale eyes were pools of emptiness.

'He was working in the prison kitchen,' he said. 'Someone walked up behind him with a carvin' knife and cut his throat to the bone.'

The silence was shocking. Terry Lynch had spoken into a lull, and two middle-aged women sitting at a table across the room were staring at us, cups poised, heads tilted and smiles frozen, looking oddly like a window display advertising PG Tips. Then the street doorbell pinged as a man walked in and the spell was broken.

'Do you think,' I said desperately, 'that you're looking at some sort of tit-for-tat thing, an eye-for-an-eye *Cosa Nostra*-style vendetta, the Gallagher mob making your lot pay for Jamie shooting one of their men?'

Lynch was looking straight through me.

'I don't know what the fuck you're talking about — and neither do you.'

★ ★ ★

'My God, Josh, what am I like?'

'A weak swimmer dangerously out of her depth in shark-infested waters springs to mind.'

'I agree. So why oh why did I do it?'

'I thought Terry asked *you*, in the car-park?'

'Well, yes, he did — but, I mean, why didn't I refuse, or just sit there sipping coffee and admiring his sporty attire while non-chalantly — '

'Reading his mind?'

'If only . . . Instead I talked myself into a corner then made sure he didn't forget that his wife had been stabbed to death and his younger brother is in prison. Except he's not, his throat was cut, and — '

'I know.'

'You do! For God's sake why didn't you tell me? Forewarned — remember?'

'I think,' Josh said, 'I'll have a Scotch.'

'Pardon?'

'A Scotch. How about you?'

I giggled. 'I thought you said *scratch*. Yes, all right, go on. With lots of ice.'

I'd recounted my tale of woe to Josh almost as soon as I walked in, catching him in his office and effectively snuffing his inspiration. Now it was midday, the sun had floated over the yard-arm and left the kitchen cool and shady and Josh had taken time out from writing a complex crime novel called *Dying to Know You*.

As an aside, I'd like to mention that I've told him many times what a super title it is. Subtle. I can think of at least two ways it could be taken. For example, does it mean what it says, that someone is dying to get to know a person they're soon about to meet? Or is it that they're dying to discover the identity of a mysterious celebrity? — an example would be those mystery voices you get on afternoon radio programmes, only this time there'd be a murder involved.

Anyway, I like it, and Josh had taken time out from writing it to put the coffee on to perc' and knock up two Danish sandwiches with rye bread, cheddar, crisp lettuce and radish, watercress that burnt the lips and luscious dollops of thick mayonnaise. The full cream version.

I was deep into mine and sporting a glossy white moustache when he returned with the drinks. He sorted my appearance with a Kleenex and, as he ruffled my hair and pulled away, I grabbed his wrist, twisted it, then planted a kiss on his palm.

'Thanks, Josh, my love. For the lunch, the strong drink, the support and encouragement that any other woman could easily be fooled into thinking was the exact opposite — but, to edge a little closer to Terry Lynch's racy lingo, what the hell do I do now?'

'We settled that before you left to bamboozle Billy Dancer.'

'I know. Nothing until . . . But that doesn't sit well with my temperament. I'm a doer. And I like things done yesterday.'

'What was done yesterday,' Josh said, 'is what started all this.'

I pushed my plate away, drank enough to lower the level of coffee in my mug then poured in the whisky. As I tilted the glass the remaining ice jingled. I popped it into my mouth where it rattled against my teeth.

Josh had finished eating and was watching me with one eyebrow raised.

'Finished?'

'I'm bored.'

'Then, while you're waiting for news of Sebastian Tombs, work out what you intend to do if it's bad.'

'I have.'

'When?'

'Just now.' I used my tongue to rattle the melting ice. 'I'm a fast thinker.'

'And?'

'I'll talk to Joanna. Gareth, her boss, works on criminal cases in Liverpool. His brother's a uniformed police sergeant here on the

Wirral, close to retirement. And I'll bet Joanna can hack into the Police National Computer system.'

Josh grinned. 'I'm mortified. I was looking forward to seeing you all dolled up in peasant blouse, satin skirt and fishnet tights, micro-recorder stuffed down your bra — '

'And wobbling off on stiletto heels to prop up the bar in one of Terry Lynch's night clubs? Don't worry, soldier, that'll happen soon enough.'

And, of course, I was right.

We were in the bedroom, white vertical blinds turned gold by the sun as we enjoyed an after-lunch doze on top of our multihued quilt, when Josh put his warm hand in the middle of my back and leaned over to switch on his radio alarm and we listened to a news reader announce that the body of missing GP Sebastian Tombs had been found at 11.00 that morning.

Both of us had been expecting the worst, despite our back-and-forth arguments. But what knocked us for six was the eerie accuracy of Josh's earlier throwaway comment.

The body had been discovered on the second floor of an establishment on Birkenhead Road, Hoylake, that catered for those people who need a bed for the night and like stumbling downstairs to a greasy English breakfast. If it was the building I knew, with crumbling brickwork and a rusty iron fire escape clinging to the back wall, then I couldn't understand why anyone in their right mind would want to stay there.

But Sebastian Tombs obviously had — and it had done him no good at all.

5

'Work backwards,' Josh said.

In a way we'd already started in that direction, because after the news bulletin had shocked us into wakefulness we'd returned to the kitchen and sat down to more cups of strong black coffee. And, surprisingly, I did know what he meant. As a cunning crime novelist he'd once told me he weaved the tangled webs that were his intricate plots by working backwards. I'd responded with the blank look he assured me he got from all aspiring crime novelists, but it really was very simple: you've got a fictional body oozing gore, so begin with the fatal gunshot or knife thrust, and trace — or in Josh's case create — the movements of victim and fictional killer that culminated in the act of murder.

Trouble is, it's easier for the novelist than it is for the real life investigator because, as mentioned, the novelist *creates* the back story. The real life investigator — official or amateur — has to uncover an existing trail the killer has done his best to obliterate.

Neither of us were equipped to do that. Josh is fifty-eight. He joined the army as a boy soldier in 1965, and left the Royal Engineers with the rank of sergeant major in 1989. Late in life. He was then forty, and getting his first real taste of civilian life at that age was one hell of a shock. We've been together for almost eighteen years, married for fifteen and I know my big, strong soldier inside out. He plays blues guitar, runs marathons with Liverpool Harriers, goes to the local gym every morning where he swims twenty lengths and on Wednesdays works out on the nautilus equipment. Is that right? I always thought it was an early American submarine! Anyway, the point I'm making is that he's lean, with muscles like fine steel cable — I've been told by an ex-army colleague I met that one of his punches doesn't so much knock a man out as cut him in half. Well, used to. But — and this is a big but — I know damn well he's never fully adjusted to civilian life, and probably never will.

My own background is different, but in its own way just as . . . well, unsettling . . . and certainly the wrong training for tracking and collaring dangerous criminals. I left university with a good degree, moved into teaching when I was twenty-one and for the next thirty years lived in a closed world populated by young teenagers. When, disillusioned with my profession, I walked out in 2003 — ten years after marrying Josh — I found myself, *like* Josh, splashing about in the deep end of a world I soon realized was as familiar to me as the ocean floor at the bottom of the Challenger Deep. Both of us had been cocooned in our careers, then abruptly dumped naked into the cruel world. We'd been on the cosy inside, looking out without really seeing. Gazing back the other way, with wistful longing for what we had been, left both of us with a dull ache.

So — where did I start?

I was faced with three dead bodies — two if you discount Ffion, four if you count Jamie Lynch and five if you count the drive-by shooting — and I'd decided it was reasonable to assume all the killings were connected. I'd got into this because my stupidity had . . . well, not exactly led to Sebastian Tombs's death, but had possibly prevented it from being prevented — if you see what I mean. So I was desperate to find the GP's killer.

But if my working assumption was correct, and four of the killings were connected, then I'd have to start the investigation much further back. Although not quite as far back as the unnamed man murdered in a drive-by shooting because he'd been shot down by Jamie Lynch, and Jamie was now dead. Case closed.

Unless, of course, the dead Jamie Lynch had been wrongly convicted.

However, assuming (I was doing a lot of that) that had been what the American's call a slam-dunk and the right man had been convicted, then my starting point was the murder of Ffion Lynch. And I did have something to go on — or at least a place to start: the Gallaghers could be going after everyone connected to the Lynchs, starting with Jamie in the prison kitchen; Terry Lynch had discovered his wife's body, on that body there had been the first of the killer's calling cards — and I, only hours ago, had been face to face with that lean, pale-eyed villain.

Brilliant? Well, no not exactly. Floundering in a mire of unlikely possibilities was more like it, and a quick rethink suggested I was badly in need of that expert advice I've mentioned.

★　★　★

'Ah, yes,' Joanna said, 'but didn't you know that in any murder case, family members are the first suspects?'

'Maybe. But according to Hood, Terry Lynch was questioned at length, and as he's obviously not been charged . . . '

'Well, we know he lied to you, because

Dancer would never have given him information about a current crime investigation. And what I think, my girl, is that you should tread very carefully.' Joanna dunked a biscuit, held it dripping over the coffee. 'After all, you're already in trouble with the police, and now you've been threatened.'

I blinked. 'What d'you mean.'

She rolled her eyes. 'God, there's no hope, is there? Look, according to you Terry Lynch glared — '

'Looked straight through me — '

' — swore at you, and — '

'And nothing. That was it. And considering my crass behaviour it's a wonder the poor man didn't give me a hot coffee shampoo and kick me . . . well, into touch.'

It was three o'clock, I was in Joanna's office, my bag was on the floor, the steaming coffee cups and packet of ginger nuts on her desk were almost buried by papers hurriedly pushed aside to make space and I could hear Gareth, her boss, droning away on the phone in the other room.

I'd left Josh in the living-room, eyes closed as he ran through intricate blues improvisations on his treasured Stratocaster electric guitar. In one of the longer pauses I promised I would do nothing drastic in the real life drama that was about to unfold without

69

informing him. Then I'd kissed him and walked out, a wailing, cascading Georgia riff ringing my ears as I chuckled up my sleeve. It was an open ended promise: Josh had neglected to insist I tell him 'first', which meant I could go ahead and beard villains in their dens and not call him until I was strapped in the chair contemplating fates worse than death.

Not that I would — go that far, I mean, like, hold back until I was actually contemplating — yet even about that I couldn't be certain because the change in me since I stumbled across the body of Ronnie Humphreys was continuing to give me cold shivers. It was like an out of body experience, me stuck up there on the ceiling looking down on this silly old lady acting like one of the Keystone Cops.

'Did you give Gareth my message?'

She'd either been glancing at whatever she was working on or daydreaming about her employer whom she considered extremely dishy, and I caught her off guard. The remains of the ginger biscuit splashed into her mug. She swore under her breath, then fluffed her hair with both hands and stood up.

'Of course I did. Hang on there, I'll see if he's off the phone.'

She was back almost at once, more thin manila files clamped under one arm.

'Go on in.'

'I'd like you to come too.'

She lifted an eyebrow. 'Moral support? Or to make sure you don't nick something off his desk? Head off down the beach looking for another corpse?'

'Ha bloody ha.'

I walked out, heard the files flop onto her cluttered desk, the soft whisper of others sliding off, the sequence of slaps as they hit the carpet. More swearing. I crossed the narrow corridor, walked through Gareth's open door. It closed behind me as Joanna, nosy as ever, followed me in like a ghostly shadow.

In his straining double-breasted brown suit and round glasses Gareth was a plump owl with bright eyes, hair sticking out like feathers caught by the breeze and a little hooked nose that could rip flesh. From behind a huge desk strewn with lots of paperwork, he was watching me with interest.

I sat down in the leather chair he reserved for clients, and smiled.

'Hi, Gareth.'

He spread his hands.

'Damn. I was expecting a female Humphrey Bogart. Hands thrust in pockets.

Narrowed eyes. A cigarette drooping in the corner of the mouth . . . '

'She wants information,' Joanna said, 'not a third rate comedy routine delivered by a — '

'Second-rate solicitor. Yes, thank you, Joanna, and hello, Penny. I believe you're now famous?'

'I will be,' I said, 'if I find the man who killed the man I found.'

'You said *if* instead of *when* — and you're talking in circles.'

'That's what Terry Lynch said — and it's why I'm here. I need straightening out and pointing. Any direction will do as long as it leads somewhere. You deal in crime. I'm here to pick your brains.'

'And that's the new you talking, the PI, the super sleuth — the *shamus*?'

'Gareth . . . '

He glanced at Joanna, held up a placating hand.

'Sorry.' He returned his gaze to me, and waited expectantly.

I said, 'There are four killings that could be linked — '

'So far.'

I swallowed, nodded. 'What I need are those snippets of information that are not common knowledge. I know I can easily get the reported stuff from the *Liverpool Echo*'s files — '

'Not if the police block access.'

'The kind of access I've got can't be blocked.'

He looked blank.

'Her son works there,' Joanna said.

Gareth looked at me, eyebrows raised. I nodded.

'His name's Adam. I think he's a sub-editor. Anyway, what was in the paper might not be enough, so I need more from you.' I thought for a moment. 'It's a bit like insider trading, isn't it? You tip me off, I use the information to my advantage.'

'Possibly. But because you slipped up when you pinched that idol, this is a race you want to win. Unfortunately, anything I give you will only put you level with the police, and they've got big computers and hordes of foot soldiers.'

'But they're visible. Villains see them coming and melt away. I'll be incognito.'

'With pretty impressive cover,' Joanna said. 'Photographer. Member of the Chartered Institute of Journalists.'

'And armed with their press pass,' I said.

'Villains,' Gareth said, 'can also smell journalists.'

'Yes, but I'm a pseud. Incognito and masquerading. No odour.'

'You're forgetting something. You've been

chatting to Terry Lynch. If he was interested in you enough to take you for a coffee, who's to say there wasn't one of his men lurking with a digital camera?'

Gareth spoke lightly, but there was no amusement in his intelligent eyes. He thought for a moment, then cocked an eyebrow at me.

'Has Josh warned you about what you're getting into?'

'Mm. He thinks it's too bloody dangerous — his words.'

'He's right.'

'But he'll get over it — and back me to the hilt.'

'Doesn't matter. You should stay well clear of this killer, Penny Lane.'

'This one?'

He rolled his eyes. '*All* killers.'

I didn't bother replying, but, well, have I told you I've got iron determination and an off-putting steely gaze?

Gareth lifted his shoulders then dropped them again with a shake of the head. 'Yes, well, if you go to the *Echo* you won't dig up much that you don't already know. Some things you do see will be linked to the various killings, but look innocent. Others will be press speculation; they'll lead you up the garden path.'

I nodded. 'I told you: that's why I'm here.'

'Right. Well, briefly recapping, that first murder has all the trappings of a gang killing leading to brutal retaliation. Jamie Lynch, Terry Lynch's younger brother, shoots dead a member of a gang run by Ernie Gallagher. Gallagher's mob retaliates by arranging the killing of Jamie Lynch, in prison. One all.' He stared at me. 'No surprises there, of course.'

'Right. Josh and I have covered all that.'

'So now on to more in-depth stuff, and awkward questions for the new PI on the block. For instance, with the score even, why was a pretty Welsh girl like Ffion Lynch murdered?'

'Why the emphasis on Welsh? Dancer mentioned that. Anything I should know?'

'Absolutely not. She was pretty, she was Welsh. I'm Welsh — born in the same village actually, though several years apart. Her brother's around as well — you'll probably meet him — but the question I asked was why was the she murdered?'

'I don't know. Maybe Gallagher didn't think getting rid of Jamie had driven home the message. By killing Ffion he was really ramming it home: lay off my men.'

'No.' Gareth absently twisted his gold signet ring, and shook his head slowly. 'The man Jamie shot dead was a wild cannon. Gallagher used him to threaten people like amusement arcade owners who were behind with protection payments. Murdering Ffion Lynch as *additional* retaliation for the death of that low life would have been way over the top — and it would have led to a bloodbath.'

'And that didn't happen,' Joanna said. 'Ffion Lynch died — then nothing.'

'So, no more deaths — but what about suspects?' I looked enquiringly at Gareth.

'Surprisingly, none at all. Oh, they went for Terry, because he was the husband and there were no signs of a break-in. That suggested someone walked in using a key, or Ffion let the killer in because she knew him. But Terry had an alibi. Anyway, some time after Ffion's death, we get another. Ronnie Humphreys is murdered. One of Lynch's men. So tell me, Penny, what the hell's going on?'

'Oh, come on Gareth, give me a break, I just don't *know* — '

'But you've got to know,' Gareth said softly. 'You've made it your business to find out, so *think*, come up with *ideas* — '

'All *right*!'

My head was buzzing. Joanna shot me a sympathetic look, then set off across the room with a swish of her skirt. Gareth called her back before she reached the door, scribbled on a slip of paper and handed it to her. She glanced at it, then went out. I heard a tap running, the click of a switch, the rattle of cups.

'All right,' I repeated, this time with less venom. 'You're right. I couldn't see where we were going but, yes, Jamie Lynch for the Gallagher man, the score *was* even, no need for more bloodletting. At least not by Gallagher — which suggests that Ffion Lynch was murdered by someone with no connection to either Terry Lynch or Ernie Gallagher.'

'Then why,' Gareth said, 'was there a card on Ffion Lynch's body pointing to Ronnie Humphreys, a Terry Lynch man? Another on Sebastian Tombs's body pointing to . . . '

He paused, tilted his head and waited.

'Well go on,' I said impatiently. 'A card pointing to . . . ?'

'I thought you might know. I certainly don't, not yet.' He spread his hands apologetically. 'Anyway, leave that for a minute. You're the PI investigating these crimes, so have another go, see if you can work something out.'

I pursed my lips, frowned, looked at nothing and tried to think. 'Maybe Ffion's killer *isn't* unconnected. Maybe he's . . . one of Gallagher's men but he has his own axe to grind.'

'With Terry Lynch and his men? And he's

going to murder *all* of them? Possible, I suppose, they're all nutters. But if so — why Sebastian Tombs?'

'Tombs was a police surgeon. He officiated at all these killings.'

'The drive-by, Jamie and Ffion, yes. But you just said this bloke had his own axe to grind. Nothing to do with the killings.'

I grimaced. 'I know. But it's all I could think of.'

Gareth frowned, then looked up as Joanna returned with three mugs of coffee, kicked the door shut with her heel and placed the drinks on the corner of his desk. Then she perched a shapely haunch on the other corner and reached across with a forefinger to move a stray strand of hair from Gareth's ear.

'OK, so let's take another look at what you said.' Gareth smiled absently at Joanna, then looked back at me. 'Tombs officiated, yes, but the only person his evidence *sent to prison* was Jamie Lynch. If this is someone bearing a grudge against the Lynch mob, Tombs helping to get Jamie Lynch locked up was a *bonus*. Same goes for Gallagher. If we're wrong and this is him taking his revenge, he'd've pinned a bloody medal on Sebastian Tombs for putting Jamie where he couldn't hide.'

'However,' Joanna said, doling out the

drinks, 'if it is someone with their own agenda, why can't it be one of Lynch's own men?'

I went wide-eyed at the beauty of it. 'Of course. Why not? We've been assuming inter-gang, but it could just as easily be internecine.'

'Which brings us neatly,' Gareth went on, 'to those juicy rumours that circulate in the murky depths of the underworld and just about everywhere else. Sometimes they slip by the police unnoticed. At other times they're noticed, but dismissed as of no use. But quite often those rumours don't surface until it's too late for them to be of use — as in the case of Jamie Lynch.'

I'd carried my bag with me into his office. It's one of those canvas, pouchy tote-bag thingies with a broad, tapering strap through which you slip head and one arm. A cross between a nosebag and a saddlebag, but settled comfortably in the wrong place for either. I'd dropped it by my feet. Now I reached down and rummaged for pen and notebook.

'Ready?' Gareth said.

'Fire away.'

'Jamie Lynch liked to beat up Ffion Sharkey.'

'Terry's wife?'

'That's right. Before she got cosy with Terry, of course.'

'And when was the wedding?'

'They got married in the Dominican Republic. Nipped over there when Jamie was arrested.'

'Those beatings. Any relevance to what I'm trying to do?'

'Well, Ffion would be bearing a massive grudge. If Terry knew about it he wouldn't have been too pleased with Jamie. And there might be others out there, fond of Ffion . . . '

I was head down, busy with the pen. 'Anything else?'

'Terry Lynch was an early suspect for the drive-by shooting.'

He watched me writing, then added, 'And although Jamie knocked Ffion about and Terry ended up with her, long before that a man called Mick Doyle had the hots for the young Welsh girl. And if you need a place to start, well, he's still around.'

I thought for a moment. 'So this bloke *Doyle* had a good reason for murdering Ffion: she left him for another man.'

'Indeed. And the police realized that: Doyle was the first one questioned, then released.' Gareth shrugged. 'But again we have to ask questions: if it *was* Doyle, why then Humphreys? And Tombs?'

I sighed deeply, slipped notebook and pen into my bag and stood up.

'I'm off. But . . . you said there was another calling card on Tombs's body?'

'That's right.'

'But you're not sure about the name?'

He looked at Joanna. 'Was he there?'

She nodded. 'Gareth's brother, Eifion,' she explained to me. 'You know he's a police sergeant, close to retirement? Well, I phoned him while the kettle was boiling. He told me that the card left on Sebastian Tombs's body didn't have a name.'

'If there was no name,' I said, 'why leave one?'

'He left a card from the major arcana of the tarot — his clever words, not mine. Anyway, the card represents the Hermit. And that *has* to be a test, Penny. In two cases the killer's directed the police to the next victim. This time he's setting them a puzzle, telling them to work *that* one out, if they can.' She hesitated. 'But what's bothering me is a nasty thought that's occurred: it's pretty clear that he's testing the police, but why has he decided to do that just when you've arrived on the scene?'

'Oh, come on,' I said, feeling a nasty tingling in my scalp. 'I'm not on the scene. I'm just a lady of middle age who stumbled on a body.'

'Mm, well, maybe . . . But as well as being known to Terry Lynch you're also a photographer with a website. That puts you in the public eye and tells people you have some very useful skills.'

She looked at Gareth. 'Something else Eifion told me: the killer scrawled a message across that tarot card. Whoever's doing the investigating — the police, or our intrepid private eye here — they've got just twenty-four hours to crack the case.'

6

'Joanna actually said that?' Josh said. 'Crack the case?'

'She's always been that way. Reads old American *Black Mask* and *Dime Detective* magazines she finds on the internet. Away from work she tends to dress like a gangster's moll.'

'If it's true, that's to catch Gareth's eye.'

'You're probably right.'

'Oh, I am. She idolizes the little bugger. When I've been in there picking his brains on legal procedures I half expect her to sashay into his office trailing her wrap along the floor as she sensually flicks the ash from a black Russian cigarette held in a slim, ivory holder.'

'I did catch her daydreaming and all starry eyed, but I still think you're exaggerating just a little.'

'Well . . . '

It was half past six and we were sitting at the table on the shaded patio finishing off an *al fresco* evening meal of cold chicken and Waldorf salad washed down with a crisp Australian Riesling. The cooling sun was on the other side of the house, a long shadow had crept across the dust bowl that was my unfinished pond, and at the bottom of the garden the old CDs I'd strung up to keep away the starlings were glinting in the evening light.

Once again I'd brought Josh up to date with developments as soon as I walked in, and he'd looked predictably sceptical when I suggested the killer was testing me. That had been part tongue in cheek on my part, of course, because I'd meant what I said to Joanna: I was a middle-aged lady who'd found a dead body, and if anyone was being tested then it was DI Billy Dancer and his merry men.

Yet, as he poured more wine and sat back in his wicker chair, Josh now returned to that theme and proceeded to scare the hell out of me.

'I think you should give up this private eye caper altogether.'

'That's what Gareth said.'

'Really?'

'Emphatically.'

'We're both right. It's either that, or prepare yourself for some very rough weather. And if you do stick with it and that twenty-four hour deadline is meant seriously, you'd better move fast.'

'Why rough weather?'

'When a crime writer works on a plot he cuts out all the bullshit. Pares things to the bone. Every action or reaction, every word of dialogue uttered in every scene — everything has relevance. And most of what happens in a crime novel is bad.'

He sipped his wine, his eyes absently on the twirling CDs.

'Up to now,' he said, 'I've not looked at real life in those terms. Frankly, the idea's always been ridiculous. But you made a chance remark about corpses and cameras when you walked out yesterday and, out of the blue, we've been clobbered by both. We've got two dead bodies. You've used a camera to take a close up of one of them, and Joanna the perceptive reckons you've been threatened. So it occurred to me — cue drum roll, American national anthem, about bloody time and all that — that the seamy side of real life is probably pretty similar to my plots. On the edge. Never a dull moment. But — more to the point — sordid and very dangerous.'

He saw me roll my eyes, and grinned deliberately to lighten the mood.

'To help you one way or the other,' he went on, 'I'm going to have to grab you by the scruff of the neck and shake some sense into you, or use my crime-writing skills to' — he looked at me and winked — 'crack the case.'

'Dancer would laugh at that. Novels are larger than life, Josh.'

'Let him laugh.' He scowled. 'What do you call what's happening to us?'

'But that's going too far, isn't it? *Nothing's* happening to us — '

'God, listen to you. You've discovered one dead body and removed important evidence; our local GP's been murdered; you've been grilled by the police; had coffee with one of Liverpool's most notorious villains and I'll bet Joanna was right: one of Lynch's men *was* lurking and your image is even now being downloaded onto a laptop.'

'Rubbish.'

'And here's something else. You think the first time anyone other than the police and close friends knew of your involvement was when the newspapers were on the streets. I'm not convinced. If this was the plot of a novel, the killer would have been watching you when you whipped out your Nikon, took those snaps and pocketed the idol. It was no accident that Terry Lynch was there in the police car-park. He was there to talk to *you*, not Dancer.'

'You mean he was lying?'

'There's one quick way to find out.'

I was sceptical, but went inside anyway and phoned the police station. Dancer wasn't there, but DS Hood was on duty and was happy to answer my question. No, Terry Lynch had not been anywhere near the police since lengthy questioning after the death of his wife. That was a lie. As for mentioning a card left on the latest body, well, he was simply making a wild guess and I should take it with a pinch of salt.

'So,' I said when I rejoined Josh on the patio, 'not so much a grieving husband — which I admit I saw no sign of — but more a suspect. Are *you* suggesting he's our killer?'

'Maybe. We are looking for suspects, so let's put him on the list. Anyway, 'grieving husband' is not the impression you got.'

'No,' I said softly, thinking back. 'I'm not quite sure *how* I saw him.' Then I thought of something else. 'You know, when I was there, on the beach, there *was* a man. In the distance. Two, actually. But the next time I looked, there was just the one.'

'If the one left standing was the killer and he sneaked back while you were playing paparazzi — '

'Paparazzo.'

' — he could've been close enough to watch over your shoulder.'

'Or she.'

He shot me a look. 'Haven't thought of

that, have we? Did Gareth come up with any possibles?'

'Just Ffion, and she was more done to than doing — I think. She must have been in the thick of mob goings on, though. I'll bet she was a tough little pussycat, wallowing in all that testosterone, and if she finally got fed up with black eyes and bloody lips, well, who knows? Anyway, she's dead and out of it.'

'So, what next?'

'Well,' I said, 'Gareth's been a big help, and so that he's fully up to date with what I'm doing — one step ahead of everyone else, if you like — he wants me to keep him informed, let him know where I'm going, who I'm seeing.'

'Can't see what good that will do him, or you.'

'I think he just wants me to know he's there for me — and good for him, I say. Anyway, this afternoon's visit to him did give me one new name. I suppose, as I *am* going to do this, that's where I should start. It takes me right back to the beginning.'

'No better place.'

'The man I'm talking about is Mick Doyle. He was crazy about Ffion, then she up and married Terry Lynch. A lot depends on how Doyle took that rejection. The obvious person for him to get back at would be Lynch, but

Ffion was a softer target and her loss would cause a lot of pain and grief.'

'Where does Doyle hang out?'

'It's time,' I said, 'to talk to Adam Wise.'

★ ★ ★

It was just gone seven but I knew he often worked late so I went into my office and rang the *Liverpool Echo*. Josh brought his half-full wine glass and perched on the corner of my desk nibbling a greasy chicken wing.

The phone was picked up on the second ring.

'Adam?'

'Hi, Mum.'

'How's Desirée?'

'What did Groucho Marx say? Better than nothing?' He chuckled. 'She's fine, Mum.'

'And you're still — '

'Together?'

'Happy. Are you both still . . . *happy* together?'

'Deliriously. And yes she's still in the Sally Army and she still plays triangles and things and, as of this morning, she's not put on any weight.'

'I'm pleased.'

'Mum, she's delicate and *too light*. Just pinging on that triangle's enough to pull her off balance. A slight breeze would waft her and her shiny little instrument into the Welsh hills.'

'I'm pleased you're *happy* — and anyway that's not why I phoned.' I hesitated. 'Did you read about me in the paper?'

'In detail and between the lines. Word around the office is there was a little yellow idol to the north of, well, wherever — and you removed it from a crime scene. I think that's called perverting the course of justice.'

'Nonsense.'

'And the grapevine says you've dumped the hi-tech Nikon, slipped into trenchcoat and fedora and turned private eye.'

'If I'd left that Buddha in place the police might have been able to save their surgeon's life. I can't forget that; I've *got* to put it right — hence the new hat, because what private eyes do is ask questions.'

'It helps to have an official certificate of some kind.'

'Or at the very least, good contacts.'

'Ah, so *that's* why you rang.'

'Yes. You newspaper boys know everything, so what can you tell me about a man called Mick Doyle?'

'One word: avoid.'

'Impossible; he's first on my list, I must talk to him.'

'Did you know Doyle was the first man they picked up when Ffion Sharkey was knifed?'

'You mean Ffion Lynch. Yes, I did. But picked up doesn't mean he was charged.'

'No, but he had means, opportunity — '

'And motive? Yes, I know. Gareth fed me bits of it, how he lusted after Ffion, and I've also been talking to a certain DI Dancer.'

'Clever guy. Tread carefully.' He paused. 'All right then, what about this? The knife Doyle was known to keep behind the bar in Jokers Wild suddenly went missing — '

'Jokers Wild — isn't that a night club?'

'Shee-eeit! Here's me trying to keep you safe and I've opened my big mouth.'

I grinned, and winked at Josh.

'Thanks, Adam, I think I'm already getting the hang of this sleuthing business,' I said, scribbling busily. 'But go on. What about the knife?'

'Doyle swore it had been stolen. I think you can guess where it was found.'

'What, Doyle's knife was the *murder* weapon?'

'Definitely. Someone walked into Terry Lynch's house and stuck that knife in his wife's chest. Doyle's prints were all over the hardwood handle. He was pulled in, questioned, released on police bail.'

'Nothing was proved. So if he's innocent, why shouldn't I talk to him?'

'Because he's got a heart like a swinging brick, the temperament of a pit bull. Also, he's edgy. Jamie Lynch shot down Nicky Nixon — '

'That was the man murdered in the drive-by shooting?'

'Right. Which brutal act is supposed to have had the Gallagher mob baying for blood.'

'Supposed to?'

'Well, no clear proof that they were on the warpath, but that's what normally happens when someone's been dissed — and you don't get more dissed than a bullet in the back.'

'But if it was a revenge thing, surely that's over? The younger Lynch was murdered in prison. Isn't that the end of it? Closure, or some such?'

'Could be. Time will tell. But that doesn't take the pressure off Doyle. Terry Lynch is still not convinced he didn't top his wife. And now you're planning on walking in on Doyle when it's common knowledge you've taken sneaky photographs of one of Lynch's dead soldiers and been talking to the CID.'

'Mountains out of molehills springs to mind, Adam.'

'I wish. At best you're a nosy old biddy with brains, at worst you're working under-cover for the police.'

He paused and I heard a hand go over the mouthpiece, the murmur of voices. When he came back on his voice was serious.

'Did you know Sebastian Tombs's killer left another message, this one with a time limit?'

'Yes. Twenty-four hours. That's why I'm in a hurry. Tombs's body was found at eleven this morning, already more than eight hours ago. But as we don't know the precise time of death, we don't really know when the killer started the clock ticking — do we?

I heard him swear softly.

'Mum, if you do go there, take Josh with you.'

'Go where?'

'You know where: Jokers Wild, off Canning Street. Near Paul McCartney's old school. But — '

'What's Doyle's job?'

'Bouncer. Not on the door. He circulates.'

'All right, thanks — and what was that 'but'?'

There was a long pause. Then a sigh.

'I've already said it, Mum: Doyle's dangerous, and he runs with a crowd of nutters. Take Josh with you.'

'Did you hear him?

Josh was busy wiping greasy fingers. He screwed up the tissue, tossed it in the wastepaper basket then drained the last of his wine. He looked at me over the empty glass.

'About me going with you? Yes, I did. I think it's an excellent idea. But . . . what about you?'

'It's a bad way to start, definitely not good for my image. Also it's hard to miss you because you're so big and striking. We'd stand out like King Kong and that woman — '

'Fay Wray.'

'Right, and at the best of times it's more difficult for two people to stay invisible.'

'At the best of times? You've done this before, then? And what d'you mean, King Kong?'

I grinned. 'No, I *haven't* done it before. But in my role of photographer I have tried to become as one with the wallpaper when taking candid shots, which takes some doing but ain't terribly dangerous. And, d'you know, I'm actually looking forward to a bit of spice in my life. I think I've been in a state of excited anticipation ever since we got news of Tombs's death.'

'Yes, well, you might be interested to know that all the best PI's have a lean mean hard man watching their backs.'

'Fiction again, Josh. Fact is a book called *Gumshoe* by Josiah Thomson. He left a teaching position at Yale to become a private investigator and spent most of his time alone in a shabby car watching empty houses and peeing in a bottle.'

'You also left teaching, as I recall. And peeing in a bottle shouldn't be a problem. If you look in the classified sections of magazines like *Yours* you'll see quaint flasks with triangular little bits of comfy plastic that allow women to do just that.'

The chicken bone hit him between the shoulder blades as he went out, chuckling.

But I knew the laughter trailing behind him was strained. The banter was normal, but tonight it was covering genuine concern. Josh was worried sick but didn't want to fuss, had taken my point that Jokers Wild was a night club where people congregated and there was safety in numbers — but wasn't quite convinced.

So after I had helped him shift dinner dishes from patio to kitchen we came together briefly in the living-room where I showed him my little Nokia and the programmed numbers that would save my life, nuzzled him gently, and we parted without quite allowing our eyes to meet.

Josh went into his office where the laptop waited with luminescent allure. I retired to the bedroom and donned a thin black polo top, dark skirt and soft Hotter shoes. A couple of quick pulls and twists put my hair into an elastic band and gave me a neat little docked pony-tail in fashionable streaked grey. I thought of buckling on a hands-free bum-bag, then opted for a smaller version of the tote bag that I could sling crosswise to give the same freedom.

The last necessity was a Fujifilm FinePix F30 compact digital camera. I was about to venture into Liverpool's night life and, because of its 3200 ISO sensitivity, with that little beauty I could take pictures in the dark.

Well, almost.

As an afterthought, I phoned Gareth, thanked him for giving me Doyle's name and told him I was driving in to Liverpool to talk to him. Then I popped the camera into the tote bag with notebook and Chartered Institute of Journalist's press pass, threw on a dark red gilet, blew Josh a kiss from his office doorway and slipped out into the approaching dusk.

7

The setting sun was in the Ka's mirrors all the way to Liverpool, transforming ordinary vehicles purring ahead of me along suburban roads into splendid chariots splashed with red and gold. I slipped on my shades and kept my speed down, chasing my car's shadow across the Wirral peninsula towards the leaden swathe of the Mersey. Beyond its sullen swell, beckoning me from the high ground, Liverpool's Anglican and Catholic cathedrals were soaring towers flooded by the brilliant light of a late summer's evening.

I took the Queensway tunnel under the river, emerged in the city centre and followed St John's Lane, St George's Place and Lime Street then pushed on through Chinatown towards the southern suburbs. I was deliberately dawdling, wasting time, circling the target at a considerable distance because I hadn't yet girded my loins — a Biblical way of saying I was suffering from cold feet — and because deep inside me a stern voice was warning me not to stroll into Jokers Wild while the doorman was still switching on the lights.

My cover story was freelance journalist with semi-official pass writing a feature on Liverpool club life that would find a home in a magazine called *Club Mirror*. Like all the best covers it was based on truth, and researching that kind of an article means talking to people.

So while the club filled up I cruised without haste down Ullet Road, on to Smithdown Road, then took the right turn into Penny Lane and made my way to the bottom end where the hospital stood opposite Liverpool College playing fields and, in a nearby terraced house, I had been born.

My father had been a philatelist who owned a tiny shop on Smithdown Road where he sold packets of pictorial colonial postage stamps to youngsters and more expensive items to serious collectors. He had been born Mark Black, which itself can be a cruel joke when application forms of one kind or another are filled in that require the surname to come first. But of course, he got his revenge. I was born, he gave me what he always called his stamp of approval by christening me Penelope, and from then until my first marriage at twenty-two I was to be that most famous of British postage stamps, the Penny Black. Many years later, of course, I would marry for the second time, and by becoming Penny Lane I went full circle and was left bearing the full name of the street where I was born.

It seemed that my life had been one long play on words — and I include my disastrous first marriage in that, as you will see — so it was fitting that I should finally settle with a man who makes his living doing just that. And if Josh's name had been Rocky, or Dusty . . .

A horn beeped behind me. I came to with a start and pushed on to the end of the street which took me, via Greenbank Lane, to a half-circuit of Sefton Park and so back where I started on Ullet Road.

Once, on the drive back to the city, I thought I saw in my mirror a dark green Mondeo that was becoming familiar. I had noticed it twice before, always behind me but never getting close. Like a lurking toothache, it threatened pain by hovering in the background and refusing to go away — or was that me being just plain ridiculous? I mean, how many green Mondeos are there out there?

Then, suddenly, I was past caring, because I had turned off Catherine Street and in the long shadow of the Anglican cathedral I was searching for a parking place where none existed. The green Mondeo — when next I looked — had become a silver Volvo and so in my muddled thinking was no longer a threat. And as I slowed on Hope Street and backed breathlessly into a space fit for a Ka, the Volvo also drifted away along with my madcap ideas of being a PI important enough to be tailed.

★　★　★

What makes a night club?

Jokers Wild turned out to be six steps leading to a peeling door bearing a painting of a capering clown with fiery red eyes, a murky passageway leading past stairs rising into impenetrable shadows, a cloakroom fronted by a counter where a thin blonde with transparent skin glanced without interest at my Press pass, then chewed gum and made an equally enthusiastic search of my handbag while I signed my name in a visitors' book over which a naked bulb hung from twisted flex.

I walked through another door into a small, low-ceilinged room boasting a semi-circular mahogany bar against a lurid matt-crimson wall. Glittering optics were backed by a huge rectangular mirror in gilt frame. Tall bar stools were of red faux leather. Tables and chairs were positioned in a concentric semi-circle while, along the right hand wall,

U-shaped banquettes embraced individual tables and were given some privacy by low partitions of padded red velvet. Each of half-a-dozen wall lights comprised three opaque glass panels bearing the same red-eyed clown transformed into a dull gnome by the weak glow from dusty forty-watt bulbs.

In the end wall another door — this one covered in torn green baize — was tight shut and had me listening for the tap of a silver-topped cane and the haunting echoes of a dark-haired singer in a tuxedo. Frankie Vaughan, one of Liverpool's favourite dapper troubadours. He had many times asked a green door what secret it was keeping; had often invited each and every one of us to come to the cabaret but, my God, he couldn't have been thinking of this place.

The room was like a hot cocoon, trapping heat and noise. I was standing there assailed by the rattle of glasses, bursts of shrill laughter, conversation loud enough to drown cicadas and the unmistakable cadence of the Beatles swinging into 'Penny Lane' when a man built like James Coburn in his *Magnificent Seven* days came sauntering towards me and I knew I'd found Mick Doyle.

Or he'd found me.

I said, 'Did you put that CD on?'

'Stan did, behind the bar. Lily read the name on your pass and rang through.'

He wore a black T-shirt and stone-washed jeans, white trainers without socks, his knuckles bore scars and tattoos and he spoke with a scouse accent as thick as Mersey mud.

Blue eyes mocked me.

'I'm Mick Doyle. Blokes like me used to be called bouncers. Now we've got some posh title I can never remember.'

'Probably Forcible Removal Operative. FRO for short.' He was grinning, tickled by my feeble wit. 'But whatever you are, you were expecting me,' I said.

'Christ, Terry Lynch *owns* this place.'

'I met him. That doesn't mean he can read my mind.'

'Wanna bet?' He winked. 'Come on, there's nobody needs bouncin' or whatever so let's go'n sit down.'

There was room at the bar, more at the tables, but Doyle led the way through the semi-circle with much dodging and weaving and to a barrage of ribald ragging. As I clutched my bag and tucked in behind him I was aware of white shirts and gelled hair; the glitter of heavy gold at wrists, fingers and low-cut necklines; an eye-watering haze of perfume and aftershave rising from flushed and glistening skin. Penny Lane was in my ears but in everyone else's eyes as they unashamedly invaded my person all the way to an empty cubicle close to the green door. My ploy of wasting time had allowed the place to fill up, but hopes of sneaking into the crowd unnoticed had been dashed by a street-wise receptionist and a barman with a sense of humour.

Doyle had ordered drinks. As I settled back against worn crimson cushions a young girl slid a wet tin tray onto the table and, even before I lifted my glass, I knew I was about to taste the Macallan. Mind readers? I looked at Doyle. He was shaking with silent laughter.

'The wonders of IT. You've both got websites. A couple of years ago your old feller won a crime diamond dagger when it was sponsored by a certain brewery.'

'The drink was still guesswork.'

'Most things are. Like, what you're doin' here.'

'A magazine's interested in Liverpool night life. Jokers Wild popped out of the box.'

'Yeah, coincidence like, the day after you find Ronnie Humphreys' body and get right up Terry Lynch's nose.'

'One was bad luck, the other bad manners. Meeting you so soon is — '

'Bad news?'

'Depends. Could be just the opposite.'

He was sitting back drinking something dark that could have been whisky and coke. There was a calculating gleam in the blue eyes, and a lurking glimmer of excitement.

'Night clubs are dull. Full of drunks an' crack heads. Gamblers in sweaty shirts who think winnin' five quid at blackjack is big time. Fat businessmen gropin' other men's borin' wives.' He twirled the drink in his glass, pinned me with his gaze. 'So maybe that's not the kind of story your magazine's lookin' for.'

'You're the expert,' I said, dipping into my tote bag for notebook and pen. 'Why don't I put myself in your hands, so to speak?'

'Fair enough. But understand this: I'm not buyin' your cover story. You got involved when you found Ronnie Humphreys with a knife in his back and you won't leave it alone. You've spoken to Dancer, and that Welsh solicitor who works crime in the city, Gareth Owen — '

'My, hasn't Terry Lynch been talkative.'

I was looking with fresh interest at Doyle, realizing that he and Lynch must be very close, wondering if Doyle was the man Josh was convinced had been out there near the police station car-park, at Lynch's behest, clicking away with a camera.

'I practically fell over Humphreys,' I said. 'Being involved was unavoidable, and it doesn't make my story untrue. I do take pictures, I do write stories for glossy mags . . . '

'Just so you know.'

'That works both ways. Let's say we're sticking to our own versions of the truth.'

'Right. So seein' as we're in the midst of death — one way or another — why don't I tell you the story of a big man who thought someone was as safe as houses, and got it wrong?' He grinned. 'You can take notes, pretend it's for the magazine.'

I smiled sweetly, pen poised. 'The big man's Terry Lynch — and the someone was his wife?'

'Lynch, yeah — but the one he thought was safe was his brother, Jamie.'

'Safe how? Wouldn't be harmed in jail?'

'Because he was innocent. Terry reckoned he didn't shoot down the Gallagher man, Nicky Nixon, and would never be convicted.'

'Why would he think that? Because *he'd* done the murder himself? Terry? He *was* a suspect, wasn't he?'

'A suspect, yeah — and Ffion certainly thought he'd pulled the trigger even after the police let him go. But whatever the reason, Terry was so sure his brother wouldn't go to jail he took Ffion to the Dominican Republic. They got married by a palm-fringed swimmin' pool in La Romana about the time Jamie was goin' down for life.'

'Bang went a beautiful honeymoon.'

Doyle shrugged. 'They were too busy havin' fun to read the tabloids. The only sun they were interested in was blazin' down from a clear blue sky. Terry didn't find out about his brother till he got back.'

He was watching me, looking for a reaction. The excitement now seething within him was palpable.

'An' that's not all,' he said, when the silence dragged on.

I scribbled in the notebook for effect, thought for a moment.

'Let me guess. Terry Lynch doesn't believe Jamie was wrongly convicted, he thinks he was framed.'

'Absolutely. He's convinced of it.' Doyle cocked his head. 'But what brought you to that conclusion?'

'All crooks are innocent. If they go down they've been . . . what is it, fitted up?'

He nodded approvingly. 'Not bad.'

'But what do you think?'

Doyle shook his head. 'Haven't a clue. But, knowin' Terry, I know what he'd do if someone *had* framed his brother.'

I was staring at him. Amusement danced in his eyes and I knew he was holding something back.

I said, 'What's going on, Mick? What aren't you telling me?'

'Ask me why Lynch is convinced.'

I sighed. 'All right, go on — why is Lynch convinced his brother was framed?'

'Because shortly after he got back from the Caribbean he got an anonymous letter tellin' him evidence had been planted to make sure there was a conviction.'

I sat back. My notebook was full of scribbles. The close, boozy atmosphere was making my eyes sting, and the words were fuzzy. Mick Doyle was nursing his drink. I sipped whisky, blanking out the laughter and talk as I turned my head from side to side to ease the stiffness in my neck and give me time to think.

As I pondered Doyle's story and began following it to several shocking but logical conclusions, a movement caught my eye. The green door opened and I caught a glimpse of bright lights hanging low over tables encircled by card players with shirt sleeves rolled up. The door swung shut. A man of about forty in a draped black suit came away with his fingers poked into empty crystal whisky glasses. He was tall, and as knobbly as a beggar's cane. Thin lips were a mean gash in dark designer stubble. Bloodshot eyes peered through surprisingly long lashes. As he lurched past our booth he looked in and leered at Doyle. His teeth were like flawless alabaster with a gloss finish.

'Bloody hermit,' Doyle muttered, as the apparition wandered towards the bar, dumped the empty glasses and made for the exit.

The hairs on my neck prickled.

'Is that your name for him?'

'Everyone's. He lives in a garden shed, eats Pedigree Chum on toast and begs for pennies on the streets.'

'Why does Terry Lynch tolerate him in here?'

'Because Ryan's family,' a different, colder, voice said, and hard muscles shunted me along the lumpy cushions fast enough to drag my skirt into a twisted tube around my hips as Terry Lynch dropped down beside me.

No sports gear tonight. Giving him a withering glance I hitched my seams back into line and noted the well-cut charcoal-grey suit, the dove-grey button-down shirt, the musk scent of expensive deodorant. He could have been a prosperous bank manager enjoying a night out on the town, but the shirt was opened almost to the waist to expose a gold necklace nestling in thick hair, heavy gold links clinked at his wrist as he put down his glass, and the sovereign rings on each hand looked enough like knuckle dusters for me to visualize dried blood in the engraved tines of Britannia's fork.

He was sitting back, looking sideways at me with speculation.

'Get what you wanted?'

'I've already told Mick I'm researching a magazine feature. It's about club life in general. From what I've seen, Jokers Wild is pretty tame. Doesn't that rule out exciting stuff like murder?'

'That sounds like a leadin' question. You goin' straight back to what we discussed last time we met. Invitin' me to snap at the bait and start blabbin'.'

'Quotes always spice up an article. And there's no denying Ronnie Humphreys was linked to you and your clubs.'

Mick Doyle was grinning. He shook his head and moved lithely out of the booth.

'He was linked all right, but no more than every other employee, every member of every club, every name scribbled in every visitors' book.'

He winked at me then turned and threaded his way through the tables to the bar. A quick word there, and he moved to the exit. The door banged behind him as he left the room.

I slid along the unpleasantly tacky seat to gain space so that I could focus on Lynch.

'You said Ryan's family. So what relation is that? Cousin? Or is he another brother?'

'His name's Ryan Sharkey,' Lynch said. He saw my quick look, and nodded. 'That's right. That walkin' lump of shite is my brother-in-law. My wife — the late Ffion Sharkey — was the Hermit's sister.'

8

When I ran along the passageway and tumbled out of Jokers Wild the night skies high above tall buildings were a deep purple veined with crimson memories of a sinking sun and I was seething with impatience and trying to move so fast I nearly broke my neck falling down the steps.

I'd found a man known as the hermit — and allowed him to walk away. The tarot card left on Sebastian Tombs pointed to the hermit, that was fact, and I could not ignore the possibility that Ryan Sharkey was next on the killer's list.

The trouble was I knew that time must be running out. I had no idea where Ryan Sharkey had gone. I had watched — yes, actually *watched* — Mick Doyle follow him out of Jokers Wild and now, when I was in desperate need of a way of getting in touch with Josh or DI Billy Dancer, my Nokia was locked in the Ka's glove compartment.

Yes, I could have used the pay phone in the night club's shadowy hall. But Terry Lynch's words had sent me rushing out into the night, and I had no intention of walking the lonely streets searching for a public phone that probably wouldn't work.

I was halfway to where I'd parked the Ka, my soft shoes carrying me like a silent shadow along a narrow street. I risked a brief stop under a light, glanced at my watch. Ten-thirty. I felt a cold shiver of dismay. Tombs had almost certainly been murdered hours before his body was discovered at eleven that morning. My own feeling was that he'd lain there in that seedy bed-sit since the previous night. If I was right, then I might have half an hour to alert the police — or already be too late.

Trembling with the need for more speed, I broke into a run — and for an instant I thought I'd run headlong into an iron lamp-post . A hard and immovable body had stepped out of the shadows and stopped me dead. My open mouth slammed into a shoulder and I tasted blood. I whimpered, recoiled, felt my wind go, my knees begin to buckle. Then an arm like a curved steel bar wrapped itself around my waist, a left hand like a fan of cold bones was clamped over my mouth and the street lights spun overhead as a hip hoisted me off the ground and I was bundled into a back entry.

I jerked my head against the fierce grip, tried to shriek, managed a strained mumble.

Breath hissed through my nostrils as, in smelly darkness, I was dumped hard, heels jarring. My head smacked back against gritty brick. I moaned, gurgling against the hand. Senses reeling, I squinted through watering eyes at a black balaclava, slits through which black eyes glittered. At the alley's opening another shadow lurked.

Then the left hand was snatched from my mouth. I sucked in air. The hand returned, fingers and thumb thrusting forward in a fork that caught my throat as fiercely as it would trap a thick snake. I gagged, felt my eyes bulge. Then my captor's other hand came swinging like a club out of the darkness. The hard palm whacked my jaw. My eyes widened in shocked disbelief. The hand struck again, backhand. Bony knuckles cracked against my nose and cheekbone. Inside my head fireworks exploded in a dazzling display of brilliant colours. My ears rang. The world spun dizzily.

I thought I was floating. I seemed to drift through eternity, angels sweetly singing, my lips curling in a serene smile. Then reality kicked in as my knees cracked against hard stone and I flopped forward with my hands skidding in something cold and slimy. My attacker came with me, a knee in my back, his hand on the back of my head. An immense weight bore down on me. In an alley where drunks had retched, on hands and knees, my arms buckled and I sank face down in cold vomit, a hard hand grinding my face into the acrid, stinking mess.

I lay there with nostrils blocked by filth, listening dully to the fading sound of running footsteps. Reaction set in. My stomach lurched. With a gurgle like a blocked drain being plunged my throat opened and, inexcusably and pathetically, I garnished the filthy mess beneath me with a warm, lumpy, liquid topping of sour Waldorf salad.

★ ★ ★

The street was deserted. As if in a dream I could hear the distant hum of traffic. Headlights flickered, and my head shot round in terror. I stumbled sideways, whacking my toe against a step. An anonymous car drove by without slowing, and out in the Mersey estuary a fog horn emitted a drawn-out moan of sympathy.

I continued walking unsteadily, scrubbing at my face with Kleenex and wincing as I touched my nose, jaw, cheek. The coppery taste of blood was on my lips. My nasal membranes were raw from being sick, my breathing a dry rasp. I had lain in filth, emerged from the alley blinking like a ragged sewer dweller, and the city air around me was tainted by my presence. I giggled, imagining a bruised and bloodied woman bobbing along in a bubble swirling with an acid-green miasma; then took a deep, steadying breath, tossed the wadded tissue into a waste bin and broke into a clumsy jog.

My heart was knocking against my ribs. The skin on my back prickled in anticipation of a fresh attack. My own padding footsteps sounded eerily like someone racing up behind me, and panic forced me to increase my pace as I tried to outdistance myself. But even as terror lent my feet wings, the overwhelming feeling was of despair; of running for the last late-night bus and watching its lights fade in the distance. Hopes of saving Ryan Sharkey were pinned on my mobile phone, the phone was in my Ka and I was racing towards it — yet I was convinced I was too late.

A police siren howled, the volume rapidly increasing. Even as I looked around, saw faint blue light flashing on high brick walls and blind windows, the sound swooped into sudden silence as if a ghetto-blaster's electric plug had been wrenched out of the wall. Then a green Mondeo sped past, tooting merrily, and in its wake I crossed over and rounded the corner into Hope Street. The breeze blowing off the river was a cool balm soothing my skin. Before me lay the street, the deep dark valley of the Anglican cathedral's cemetery, the soaring floodlit tower that touched the stars and beyond it the land falling away to the glitter of the Mersey and the smudged shadow of distant hills.

I saw my car, and slowed to a breathless walk.

I had parked it against the kerb in the light of the setting sun; now it was the reflection of the cathedral's floodlights glinting on its glossy bodywork. But there was something wrong. My pretty red Ka was squatting low, the sun-kissed shell of a giant turtle with its legs tucked beneath it on the sand. As I drew near and circled it in nervous disbelief I saw that all four tyres had been slashed.

With a sob of anger I found my keys, opened the door and slid inside. I dropped with a bump; with the tyres flat it was like sitting down just as someone snatches away the chair. Almost weeping I dug out my phone, switched on, found the card given to me by DI Dancer and keyed in the number.

I didn't expect him to be there. I glanced at my watch as the phone continued to ring and saw that it was now almost eleven: the grievous bodily harm wreaked on me had whiled away thirty fascinating minutes. When

116

the thought caused me to snigger I realized I was slipping close to mild hysteria. I was losing it, which made me much more vulnerable. Fear came sneaking silently out of the darkness like a returning footpad. I quickly stretched to lock the doors and swallowed another bubbling snigger — just in time. The phone was picked up. I was through to Dancer's direct line.

He was breathless.

'We're closed,' he said, 'I was on my way out. What d'you want?'

'I've found the hermit.'

There was a strained silence.

'What bloody hermit?'

'There was a tarot card left on Tombs's body — '

'I know that, but you're not supposed to. So why don't you forget all about it and go — '

'No, please, listen to me. I know I *shouldn't* know about that card, but I do — and I've found the man it was alluding to and we both know he's in real danger and time's running out and — '

'Stop right there — '

'I can give you his description, and his name, and if you look on your big computer — '

'Jesus Christ,' Dancer said. 'I want you to

shut up, Penny, right now, and listen hard to what I have to say. Will you do that?'

'Yes. But only if — '

'Only nothing. I don't know where you got your info, or where you are now — '

'I'm in Liverpool. I've been crawling around in an entry. I'm filthy, and I'm bruised. At the moment I'm sitting in my car looking at the floodlit cathedral. Near a night club called Jokers Wild. But I'm stuck, because someone's ruined their good Stanley knife on my tyres.'

I could hear him breathing. I could almost hear him thinking — if that's not ridiculous. But it was that kind of a night, and I was higher than a kite . . . and now the mischievous giggle again bubbled within me because I was waxing poetic and I think I knew, with a terrible foreboding, exactly what was coming.

'If you're that close to the cathedral,' Dancer said, 'you must have heard the sirens.'

'Police cars? Yes, I did, just a moment ago.' I swallowed. 'What's happened, Billy?'

'A man walking home took a shortcut and tripped over a body lying in an alley.'

I moaned softly. 'Was it the same . . . ?'

'MO? He'd been stabbed, yes.'

'And another card had been left about his person?'

His chuckle was chilling. 'Delightful turn of phrase. But, yeah, there was another card.'

'Whom did . . . ? No, I won't ask that. But . . . has the dead man been identified?'

'Whom!' The chuckle again, warmer this time. 'Yes, he has.'

'Poor devil. His name was Ryan Sharkey, wasn't it? He lives in a shed or something, and I'm convinced he was the hermit of the tarot card because that's what everyone called him, but you know that, don't you?'

'No, Penny, I don't,' Dancer said. 'But, hermit or Kermit, he's definitely not the dead man. Ryan Sharkey is involved, but he was the man who *found* the body. He was on his way home from Jokers Wild — but, now then, that's something *you* know all about, so I really do think we should have another talk.'

9

Day Three — Wednesday 20 September

I'd once experienced the force of a power shower when I visited my eighty-year-old father in his sheltered accommodation, quite near Strawberry Fields, but a home of a very different kind from that famous establishment and situated on the other side of Liverpool's Calderstones Park. The force of the hot water had almost beaten me to my knees, left me lobster-pink and as limp as the warm plastic curtain; my father had gone up in my estimation, but I'd vowed never again to visit his shower.

That night, home safe after a fearsome beating but reeking like a yacht's head on a Biscay crossing, I would have sold my soul for a repeat performance and remained under the fierce spray until Josh dragged me out kicking.

Instead I sluiced myself clean under my own, gentle electric shower, then soaked for forty-five minutes in a hot bath, the only light the glow from an amber aromatic candle, my eyes closed and a glass of red wine held daintily poised above sumptuous mounds of perfumed Royal Jelly foam. When, clean, glowing and cosy in my pink towelling bath-robe and fluffy slippers I walked into the living-room, my big handsome crime writer had lowered the lights to intimate, placed mugs of steaming Ovaltine and plates of hot buttered toast smeared with honey on the coffee table, and one of those CDs you can pick up for a couple of quid from Oxfam or Barnardos was playing softly in the background — I think it was *Soulful Sax*.

It was half-two in the morning. A couple of hours since Josh had picked me up in the Range Rover and arranged for my Ka to be collected and repaired. Everything was sorted. At last, I could relax. I pulled up my legs, curled myself into a corner of the settee and sank into deep, soft cushions. The hot mug was clutched in my hands. Josh was watching me with smoky blue eyes. A faint wry smile played about his lips.

'Which is the real Penny Lane?'

'Hmm?'

'Is it the fluffy kitten with damp hair looking all hot and sleepy on the settee — or the slim woman dressed in black who sneaks into seedy night clubs and gets beaten up by a thug in a back entry?'

'A hot shower followed by a good soak

does wondrous things for the battered female frame. I don't really know, Josh. Sitting here like this, it seems perfectly possible to be both.'

'Forget it. You dipped your toe in shallow waters, Pen, and came off second best when the punches were flying.'

'Isn't that a mixed metaphor?'

'It's the truth. First time out in the big bad world, and you came a cropper.'

'I disagree. I returned, battered, yes, perhaps a little less attractive — '

'And stinking like a camel.'

'That too; but smells wash off, and you must admit I brought with me some intriguing information.'

'Maybe, but talking of smells, are you going to get medical advice? Some shots against . . . what d'you reckon, beriberi, yellow fever?'

'Who do you suggest I see? Our usual GP's not available.'

'You're right. And with that man's violent death hanging over you like a dark cloud, I know that first thing tomorrow morning you're going to share the intriguing information you've gathered with DI Billy Dancer.'

I'd told Josh everything that had happened that evening as I soaked in hot, scented foam and sipped rich red wine. He had perched delicately on the toilet seat, and when I ran out of steam — sorry! — he'd rolled his eyes and walked out. After that he'd obviously thought long and hard while preparing supper. Now he was suggesting the obvious: take what I had to the police.

I wasn't so sure.

'I don't know what to do,' I said. 'Isn't talking to Dancer sending the wrong signal to the baddies when they find out? Proving them right, sort of thing? Making me into . . . what is it, a snitch, a grass, a police nark?'

Josh sipped his Ovaltine but over the mug's rim his crinkled eyes told me he was trying not to smile. With the hot drink in his hands he couldn't steeple his fingers, but I could still see the way his mind was working. The protective husband within him wanted me to give up sleuthing with immediate effect. The crime writer that was his other half was twisting his arm up his back and telling him to look and listen because there was a real life plot unfolding before his eyes.

'What bothers me,' he said, 'is that all the information you got tonight was dropped in your lap. You walked into Jokers Wild and within minutes Mick Doyle was feeding you a story that makes his employer a prime suspect for multiple murder. First Ronnie Humphreys, then Sebastian Tombs, and now . . . who's the latest, do you know?'

'Not yet. Dancer didn't give me a name.'

'Never mind. We know there's a third body to add to the most recent murders, and Mick Doyle seems to be pointing to the killer.'

'Mm. That's the way I saw it at the time. Then I began to have second thoughts because it was all so obvious, all much too easy.'

'Not at all. Look at the story. Jamie Lynch was charged with murder, convicted, and sentenced to life. Then, according to Doyle, shortly after that Terry Lynch got a letter telling him his brother had been framed.'

'Yes. Just days after he got back from a wonderful honeymoon in the sun.' I sipped my Ovaltine, frowning at the thought. 'It must have been truly awful. And Jamie's fate turned out to be much worse than a long prison sentence, didn't it?'

Josh nodded. 'He died. Horribly. His throat was cut, in prison.'

'So if somebody did frame Jamie Lynch, and *put* him in prison, that person was guilty of . . . what?'

'In Terry Lynch's eyes, guilty of Jamie's murder.'

'And what we're seeing is Lynch hunting that killer?'

Josh frowned, sucked his teeth.

'The quick answer is, yes, of course.

Trouble is, everything is based on information that came from Doyle. And when you look at the victims, suddenly there are holes all over the place.'

'Why?'

'Ffion Lynch, for starters. Terry Lynch had an alibi, so where does her death fit in?'

'Put that one down to gang culture, payback for Nicky Nixon. Instead of Ffion, look at the victims we can link to Jamie. Where are the holes?'

'Well, Sebastian Tombs is definitely odd man out.'

'No he's not. When I was talking to Gareth we worked out that Jamie Lynch was the only person Tombs's evidence had sent to prison.'

'Right, so you believe Terry Lynch murdered Humphreys because he framed his brother, and Tombs because he was involved in the forensics?'

'Believe is too strong, because I've really only got Doyle's information to go on. I do think it's possible.'

'Then why this latest victim? If the two men linked to Jamie's death have been disposed of, what did this man do? Why was he murdered?'

I leaned across to put my sticky, crumby plate on the coffee table, then sank back hugging my still warm mug of Ovaltine.

Josh's questions had sent my mind racing at a speed that was sickening. Suddenly I was recalling little things I had forgotten, spotting others I'd missed, and the horror that swept over me chilled me to the bone.

'I . . . think I know his name. This . . . this latest dead man.'

'Go on.'

'Well, a tarot card gave me Ryan Sharkey — '

'No, *Doyle* gave you the hermit, Terry Lynch gave you Sharkey.'

'Yes, all *right*. So, anyway, I saw him come out of the back room. Doyle told me how he got that nickname. I watched the poor man take a handful of empty glasses to the bar, and walk out of the club. Then Terry Lynch arrived and told me this . . . hermit chap . . . was his wife's brother, Ryan. A little later Doyle got up — and *he* left the club. Josh, I watched him leave, only minutes after Ryan Sharkey had walked out, but I was talking to Terry Lynch and, stupidly, I didn't see the connection. When I did, well, I jumped up, made some excuse and raced out of Jokers Wild only to make a complete fool of myself.'

I managed a helpless shrug.

'And this connection was what?'

'Sharkey was the hermit, Doyle the killer. Doyle had given me everything, even winked at me when he walked out.'

'But the hermit didn't die.'

'No. And just now you asked about the latest victim, asked me what he'd done — and I think I know.'

Josh nodded gravely. 'He'd opened his mouth, hadn't he?'

'Yes. He sat by me in Jokers Wild and he gave me information that sealed his fate. I did get the connection but the wrong way round: *Ryan Sharkey* is a killer, and I'm pretty sure the man lying dead in the entry was Mick Doyle.'

In the sudden silence, the doorbell rang.

★ ★ ★

Detective Inspector Billy Dancer breezed in with his thin suit flapping like the sails of a yacht in the doldrums. He was accompanied by the same fair-haired uniformed constable I'd seen at Hoylake Police Station carrying half the force's equipment on her hips. She was slimmer tonight, but the two police officers walking ahead of Josh into the living-room bore on their clothing a chill that was part cold night air, part an aura of menace that turned my mouth dry and set my pulse thumping like that of a frightened rabbit caught in the headlights.

127

Dancer accepted a whisky from Josh, and sat in the chair he'd vacated. The young constable drifted across the room to stand near the window. Josh swiftly whipped away dishes and mugs and returned from the kitchen to sit on the other end of the settee.

I met Dancer's gaze with trepidation. He meditatively sipped the smoky Islay spirit, pursed his lips, then shook his head and sighed.

'What were you doin' at Jokers Wild when I told you to stay away from crime?'

'I was working on an illustrated article on Liverpool night clubs. For a magazine called *Club Mirror.*'

'So tomorrow when I phone the magazine's editor, he'll confirm that?'

I shook my head. 'No. I was doing this one on spec.'

'Convenient.'

'No, risky. It might not sell.'

'Not the only risk, though, was it?' he said, looking pointedly at my damaged face.

'This happened well away from the club. It could have been a random attack.'

'But you don't think so?'

I hesitated. 'No.'

'Because not only were you attacked, but somewhere around the same time you were up to your old tricks, weren't you? I mean, on

128

top of hobnobbin' with known criminals, and working on illustrated articles without takin' any pictures.'

I frowned, wondering how he got his information.

'I'm puzzled. What tricks are those?'

'Contaminatin' a crime scene. Only this time instead of removing evidence you left your callin' card.'

'What, at *my* crime scene? Where I was attacked?'

'The other one. The one where a man died. Which I'll admit could've been the same one, seein' as you told me you'd been crawlin' round in an entry and this feller died in one.'

'Yes, but I don't understand the bit about me leaving a card. I know you said the *killer* left a card — '

'Isn't that what I just said?'

'No, what you *just* said was *I* left my calling card.'

'So put the two statements together and you come up with . . . ?'

I looked at Josh. He was supposed to be frowning with concern, or utter confusion, but all I could see was intense interest and almost as much amusement.

He said, 'DI Dancer's saying you're the killer, Pen. Ask him why.'

I said, 'Why am I the killer?' It came out like the squeak of a very tired mouse.

'Because you were there, with him, before he died. You took a very nasty picture — '

'I did not!'

He slipped a hand into the pocket of his alpaca suit, pulled out a transparent plastic bag containing a digital camera and dangled it in the air. It looked like a Fujifilm FinePix F30. In a flurry of pink bath-robe and flashes of naked flesh I dived off the settee and grabbed my handbag from where it was hanging on the back of a chair. Opened the zip. Rummaged inside.

No camera.

'You see.'

Without removing it from the bag Dancer switched on the camera and waved me over. As if wading through deep water I crossed the room and looked over his shoulder. The camera was in display mode. The pictures had been taken using flash. The first shot was of a man standing against a rough brick wall. He was dark, burly and unshaven. His eyes were wide with fear. In the next shot he was lying flat on his back in a pool of water. Blood had trickled from his nose. His eyes were still open, but the fear had gone and so had any sign of life.

I had my hands clamped on the back of Dancer's chair to stop myself shaking. I looked across at Josh.

'I was wrong. The dead man's not Doyle.'

'Recognize him?'

I shook my head.

'His name's Joey Farrell,' Dancer said. 'Another of Terry Lynch's merry men.'

'Where did you find my camera?'

'You mean where'd you lose it?' He watched me stumble back to the settee and collapse against Josh. 'It was lifted from your bag when you were signin' the visitors' book in Jokers Wild. The anorexic blonde confessed. Where we found it was alongside Farrell's body. An' my guess is when we check it for prints the only ones we find'll be yours.'

'But I didn't kill him. You know that. The camera was stolen and — '

He stopped me with a dismissive wave.

'What was all that about Doyle?'

'I'd tried to put two and two together, but I came up with the wrong answer.'

'The card left on Tombs's body pointed to a hermit. What's that got to do with Mick Doyle?'

'When I was with Doyle in Jokers Wild, he told me Ryan Sharkey was the hermit. But when you told me Sharkey *found* the body,

131

and I knew Doyle had followed him out, I — '

'Came up with the wrong victim.' He nodded. 'Actually, you were right, the hermit did die. Joey Farrell didn't have a permanent home. He moved around, stayin' in squats. When he got turfed out of one he'd move to another . . . an' then another . . . '

Josh nodded slowly. 'A hermit *crab*,' he said, and gave my arm a reassuring squeeze.

I said, 'If the blonde confessed to stealing my camera, she must have told you what she did with it.'

'She says she gave it to Ryan Sharkey when he was on his way out of Jokers Wild,' Dancer said. 'Sharkey backs her up. Not only that, he admits he took that second picture, the one of Joey Farrell lyin' dead in a pool of water.'

'Then if he took that picture,' I said, 'he must have taken the picture of Farrell when he was alive.'

'Why?'

'Because it was on my camera, and the camera was in my possession until stolen by that blonde girl.'

'You're sure?'

'Absolutely.'

'That's a shame,' Dancer said, and now there was a glint in his eye. 'See, as you say,

Ryan Sharkey only had the camera in his possession, what, an hour at most. Yet accordin' to forensics, when that second picture was taken, Joey Farrell had been dead at least a couple of hours.'

10

'What we've been forgetting,' Josh said, 'is the important matter of an anonymous letter.'

'I know. That was bothering me when I was trying to get to sleep. Who sent it? Why did they send it? And what is this person, or persons, doing now?'

'That's the *really* intriguing question, and it's got sinister connotations,' Josh said. 'What *are* they doing now?' He stared hard at me. 'And there's another.'

'Go on.'

'Why did you withhold information from Dancer?'

'What, the bit about the anonymous letter?' He nodded.

'We were talking about dead bodies and me being a killer and taking photographs . . . ' I shrugged. 'I really did forget all about it.'

It was eight o'clock. Morning sunlight was streaming through the kitchen window. True to our agreement I'd phoned Gareth as soon as I crawled out of bed and brought him up to date with what had happened. He was sympathetic — even apologetic — because he felt that by giving me Doyle's name he'd sent me rushing headlong to my fate. I'd consoled him, told him not to work Joanna too hard, and rung off.

Now I was at the breakfast bar munching muesli with an aching jaw while absently rubbing the bruise on my cheekbone that had spread downwards and upwards and was gradually turning purple. Half an hour earlier the spray from my gentle shower had cruelly exposed in my elderly body aches and pains I didn't know existed. When I wiped condensation from the mirror and cleaned my teeth I'd been gazing at my reflection through one good eye and one moving towards red and bloodshot.

It had been almost four in the morning when DI Dancer departed, very soon after dropping his bombshell. He'd said nothing more and I knew he was leaving me to stew, definitely hoping I'd remember something useful after a night's sleep, but possibly praying I'd disappear without trace and leave him to get on with the job.

Yet about that last bit I wasn't too sure. I was beginning to like the gaunt, untidy detective, and when he looked at me I'd seen in his deep-set eyes all kinds of conflicting emotions: interest, frustration, speculation — possibly even a hint of growing warmth. Anyway, I was pretty sure he'd peeped into my background. If so then he knew I was no fool and, in the work he did, information that helped a case was welcome regardless of the source. So, dish out warnings to the interfering busybody, but handle her as he would a friendly gift horse.

My train of thought was disturbed by a clatter as Josh carried his empty dish and spoon to the sink, then opened the kitchen door and let in the early morning scent of dew-soaked grass being warmed by the sun. He detoured on the way back. When he returned to the breakfast bar, our cups were filled with hot coffee and his eyes were gentle and studying me with concern.

'Dancer doesn't really believe you're a killer, Pen.'

'Oh, I know that. I think what he's trying to do is drill into my stubborn brain just how dangerous these men can be. How cunning they are. The way they can come at you with something totally unexpected. Well, after last night I don't need convincing. I was dragged into an entry, punched in the face, thrown to the ground and my face was rubbed in another man's vomit — or men's.' I shuddered. 'And that, I suppose, was just a warning.'

'But you're going on?'

'Absolutely. Nothing ventured, and all that.

The trouble is, I haven't got a clue what to do next.'

'Maybe I can help.'

'You're precious. I don't want you involved, because these boys are real live hard cases.'

'And I'm lean, mean, ex-army, a marathon runner, regular at the gym — '

'But not today.'

'Give me a chance, we were up till all hours — '

'See what I mean. You think you're superman and one late night — '

'What if I say you *can't* stop me helping?'

'It's still no.'

'And I adore you for your concern, Penny, but you're too late.'

I reached for the coffee. Savoured the aroma, the taste of the hot, strong Kenyan. Looked at Josh, his tousled mop of grey hair, his dancing blue eyes.

'Explain.'

'You first. If you're not the killer, how did someone else take those photographs when you had the camera in your bag?'

'Forget film, think digital, Josh. They photographed Farrell alive with another camera. Then they murdered him. When they pinched my camera they threw away the memory card, inserted theirs and took the second picture.'

'Which means — thinking digitally — that the police can look at information on that memory card and discover which camera the crooks used for the first picture, and the time it was taken. And the time the second picture was taken using your camera.'

'Yes. Dancer knew all that last night. He was just having me on. However, he must also realize that knowing the camera used won't do them much good unless they can trace it.' I smiled, and raised my eyebrows. 'Right, now it's your turn.'

Josh grinned smugly. 'Last night I went to the B & B where Sebastian Tombs died.'

'You're kidding.' Taken completely by surprise, I stared at him. He stood firm. I said, 'All right, but if you did go there you wouldn't have got near the place. It's still a crime scene — isn't it?'

'Well, yes, it is. But I'm a crime writer, it's my job to pitch characters into impossible situations and help them wriggle out of tight corners and — '

'Yes, all right, big head no bread in the house. So what did you do?'

'I trotted up the rusty iron fire escape.'

I groaned. 'Of course. That's the first thing I thought of when I heard where Tombs had died. Not as a way for me to get in, but a way for the killer to get out.'

'He probably used it,' Josh said. 'And so did the girl. Once to get out, once to get in.'

I frowned. 'What girl?'

'The girl who was there in the room that evening, with Sebastian Tombs. She watched him fall asleep, then got out via the fire escape. It wasn't until yesterday afternoon — when she rolled out of bed — that she realized she couldn't find her purse. And by then Tombs was dead. So she had to wait until last night to go back. That's when she used the fire escape to get in.'

'Waste of time. If she'd left her purse in Tombs's room, the police would have found it.'

'Actually, I found it. She'd dropped it well away from the B & B. It was some way down the road, up against a hedge and half-hidden by a waste bin. I looked inside. Her photograph was on her driving licence. So when she walked in on me, in Tombs's room, I recognized her and knew her name.' He paused, and I knew it was for effect. 'Of course, I already knew her by sight — and so do you.'

And I was about tell him to bloody well get on with it and stop acting like a pompous, conceited prat when we both heard a muted click outside the house that snapped our gaze towards the open kitchen door.

I realized I was holding my breath. Carefully, I exhaled, aware of the sudden uncomfortable pounding of my heart. My ears ached as I strained to listen. I took several rapid breaths, glanced quickly at Josh then back at the door.

'Aren't you going to do anything?'

Unconcerned, he'd turned back to his coffee.

'It's broad daylight, Pen, all self-respecting crooks are still abed. It's probably the milkman — '

'I can't hear bottles. Anyway, he's been, you had fresh semi-skimmed on your muesli.'

'All right, the window cleaner.'

'Not due till next week.'

Something scraped on stone. Josh turned. Both of us saw a shadow lying across the paving stones edging the lawn. Unmoving. The clear outline of head and shoulders.

Josh slipped silently from his stool, padded towards the door and stood to one side. He looked across the room at me. Waggled his hand in the universal drinking motion.

I turned back to the breakfast bar. That put the danger behind me. Last night's memories rushed back, capering like shrieking ghouls. The skin on my back crawled. I tried to lift the full coffee cup to my lips, but my hand was trembling. Grimly I held the cup with both hands and lowered my face, lips pouting. I didn't make it. I was almost there when a sudden scuffling brought me spinning round on the stool. Hot coffee splashed my hands. The cup fell to the floor and shattered.

In the garden doorway, outlined against bright sunshine, Josh had a young man in a headlock.

It was my son, Adam Wise.

★ ★ ★

Whenever I see Adam I am torn between intense feelings of love and loathing, the first emotion aroused by the son I adore and the second by a man who lives 12,000 miles away and whom I haven't seen for more than twenty years.

Adam is so like him at times it almost breaks my heart.

I met Peter Wise one lunch hour when we were both newly qualified teachers working in a south Liverpool comprehensive. Blond-haired Pete, with the sweet fresh skin of a wartime land girl and the devil dancing in his eyes. A lovable rogue. Why is it young women find them so irresistible?

From the moment he walked into the common room and touched my shoulder as he leaned over to look at the essays I was marking, I was lost. We went out together that night, then every night thereafter in the dizzy, bubbling six weeks before we rushed into marriage. I was twenty-two, Peter twenty-five, it was 1974 and I had moved from being an expensive postage stamp to become the first half of a proverb: *penny wise and pound foolish* — wrong in my case, because it was my very worst decision, but the 'pound foolish' bit could have been coined especially for Peter.

Unfortunately, as I was to find out, the inability to handle anything financial wasn't my new husband's only fault. Adam was born in 1977, Jacqueline two years later. And one pleasant evening three years after the birth of his daughter the blond-haired devil with the morals of a Fagin went out for cigarettes and, a couple of days later, bought a packet of Marlborough at a tobacconist's in George Street. You know, the one in Sydney, Australia.

No, I didn't miss him. The marriage had been going downhill from day one — God, how I hate that term — and so as a single mum I muddled through coping with rebellious teenagers at work and a young family at home and I thought I'd done wonderfully well until 1994 when my sixteen-year-old daughter walked in from school and told me she was flying to Australia to live with her father. They'd been corresponding without my knowledge. She had a plane ticket in her purse. The flight was already booked.

The man I'd longed to forget was suddenly inextricably linked to the family he'd deserted. My daughter was with him, which made damn sure I had to be, at least in spirit. I couldn't even get away from his blond good looks; my son, his spitting image, grew up quickly and put paid to even that forlorn hope.

★ ★ ★

'I warned you about Doyle, Mum. In words of one syllable.'

'Two, actually. Av — oid.'

He grinned. 'Means the same however you say it. And by the bruises and that lovely black eye it looks as if you jumped in face first.'

'Yes, but that happened in a separate incident. I walked out of Jokers Wild, and a few minutes later I was dragged into an entry and slapped about the kisser.'

'Kisser?' Josh was grinning.

'Yes. That's private detective speak. Ask Joanne. Anyway, my attackers could have been anybody.'

'Wearing balaclavas? And what was the reason for the attack? Why weren't you robbed — or something?'

He was being discreet. I gave him an appreciative smile, then shrugged. 'I don't know.'

'Where was Mick Doyle? Still in the club?'

'No. He walked out earlier. That was why I left in a hurry.'

We'd moved from kitchen to patio and were sitting by the table, under big yellow and lime-green parasols, sipping coffee freshly brewed by Josh and listening to the lazy droning of bumble bees.

I quickly filled Adam in on what I'd heard, been told, what I'd deduced, and how I'd got it all so badly wrong. Even as I spoke I sensed that he already knew most of what had happened, and I wondered what had dragged him from his desk at the *Liverpool Echo* all the way across the water to Heswall. Eventually, reluctantly, he told me he'd come because he'd heard the stories and he was worried and wanted to check on my condition without dwelling too much on my obvious scars of battle. He certainly hadn't anticipated walking into a vicious assault, I thought, smiling inwardly at the recollection.

My ex-soldier's attack on him had been instinctive. First there'd been the menacing shadow then, moving with silence and stealth, a man had loomed in the doorway. Josh grabbed him by the throat before he recognized Adam. As soon as realization dawned, they broke apart and laughed till they cried. They've been good friends for years. And Adam's stealth on his way in through the garden was quickly explained: he'd been afraid of disturbing a family of house martins, who had fascinated him as they dipped in and out of their nest under the eaves.

'So that's what happened to me,' I said, 'but I'm not the only one who's been living dangerously. Last night Josh poked his nose into a crime scene, and just before he tried to throttle you he'd said something very interesting.'

I looked at Josh, leaning back in his wicker chair, bare feet resting on an upturned plant pot in the warming sun.

'So, go on,' I said. 'If I know this girl by sight, where have I seen her?'

'She was sitting at the bar when we walked into the Golden Fleece looking for Sebastian Tombs.'

'What, the girl who looked as if she'd — '

'Forgotten her skirt? Yep, that's her. That was her hooker's garb.'

'Incredible. We were sitting with DI Dancer

discussing the man that girl had just . . . well . . . '

'Had nothing. I told you, Tombs went to sleep and she walked out. And it wasn't just, either; she got involved with Tombs long after we left the Golden Fleece.'

He reached for his coffee, decided against it and left it where it was.

'D'you remember the bloke sitting at the bar with her?'

I rolled my eyes. 'Definitely. Rings and things all over his face and — '

'Extremities? Organs?' Josh grinned. 'He put her up to it. She's short of money, and thought paid-for sex might be a good idea. But it was always a non-starter. She took one look at Tombs, old enough to be her grandfather, started shaking like a leaf and as soon as he passed out she bolted for the exit.'

'So what did you get up to last night?'

'Well, I went there as much to soak up atmosphere as look for clues. The poor girl nearly died when she found me in that room, went white as a sheet, but I quickly held up her purse and after that she calmed down and we clattered back down the fire escape and walked and chatted.'

'What does she do?'

'She studied photography at uni. Got a degree of some sort. I think. So I told her you were thinking of diversifying into wedding photography, and if you did you'd be looking for an assistant.'

'I've already diversified,' I said.

Adam shook his head. 'Yes, and look where it's got you.'

'I'm fine. Honestly. And I did learn something, last night. For a start there's that anonymous letter, and what it said.'

'Which was utter nonsense,' Adam said. 'There might have been a letter, but I can tell you now that the case against Jamie Lynch was rock solid. Planting evidence to convict him would have been daft. There were half-a-dozen eye witnesses to the drive-by shooting, and the murder weapon was found in a skip, plastered with Jamie's fingerprints.'

'Josh and I discussed this last night. We had some misgivings — you know, doubts about what Doyle told me. But if he was lying, what the hell is he up to?'

'The quick answer is he's pointing the finger at Terry Lynch.'

'We'd figured that out — but why?'

'Same quick answer: Doyle is the killer.'

Josh had climbed to his feet and wandered away and was a tall, lean figure in jeans and T-shirt as he walked barefoot through still damp grass around the dry water-hole that was my nascent pool. But he was all ears, and now he turned to look sceptically in our direction.

'Knee jerk reactions are rarely reliable. We need to know more. When we do, my bet is you'll find those quick answers are well wide of the mark.'

After that sobering thought we were quiet for a while, all of us lost in thought as we enjoyed the summer sunshine. I was experiencing gradually mounting excitement as Josh's talk of the young photographer led me down familiar paths that had suddenly taken on new meaning. I'd always considered wedding photography, not least because from *Professional Photographer* magazine I knew fees could be as high as £5000 for a weekend's work. All right, that sort of cash is unlikely to come to an elderly lady without portfolio — the photographic kind — but the point was that I remembered turning down a request to photograph a wedding in Chester. That had been Monday afternoon, only hours after I'd discovered the body on the beach. At the time, the names of the couple getting married had meant nothing.

'Josh,' I said quietly, 'I think I'll go and see your young lady, and if she impresses me we'll do that Chester wedding.'

He was back, treading gingerly on the hot Cotswold flags, hands on hips and the sheen of perspiration on his brow.

'Why?'

'Did I tell you the name of the bride to be?'

'Diane . . . Diane Gallagher, was it?' He cocked his head. 'Oh, come on. Surely you're not thinking what I think you're thinking?'

'Ernie Gallagher lives in Chester, and we know he's Terry Lynch's rival. If I'm on the right track, the opportunity's too good to miss. A wedding photographer gets unrivalled access, the freedom to wander at will inside private houses taking intimate shots of bride, groom and, well, the chance to do a bit of snooping.'

'Granted, but there must be dozens of Gallaghers in Chester. Ordinary, honest folk. Hell, I think I know one, he runs a tobacconist's shop in the rows above Watergate Street.'

'Could be a relative. Even crooks have families. And some of them run legitimate businesses.'

Josh was shaking his head, but Adam was less dismissive.

'It's a common enough name,' he said, up out of his chair with car keys jingling, 'but if you're right, you get the same warning you got last night: avoid.'

'Avoiding won't get results,' I said. 'Josh, this lady you met last night, what's her name?'

'Annabel. Annabel Lee. She gave me a card. Looks as if it was done on a computer.' He smiled. 'I won't comment on her morals, but she really is serious about breaking into photography.'

'Maybe she's already done so, in ways you really will not appreciate,' Adam said.

He'd stopped jingling his keys. When Josh and I looked at him, my son's face was grim.

'Annabel Lee,' he said, 'is Terry Lynch's niece, the daughter of his sister, Nellie Lee, married to a bloke whose first name, would you believe, is Bruce. And, as you know, last night someone who knew a little bit about cameras was juggling with digital memory cards in an entry where a man was lying stabbed to death.'

11

Reaction always takes time to creep up on me. A few minutes after Adam drove away and some twelve hours after the beating I went weak at the knees and all swimmy in the head and was carried bodily to bed by Josh. I slept for almost four hours. At two o'clock, looking snazzy in white T-shirt and lycra tracksuit bottoms but ruining the trendy image with fluffy pink slippers, I shuffled into the kitchen where a lunch of crisp cold salad and fresh orange juice was hiding under a serviette on the breakfast bar. Josh's office door was closed. There was a note under my plate: he'd gone to the gym to work out on the nautilus machines, as he always does on Wednesday afternoons.

I ate at my leisure, alone with thoughts that struggled in vain to reach the surface.

Half an hour later I'd rinsed the dishes and was yawning at the kitchen window when the phone rang. With his usual consideration and forward planning, Josh had left the cordless handset by my lunch.

My 'Hello' came out as a mumble.

'Penny?'

It was Gareth. I pictured the owlish solicitor at the desk in his office and somehow Joanna, the crime buff, sneaked into the picture, perched in his lap like a sultry Bonny Parker nuzzling an undersized Clyde Barrow. I found myself grinning as I looked out across the sunlit garden.

'Afternoon, Gareth. If I sound dozy, it's because I've just woken up.'

'Nevertheless, I detect a smile in your voice. The morning after the night before has stretched well into a lovely afternoon and done you a pile of good.'

'Well, after I called you I had the strength to eat breakfast with Josh. Then Adam turned up, and when he'd gone events sort of snuck up on me.'

'They're about to do it again.'

'God, what's happened now?'

'First, let me ask you a question. You had coffee with Terry Lynch in The Thirsty Goose, and I know you spoke to him and his *aide de camp* last night at Jokers Wild. What d'you reckon? Thinking of the most recent murders — Humphreys, Tombs, and Farrell — that's the dead man in the entry, in case you don't know — could Lynch be the killer?'

'Mick Doyle would like me to think so. He seemed to be pointing the finger, which makes me suspicious.'

'He'd make a copper suspicious if he asked him the time. But if we ignore Doyle's attempts to sway you — what's your feeling?'

'Confusion, mostly. But if asked to pluck a murderer out of the mire, I'd say Terry Lynch would be the most likely candidate.'

He chuckled, but if he'd detected a smile in my voice I knew just as clearly that there was none in his. The phone has that unique quality of cutting out all outside distractions and letting listeners concentrate on the voice. Gareth's voice, even in laughter, was coming across as odd.

'Gareth, what's happened? What's going on?'

'There's something I neglected to tell you — well, didn't bother telling you, actually, because I thought it unimportant.'

'You *thought* it was unimportant. But now you don't. So tell me. What have you found out?'

'It's not what I've found out, it's what I've done.' He paused. I realized his breathing was shallow, too rapid. Hearing was the only sense I was using, yet my skin was prickling and I could feel the tension coming down the wire.

'When Jamie Lynch was tried for murder,' Gareth said, 'I was counsel for the defence.'

'Oh, Gareth, no, not you. He was sentenced to life, the defence *lost* the case . . . '

153

I broke off, thought rapidly, reached the obvious, awful conclusion, and with my eyes squeezed shut and my face all screwed up as if expecting a violent blow — which I was — I asked the question.

'Why now?' I said. 'I mean, why tell me now? Why, suddenly, is it so important?'

'My brother, Eifion, was on the phone just five minutes ago. He was telling me about the card found on Farrell's body. Apparently our killer's dispensed with credit cards and the tarot, and gone all artistic. He left an excellent depiction of a bright red Welsh dragon, all dolled up in a lawyer's wig.'

'Damn. But those wigs sit on all kinds of heads. Couldn't it be pointing at the judge, the man who *sentenced* Jamie Lynch?'

'I don't think so,' Gareth said, and now there was amused resignation in his voice. 'The judge was English. He suffered a heart attack and died, a week after the trial — so I'm afraid that leaves little old me.'

12

As soon as I'd said goodbye to Gareth — after advising him to talk to the police (which I knew he wouldn't do), and inviting him and Joanna to dinner that evening — I hunted around for the yellow Post-it note with the telephone number, and called the Gallaghers in Chester. Without expecting any success I told them that if they hadn't already hired a photographer, I'd be delighted to cover their wedding. They jumped at the offer. The wedding was three days away, they hadn't found a photographer they could trust, and my quoted fee was accepted without quibble.

The man doing the hiring was Ernie Gallagher. It was his daughter's wedding. We agreed to meet before the weekend without making any firm plans, and that was half the job done.

My next step was to hire Terry Lynch's niece.

According to the business card she'd given to Josh, Annabel Lee lived in rented accommodation in Parkgate, a riverside village just a few miles from Heswall. The

River Dee has been silted up for years, so riverside tends to mean situated alongside a vast expanse of reeds and grass flourishing on the rich alluvial deposits. But riverside in Parkgate can also mean expensive and, as I drove down Boathouse Lane in Josh's Range Rover and turned onto The Parade, I was wondering how a young girl desperate enough to risk selling her body could afford up to £600 a month for a small terraced house.

Or was I being naïve? Why assume Sebastian Tombs was the first to pay for her favours?

I'd phoned ahead before leaving Heswall. I do hate wild goose chases. Annabel had been absolutely staggered that I'd bothered to call, agreed breathlessly when I told her why I wanted to see her and suggested meeting within the hour, and I'm pretty sure she was eagerly peeping through the vertical blinds when I pulled up outside what turned out to be a delightful white stone cottage. So, up that rent estimate to a thousand a month.

As I climbed out of the Range Rover I was still trying to work out how to combine a murder investigation with a job interview. And I got a distinctly eerie feeling when the young woman I remembered from The Golden Fleece answered my knock and I

156

followed her from a cosy living-room through an arched opening into a rear eat-in kitchen overlooking a tiny walled garden. The tiny skirt she'd been wearing that night had been replaced by expensive jeans, something flowery and sleeveless from Top Shop fitted her like a second skin and her hair, lustrous and flowing, would have hidden most of a modest mermaid's top half — but this young woman was the niece of Terry Lynch, a man I suspected of murdering several people and now holding a pistol to the head of one of my best friends. It seemed I was automatically assuming she was guilty by association, which was ridiculous. Yet I was finding it impossible to control my feelings. Annabel was related to Lynch, that close link was making me uneasy, and I think she sensed a coolness in my manner.

Sensed it, but got the reasons for it all wrong.

'I know exactly what you're thinking,' she said, as we sat either side of a pine table where a cafetière sat snug under a colourful knitted tea cosy alongside two china mugs. 'I don't blame you, but you've got it wrong. I've already told your husband, and he should've told you. It was a one off, a big mistake, and it went nowhere. I walked out on Tombs, came straight home and stood under a hot shower until I turned lobster and *still* I didn't feel clean.'

'Don't worry about it,' I said, mentally empathizing and warming to the young woman as I recalled resorting to the same remedy for a different but no less stupid reason.

'Josh did tell me. He also told me the young man we saw you with arranged the . . . what do they call it . . . assignation?'

'Bit posh. More like he fixed it so I could turn a trick. I think he had Tombs down as a champagne trick — and in case you don't know, that means a rich client. Anyway, the young man was Gordon, a beady-eyed amateur pimp with an inferiority complex who uses safety-pins to keep from fallin' apart at the seams.'

'Sounds a bit like me. In at the deep end, and not much of a swimmer.'

She gave me a strange look, and I suddenly realized that unless Josh had given the game away she knew nothing about my hunt for Tombs's killer, or who I had earmarked for the role. Which meant she'd be confused, and wary. My name had been in the newspapers. I was the woman who'd found a body on the beach. She probably knew Ronnie Humphreys was linked to her uncle, Terry Lynch, so she'd be wondering what the hell was

158

going on; thinking, why *has* this woman come to see me?

'I blame myself for Sebastian Tombs's death, so I'm sort of looking into it,' I said, offering an explanation without giving too much away. 'Naturally I'm intrigued by the way things went that night. I mean, you visit a police surgeon in a run-down B & B establishment, and a few hours later he's dead.'

I studied her face for reaction, saw none and said, 'Anyway, you know why I'm here. I may be an amateur PI blundering from one clue to another, but I'm a photographer first, and it's *those* I'm really interested in.'

I swept an arm behind me to indicate the prints artistically displayed in plain frames on the white walls of the living-room. I could see informal portraits in settings ranging from meadows to moody interiors, Scottish castles against wooded backdrops done in infra-red I guessed had been created on the computer, coloured prints of flowers that would win prizes anywhere and be snapped up by photo libraries.

I could sense her watching me as my eyes moved from print to print, lingering on a display of talent I secretly admitted exceeded my expectations. When I returned my gaze to her, her cheeks were pink, her eyes both proud and shy.

'What camera have you been using?'

'A Nikon D50 with a Sigma lens for the most recent, various film Nikons before that.'

'And doing your own darkroom work?'

She grinned. 'In the bathroom. Now it's all computer and Photoshop Elements, upstairs in the spare bedroom. I don't need the full Photoshop suite because all I do is minor stuff. I don't believe in too much manipulation.'

'How d'you back up your files?'

'To a portable hard drive. 80 gigabyte. For temporary stuff I use a couple of one gigabyte memory sticks — flash memory, you know?'

I nodded. 'And what about your qualifications?' I quickly held a hand up as her eyes clouded. 'Not that it matters. I mean, those prints are brilliant, and if they're genuine — ' I broke off, and managed to bite my lip, roll my eyes and shake my head. 'I'm sorry, that really was unforgivable.'

Her gaze was rueful. 'Par for the course as far as interviews go — if that's what this is. Those prints are all my own work, and I went to Bangor Uni but dropped out so I've got no qualifications. But that was my choice, wasn't it? I figured, why waste time? I can do the work, so let the results do the talking.'

'Are you selling many?'

'A lot. Most of them from a market stall

run by a friend of mine. Once or twice I've been asked to take a special photograph, and then I'll charge a bit more.'

'A good policy,' I said 'Never undersell yourself.'

She nodded as if this was old hat, then plucked the tea cosy off the cafetière and poured two coffees with a steady hand. I said yes to milk and sugar, waited until she'd finished, then raised an eyebrow and sprang my surprise.

'Are you free this weekend?'

She paused, the coffee mug on its way to her lips.

'Could be. Depends what for.'

'I was asked to cover a wedding in Chester. I've accepted, but I can't do it on my own.'

Her eyes widened. 'And you want me to assist?'

'No.'

The small frown furrowing her brow told me she was baffled, and I could feel laughter bubbling like champagne.

'Then why tell me?'

'Because *I'll* be assisting you. You'll take all the important photographs — the cars when they arrive, inside the church, outside when it's all over. If I do anything it'll be backup, and possibly some candid shots before the bride leaves home. At the reception it'll be

161

over to you again.' I let all that sink in, then said, 'You'll be working with a Nikon D2Xs.'

'Christ, I've never touched one — never even *seen* one outside a shop or a magazine.'

'Well, if you want to do this you'll have to be an expert by the weekend.'

'And it'll be your camera? Or one of them?'

'Of course. And if things work out, and you stay with Penny Lane Panoramas . . . ' I spread my hands, leaving her to finish it.

She finally got the coffee mug to her lips, sipped, watched me over the rim.

'If you agree to do the wedding,' I said, 'I'll pay you one thousand pounds.'

She choked, almost dropped the mug, then put it down and fumbled for a tissue as hot coffee slopped over her hands. When she'd caught her breath her blue eyes were damp and, as she dabbed at them, I knew she was trying to hide genuine tears of . . . well, disbelief and delight.

'I'll pay you that much,' I said, 'because it's a big wedding. The young lady getting married is the daughter of a man called Ernie Gallagher.'

'Well, I don't know her,' she said, absently dabbing at the pools on the table, 'but I've certainly heard of him. He's a crook, isn't he?'

'Yes, he is. One of his men was shot. Jamie

162

Lynch went to prison for his murder. But you'd know that, of course. Wasn't Jamie your uncle?'

'One of them.'

'Who are the others?'

'They're Lynchs as well. Ray, and Terry. My mother's got unmarried sisters, so it's aunts on her side.' She smiled. 'Ray Lynch was one of the people I took a special picture for. He was delighted. I framed it for him, so he's probably got it on his wall.'

'I know Terry,' I said. 'I spoke to him last night, in his club, Jokers Wild.'

'Is that where you got the bruises?'

I smiled. 'I thought I'd hidden them pretty well.'

'Not bad, except for the eye. And there's not much you can do about that, unless you wear a patch.' She waited. 'So, was it?'

'At the club? No. I got mugged when I was walking back to my car.'

'Tough. What did they get?'

'Nothing. I think the muggers must have been disturbed. They knocked me down, and the next thing I knew I was on my own. Purse untouched.'

'Lucky you. I wish I could say the same for Uncle Terry. I mean, he's no angel, but that doesn't mean he deserves to be robbed.'

'Terry Lynch *robbed*. Who on earth managed that?'

'Well, they've not actually *managed* to get their hands on any cash yet. And when they do, I suppose the bank will cough up.' She looked me straight in the eye. 'See, someone's sneaked into his office and stolen one of his credit cards.'

13

'You may be seeing this commission to photograph a Gallagher wedding as a feather in your cap, cleverly worked infiltration into the enemy camp,' Gareth said, 'but what if it was planned — and not by you?'

'I'm not sure I understand.'

'When's the happy day?'

'Today's Wednesday, the wedding's Saturday — call it two clear days.'

'If you were getting married, would you leave it that late to hire a photographer?'

I looked at Josh. He was at the head of the table, sipping a rich Merlot out of a crystal glass and looking at Joanna, who was looking at Gareth, and looking . . . well . . . smitten. Food had been scoffed, dishes were in the kitchen, and uncountable years ago it might have been the sergeant's mess and Josh would have been sitting in his Number One Dress uniform, *sans* females, and laughing raucously with his fellow NCOs between puffs of an expensive cigar.

But of course — and, in Josh's opinion, almost certainly alas — those times were over. It was me sitting at the foot of the table, not some red-faced drill sergeant, and I was toying with the stem of my wine glass while wondering exactly where Gareth was going.

Still watching Josh, I said, 'What d'you reckon? Do you think I've walked into some kind of trap?'

He pulled a face, and rocked his head from side to side to indicate uncertainty.

'Hard to say. I do think he was cutting it a bit fine. My guess is if you hadn't phoned, Gallagher would have phoned you.'

'With an offer you couldn't resist,' Gareth said.

'But why?'

'For some reason we haven't yet worked out, he wants you to photograph his daughter's wedding.'

'But I don't do weddings. He knows that, because I told him.'

'When?'

'Monday afternoon.'

'Didn't that strike you as odd? The request to photograph a wedding coming from a man named Gallagher, only hours after you'd discovered a dead body linked to his main rival?'

I sighed. 'Yes, I see what you mean. It would have done, if the name had meant anything. At the time, it didn't. Now it does — and you've got me worried. But I still don't see what this has to do with photography.'

'But that's the whole point,' Gareth said. 'We have absolutely no idea what he wants. Photography may be the last thing on his mind.'

'It's still a bloody marvellous opportunity,' Josh said softly.

'To do a bit of snooping, and to diversify,' I said. 'Yes, it is. And I think the photography part is what's exciting me — anyway, I've taken Annabel on now so I can't very well back out.'

'You've told her?'

I nodded at Gareth. 'This afternoon.'

'Well, you're right about it being a good business opportunity, but you still have to consider the dangers. Knowing the people involved, is it really worth the risk?'

'In view of the latest juicy bit of news,' Joanna said, 'it's one it would be foolish to turn down. I know Terry Lynch was your prime suspect, Penny, but look at him now. A killer's been leaving cards on bodies, and now Lynch's credit card's gone missing. OK, so it may mean nothing, could be a genuine theft and even now someone's down in London's West End maxing out the card. But if it's not, it looks as if our killer is about to point to Lynch as his next victim — and Lynch can't be both victim *and* killer.'

Gareth was looking uncomfortable.

'Next but one victim,' he said. 'According to precedent, Lynch's card will be left on my dead body.'

'God, will you listen to yourself,' Joanna said, impulsively reaching across the table to grasp the solicitor's hand. 'Your life's been threatened, yet still you talk like a bloody lawyer.'

'I am a lawyer, it's me he's targeting,' Gareth said, 'and I can understand why. I was defending counsel, and I blew it. But why Terry Lynch? It was Lynch's brother who went down, then had his throat cut in prison. So where's the link? What do Terry Lynch and I have in common that would drive a mysterious killer to murder us?'

'What about Mick Doyle? I can see him wanting Terry Lynch out of the way,' I said, 'but what about you? Have you ruffled Doyle's feathers, incurred his wrath in some way?'

Gareth shrugged. 'Maybe. Doyle might have a record, almost certainly has, but if it was something serious and I was involved I'd remember it — and I don't.'

'The truth is,' Josh said, 'we could rule both those men out and put this whole nasty business down to Ernie Gallagher.'

'Or not,' I said. 'To put it bluntly, we haven't got a clue who's doing what to whom.'

I finished my wine, nodded when Josh waggled the decanter and, as he came around the table to pour, I turned again to Gareth.

'What about the police? If this wedding turns out to be nothing more than church bells and confetti, I'm left with Terry Lynch and Mick Doyle. Are Dancer and his boys thinking along the same lines?'

'If they are, they're not saying. I know they've interviewed just about everybody in sight — and that includes Ryan Sharkey, who was in the wrong place at the wrong time.'

'As was I,' I said, thoughtfully touching my bruised cheek.

'But was he?' Joanna said. 'In the wrong place, I mean. Apart from our feisty PI there, Sharkey is the only person we can definitely place within touching distance of a dead body. And from what I've heard, he's certainly crazy enough to put killing on his CV.'

'But nowhere near clever enough for this kind of vicious campaign,' I said, 'and you're talking to someone who's been close enough to meet his vacant gaze.'

'Ah, well now,' Gareth said, 'that, you see, is where you're wrong.'

Josh is the kind of man who hates his wife to be tied up in the kitchen on evenings when we're entertaining guests — if you see what I mean. Me, well, I'm happy to go along with his wishes, so in a superb Ercol buffet type thing we keep crockery carefully chosen so that no matter what meal comes through the back door all packaged and wrapped and piping hot, we've got the dishes to suit.

Tonight it had been Chinese from the local takeaway. The various greasy little packages were craftily delivered via garden gate and kitchen door, silently unwrapped, and the spicy delicacies carried through by Josh and served from and into decorative Oriental dishes bought at a Barnardos charity shop for thirty quid. Joanna, bless her, insisted on praising poor exhausted me as if I'd spent the entire afternoon toiling over a wok.

Gareth looked puzzled. But then, he had his mind on other things.

And so did I. Minutes after he'd dropped his intriguing statement into a pool where confusion and indecision were threatening to sink I led the way through to a warm conservatory lit by candles and a rising full moon and served coffee actually made by me and we sat in wicker chairs to nibble after dinner mints and, with a little clearing of the throat, I got back to business.

★   ★   ★

'So, what exactly did you mean, Gareth? Are you saying Ryan Sharkey is no fool?'

'Sharkey is a university graduate with a black belt in Karate.'

'Well, according to Doyle he lives in a garden shed and eats Pedigree Chum on toast.' I faked a shudder. 'He also works in Jokers Wild for his brother-in-law, Terry Lynch.'

'Does he?'

'Work for Lynch? Well, I saw him carrying glasses, so I assumed — '

He grinned. 'You know what they say: to assume makes an 'ass of u and me'.'

'Very clever. But if I'm wrong, what *was* he doing?'

'Gambling. Drinking. Passing the time until the witching hour when he could change into his walking-out clothes.'

'Which are?'

'Depends on his mood.' There was a glint of amusement in his eyes as he watched me. 'Most nights it would be a tight dress and stiletto heels. Liberal applications of foundation, blusher, glossy lipstick. False eyelashes long enough to cause a draught.'

'Dear God,' I said softly. 'If that's what he was planning when I saw him, a shave would have come first.'

Josh and Joanna had been listening with interest. Now Josh leaped in with a question for Gareth.

'You seem to have proved Sharkey *could* be clever enough to be the brains behind the murders — but where's his motive? I mean, what else do you know about the man?'

'Very little,' Gareth said ruefully.

'But we do know for certain that he was there with Joey Farrell's body,' Joanna reminded us.

'Which has to make him a suspect,' I said. 'Still waters run deep — or something like that.'

'Never judge a book by its cover,' Josh suggested, and toasted me with his glass when I glared.

Then the phone rang.

The handset was in my office. I was nearest. I scraped back my chair, hurried through kitchen, lounge and hall, snatched the phone up on the fifth ring and said a hasty 'Hello?'

Heavy breathing. Then:

'Annabel's a nice-lookin' kid,' a male voice said, so softly I had to strain to hear. 'But next time you talk to her, ask her who was paid to open Sebastian Tombs's door so his killer could walk in.'

14

'The voice wasn't disguised, but that doesn't mean I recognized it,' I said. 'Liverpool accent, definitely, male and not young — but after that I'd be guessing.'

'What about the message?'

'Annabel *is* nice-looking. But the whole time I was talking to her I saw no sign of wickedness in those clear blue eyes. She's not just nice, deep down I know she's *good* — and one anonymous phone call isn't going to change my mind.'

'Not many things can,' Josh said, 'but your big fault is you're an old softy. If you take a liking to someone you see nothing but goodness and completely ignore obvious signs to the contrary.' He hesitated. 'No, not ignore. Overlook — and always deliberately.'

'It's called giving the benefit of the doubt,' I said. 'She deserves that much, at least.'

Josh snorted. 'I hope you're right. She's now working for you. If there was any truth in the phone call, you could be in danger.'

'Why?'

'Because if she helped a killer once, she could do it again.'

'Yes, but she didn't approach us. You mentioned I might be diversifying into wedding photography, and if I did I'd need an assistant. Then *I* arranged to see *her*.'

'Doesn't matter who did the approaching and the arranging. When I'm writing a crime book, my characters often move in unexpected and independent ways. Same could happen here. We approach Annabel Lee, and she sees possibilities. Your caller told you she was paid to open Tombs's door, and now we pop up and another door opens, this time for her.'

I was sitting up in bed applying expensive anti-ageing skin cream that after two months' use had made me look no younger. Josh was sitting on my stool, his back to the dressing-table, eyeing me like someone watching a clumsy plasterer trying to fill cracks.

Soon after the mysterious phone call, our two guests had left in Gareth's Mercedes C200. Josh and I waved them off, then returned to sit in the conservatory ignoring everything criminal as we finished off the third bottle of wine — the third between four of us over a couple of hours, in case you're wondering. Gradually we had slipped down until we were almost horizontal in our cushioned wicker chairs. The feeling was of floating weightlessly in warm moonlight. Then, as if by magic, sleep had become an irresistible siren call to bodies made lethargic by excellent food and drink — no, age doesn't come into it — and when Josh had locked up we drifted silently hand in hand along the shadowy hall to the bedroom.

Now, the delightful Annabel Lee stubbornly refused to go away. By the time I'd finished plastering the cracks, I knew why.

'I don't know if you're right or wrong about the girl,' I said, 'but I do think I'm cut out for this work. I'm convinced I could be very good at it.'

'If you mean investigating crime and not dealing with wrinkles,' Josh said, leaving the stool, jettisoning his dressing-gown and slipping into bed, 'where are the results to justify your confidence?'

'Bugger results, for now,' I said elegantly. 'They'll come to me the way one of your plots unravelled, because I know I have the knack. The challenge gives me a buzz, and I'm intrigued by the puzzle.'

'For intrigued, read baffled.'

'No. Sod off. I've already got three suspects, I'm about to invade the premises of a possible fourth — '

'And you've been infiltrated by a fifth-columnist, Annabel Lee.'

'If you're right, what can she do to disrupt? Gallagher already knows I'm on my way.'

'More to the point, what can *you* do? You're going to storm a known criminal's premises armed with a camera. Approved access will be to those areas occupied by the bride-to-be. Even if you could sneak into Ernie Gallagher's study, what do you hope to find?'

'Evidence. Clues.'

Lying back on his pillow, Josh grinned.

I punched his arm.

'All right, so I don't know. And maybe this jaunt has nothing to do with crime and a whole lot to do with earning money to keep a mid-list writer in the manner to which he's accustomed — and don't you dare bloody laugh. Anyway, whatever the reasons, it's my first stab at wedding photography.'

Josh chuckled. Then grimaced.

'What?'

'I thought stab was a funny word to use, after what's happened. Sort of amusing, an unintentional pun. Then I thought, no, maybe that's not it at all, maybe it's you being prescient. Maybe something bad is going to happen.'

'Oh, come on.'

'No, seriously. I know we've been joshing around — and, yes, that's an *intentional* pun — but what you're doing is dangerous. With a capital D. Remember going to Jokers Wild, and what happened later in that entry? Christ, your eye's still bloodshot, the bruise is positively glowing through that thick layer of grease — '

'Thin film of cream — '

'And even knowing the deadline you were unable to prevent a murder. Now Gareth's under sentence of death. If you're so good, shouldn't you be hunting for the man who planted the card bearing his name?'

'Not a name, a picture that might or might not be pointing at Gareth. And I am. Hunting that man. That's why I'm photographing the Gallagher wedding.'

'It's a shot in the dark.'

'All right, Mister Crime Writer, then what do you suggest? The wedding's Saturday. Tomorrow's Thursday. What can I do in those two days?'

'I don't know. I'm worried. While you're pratting around — '

'Now just you hang on a minute — '

'All right, so that was unkind — '

'Chauvinistic — '

'And completely wrong. Yes. I'm sorry. But while you're out there doing your best to find the killer, what d'you think he's doing?'

'I hadn't thought about it. Planning the next, I suppose.'

'And looking for you. Or at least keeping a very close eye on what you're doing.'

'You think so?' My voice had turned into a mild squeak. I tried clearing my throat.

'They were six steps ahead of you at Jokers Wild,' Josh said softly. 'Your camera was nicked. The memory card was changed. It was used to photograph the man whose life you were rushing to save.'

'I know. I've thought of that.' I sighed. 'But I meant what I said. I like this work. If the challenge gives me a buzz, then the danger makes me go all tingly — and that's not a bad feeling.'

I reached for his hand. He grasped it, my big, lean strongman of fifty-eight who in his imagination fancies his chances in a bar-room brawl, and I knew he was feeling all masculine and protective and in that instant I got a premonition and I knew that before I'd solved this as yet unfinished spate of killings, Josh's strength — his true strength, not the testosterone thingy and the bulging muscles — was going to come in handy. But not yet. What I needed now was some kind of an investigative map with an unerring compass pointing me in the right direction; some scribbled notes offering an inexperienced but enthusiastic PI several options . . .

'Two days, Josh,' I said, dropping my voice

a couple of tones to add power. 'I'm seeing Annabel Lee to talk cameras, but that will take minutes and the rest is time wasted unless . . . Come on. Give me a bloody clue.'

'Well,' he said, gravely dropping *his* voice a couple of tones which threatened to send us off into fits of giggling, 'you said you've got three suspects, but so far you've only spoken to two. I think you should go and talk to Ryan Sharkey.'

He was right. Obvious really. So of course, I did. But that was late the next morning, and in the wee small hours in between with the moon peeping in through a gap in the curtains, Josh got a lot of that thick grease he'd mentioned transferred from my face to his. Now, come on, think about it. Even an amateur PI like me, with little experience, could work out how that happened.

15

Day Four — Thursday 21 September

The next morning, early, Josh hopped aboard the Range Rover and set off for the fitness centre in track suit and trainers to do his twenty lengths. I phoned Annabel Lee, caught her tucked up in bed (alone, she pointed out), and arranged for her to call round that evening to talk about top-of-the-range Nikons and wedding photography. And a small matter of her dishonesty, a sensitive topic I tactfully didn't mention.

Then I phoned Adam, at home.

'Ryan Sharkey,' I said. 'Where can I find him, how do I get in touch? I've heard he eats dog meat and lives in a shed, so what can you tell me that might help me avoid contracting rabies and dropping clangers.'

'For a start, your information's wrong.'

'Which bit?'

'He owns a flat at the Albert Dock and eats in expensive restaurants. He's a professional gambler, Mum. Very successful.'

'I'm surprised. Gareth Owen seems to believe he cross dresses, and the little solicitor's usually accurate, and truthful.'

'Not this time. Sharkey once turned up at a fancy-dress ball dressed as Madonna, and looked ravishing. A one off, but I suppose people have long memories.'

'More of the snide comments on his character came from Mick Doyle. Why would *he* want to blacken Sharkey's name?'

'Because Sharkey's linked by marriage to Terry Lynch. That makes him an untouchable.'

'But Doyle *works* for Lynch, at Jokers Wild.'

'And at Lynch's other clubs. Doesn't mean he has to like him. It's a paying proposition; he almost certainly conspires with the managers to help skim profits.'

'OK, so if Sharkey is solvent and successful, why call him the Hermit?'

'Look it up. It goes way back to when it meant an early Christian recluse. Now it simply means someone who lives alone — which Sharkey does.'

'Right. And, as you're an ace journalist with your finger on the pulse, you can give me an address and telephone number.'

I heard him tapping at a keyboard. Silence. Then he gave me the information which I scrawled on a Post-it.

'Why d'you want to see Sharkey?'

'He's a suspect in a murder enquiry.'

I put the phone down to a squawk that sounded like a cat with its tail trapped.

Then I phoned Ryan Sharkey.

★ ★ ★

My Ka had been returned the previous evening with four new tyres, and less than an hour after my phone call I was parking it in the residential area of Liverpool's Albert Dock. Sharkey had told me I'd need to be buzzed in. I located his number, pressed the right button, and was whizzed up to what seemed like a very high roof in a lift that was all panelled wood, soft carpet and perfume.

The interior of his flat made the luxurious lift look like the garden shed he was supposed to live in.

'Impressive,' I said, walking ahead of him from tiny entrance hall to a living-room like Wimbledon centre court kissed by the morning sun.

'Opulent but tasteful,' he said, watching my reaction. 'Classy but understated.'

'Couldn't put it better.' I cocked my head. 'I'm Penny Lane; I know you're Ryan Sharkey, but you look . . . different.'

The black draped suit from Jokers Wild had gone and he was dressed in baggy fawn

183

lounging pants and a dark green singlet. He was still as knobbly as a yokel's stick, but the sleeveless vest made it clear that a lot of the odd shape was down to his highly developed musculature — someone less refined than me might call it beefcake, and be apt to drool.

Amusement lurked in his eyes. He waved me to a plush recliner, sat down opposite me with his sleek black hair highlighted by sunlight streaming at an angle through French windows that opened onto a small balcony overlooking the river.

'So, what do you want with me, Penny Lane?'

'What would you say if I told you I was planning an article on professional gamblers?'

'I'd start by talking to you about standard poker games like Five-Card Draw, Five-Card Stud with Joker, then move on to Seven-Card Stud variations like Betty Hutton — where nines and fives are wild — or Doctor Pepper where the wild cards are tens, twos and fours. There's also Baseball and Football — '

'Actually, I'm here to pick your brains. You found a dead body, so did I. That makes us ghoulish soul mates. I thought we might share secrets.'

'My pleasure.' He grinned. 'But first, let's share a drink.'

He swung lithely out of his chair and

padded to a cocktail cabinet where he tinkled ice into two champagne glasses and filled them from a bottle of Sheridan's coffee layered liqueur. He handed one to me, and sat down. White over black; the taste, when I sipped, was like up-market Bailey's dusted with the finest Brazilian ground coffee.

'It's said to be delicious with hot percolated coffee,' he said, 'but I can't be arsed.'

'Indolent.' I said. 'And a bit of a poseur.'

He chuckled. 'So what's this about secrets?'

'I found a dead body and made a bad mistake. I'm trying to put that right by solving the crime, but I'm nowhere close and the bodies are piling up.'

'Why come to me?'

'After Lynch and Doyle, you're my only suspect.'

'Straight to the point. OK, so what you're saying is I didn't find Farrell's body, I murdered him. If I murdered Farrell, I must have murdered Tombs, and Humphreys. And you want a confession to ease your conscience.'

'The truth is, I don't know what I'm saying. That's why I talked of picking brains.'

'What about my sister, Ffion? I'm unlikely to have murdered her, and if I didn't, why would I murder the others?'

'Are you saying Ffion's death is connected?'

He played with his glass, tinkling the ice.

'Not necessarily.' He dipped his finger into the liqueur, tasted it, and said, 'Do you know the full story?'

'Starting where? With the drive-by shooting?'

'Which led to a prison sentence for Jamie Lynch, yes. Then he was murdered in the prison kitchen. Ffion died next, and that's when the first card was left — you know about those?'

I nodded.

'OK, and that card led to Humphreys, he should have had stowed about his person a little yellow idol' — he winked at me — 'which pointed to Tombs and then, more cryptically, the card on Tombs led to Farrell.'

He was looking thoughtfully into his half-empty glass. I waited. He pursed his lips and I thought I caught an almost imperceptible shake of the head. Then he placed his drink on the coffee table, and looked up.

'So, who's next?'

'Have you heard about the latest card? What was on it?'

He nodded. And, with considerable interest, I wondered how.

'Right, so according to the crude drawing on that card,' I said, 'it's someone Welsh, who wears a lawyer's wig.'

'Logically, that's Gareth Owen, solicitor. Well known in the city. His loss in court put Jamie away for life.'

I nodded. 'Have you any idea what's going on? Is your sister's death a link in the chain? Are we looking at gang killings, or something much more personal?'

'Personal.'

'What makes you say that?'

'Because gangs always kill to impress. In your face. No hiding. The way Jamie Lynch went about it was pure gang warfare — or at least serious trouble between two men involved with gangs. After all the other murders the killer's staying out of sight, so it's been personal all the way.'

'Yes, but why? What brought about the change?'

I'd finished my drink. He took my glass and refilled it, and I tried to recall what I knew about the alcohol content of Sheridan's. While I was doing that — and melting at the taste — Ryan Sharkey topped up his own drink and crossed to the window.

'It has to be Jamie,' he said softly, his back turned. 'It's all down to his death, but if that's true then it leads to one logical conclusion — and that conclusion, when looked at more closely, doesn't make sense.'

He swung round. Took a long drink. Grinned again, the look now ferocious.

'Are you with me?'

'I think so. You're suggesting these murders have been committed to avenge Jamie's death. If they have, then logically Terry Lynch is our mysterious killer — '

'Or Ray.'

I thought quickly and realized that, despite Annabel giving me his name, I'd been ignoring Terry's brother when looking for suspects. I shook my head and grimaced.

'Of course. But anyway, that doesn't change anything. The first victim after Jamie died in prison was Terry's own wife, Ffion, so surely the revenge idea goes out of the window.'

'Not at all. My sister was a tough kid, well capable of arranging a prison hit.'

I nodded, suddenly recalling what Gareth had told me.

'And Jamie used to beat her up, didn't he?'

Sharkey nodded.

'Right, so Ffion arranged Jamie's murder, Terry or Ray found out what she'd done and murdered her — and I suppose that's the bit you believe doesn't make sense: you can't see either of them murdering Ffion?'

'Oh no, that bit's perfectly reasonable. Men like Terry — forget Ray for the moment — if a woman stepped out of line, men like Terry would squash her like they would a bothersome fly.'

'Then what are you talking about? What doesn't make sense?'

'You know what doesn't make sense, you must have talked it over with Gareth and your husband and at least got that far. Look, if Ffion arranged Jamie's murder and paid with her life, why are the killings continuing? OK, I can see why the killer or killers would want to get rid of Sebastion Tombs and Gareth Jones, police surgeon and bungling solicitor who helped put Jamie away — but coming between those two we've got Humphreys and Farrell. What have they done? Where the hell do they fit in?'

'And if we don't know the answer to that,' I said, 'we can't possibly know when or where it will end.'

Sharkey shrugged. There was something in his eyes I couldn't read. As he took my empty glass and carried both over to the cocktail cabinet, I thought back over what he had said. Right in the middle, there was something I'd almost missed.

'You said 'killer or killers', Ryan. D'you think there could be two out there? And I'm not talking about Terry and Ray. I mean two different killers, with two different reasons for doing what they're doing?'

Sharkey nodded. 'I think it's a possibility, don't you? We're looking at one excellent

189

motive, but that one doesn't explain all the deaths. All right, if there's a second killer out there he'll be killing for a different reason, and suddenly everything makes more sense.'

'Mm, I see what you mean. If the first motive covers Ffion, Tombs and Gareth Jones, we're left with Humphreys and Farrell. If we can link those two in some way . . . '

I looked at my watch. Eased myself reluctantly out of the wonderfully relaxing recliner.

Ryan Sharkey grinned.

'Got enough for your gambling article?'

'That's the problem isn't it?' I said as he saw me to the door. 'The only gambling I'm doing is with other people's lives, and I can't seem to get it right.'

We shook hands in parting, which was a bit of a surprise considering my opinion of Ryan Sharkey when I'd first seen him in Jokers Wild, but even when my hand was clasped in his it was his eyes I was watching. I knew there was something I was missing, something of great importance; there was a clear message there I found impossible to read, and all the way from Liverpool back to the Wirral my failure kept popping up to haunt me.

It was to be another thirty-six hours before realization dawned, and by then it was damned near too late.

16

After a quick lunch under the yellow and green parasol on the patio — sliced cheddar and beetroot on buttered Ryvita washed down with fresh orange juice with all the floaty bits that stick in your teeth — Josh and I headed for our respective offices. He'd been tossing up whether to go for a long run, because he'd been too busy to do any training for almost a week and there was now just a month to go before his next marathon with Liverpool Harriers. But crime writing, as he so frequently tells me, fills every waking minute, the subconscious takes over when the eyes close in sleep, and a day's writing missed always leads to another wasted half day spent getting back into the rhythm.

He was reaching the bloody climax of *Dying to Know You*, and was keen to press on.

Me, I just wanted to forget.

Not because I was scared of what I'd missed when gazing into Ryan Sharkey's soulful dark eyes, but because the neatest trick I know for remembering is to concentrate on something else.

So I spent the first half of the afternoon on Penny Lane Panoramas. Several orders had been posted on my website, and I responded to those then located the required files and gathered together what I needed for printing.

Most of my framed prints go to corporate buyers. Private clients tend to buy unframed prints on expensive art paper. I had orders for three of those, all moody landscapes and, curiously, all three orders specified gloss paper rather than the textured kind like that used by watercolour artists. From experience I know I get the best results with a fairly new paper called Chaudigital Da Vinci Fibre Gloss. It has a weight of 300gsm, a coated fibre surface and is absolutely gorgeous. My clients wanted A3+ black and white. On my Epson Stylus Photo R2400 printer I used the advanced mode for warm hues, and by coffee time at three o'clock I had all three large prints set aside to dry.

Josh's door was still closed. I told him what I was doing — in a muted shout, if that's possible — then boiled the water, poured it on Carte Noire instant and headed for the patio.

It was still sunny, but the long range forecast was for rain and I was beginning to worry about the Gallagher wedding. Photographers are always advised to visit the church before the big day and select a number of locations so they're prepared for the vagaries of the British weather. Because of the late commission, I didn't have time — well, I did, but like Ryan Sharkey I couldn't be arsed (sorry) — so I was prepared to wing it, as the Americans say. Or, rather unkindly, I suppose I was being indolent — more of Ryan Sharkey — and happy to leave everything to Annabel Lee.

Of course, when Sharkey and Terry Lynch's niece popped up in my thoughts as soon as I sat down I realized at once that concentrating on other things had done nothing to solve the mystery of what had been lurking behind Ryan's steady gaze. I was no closer to unscrambling the message, and that was the way it remained all through dinner with Josh, cheese and biscuits, coffee, and a couple of delicious After Eights with a glass of tawny port as we sat watching Channel Four news.

When Annabel Lee rang the bell towards eight o'clock, Josh was back in his office and I was close to tearing my hair.

★ ★ ★

I said, 'You didn't go with Sebastian Tombs for sex, did you? You went with him to unlock the door for his killer.'

Her face went white and she had spun on her heel and was heading for my office door before I'd finished speaking.

'Annabel!'

She stopped.

'Why don't you sit down, and explain?'

She was slender in white T-shirt and faded jeans, brown toes poking out of Jesus sandals, blonde hair tousled and eyes wide with fright and a body as taut as piano wire. I was standing by the desk. Too dominating. I sat down. Her breath was released softly. She took the other chair and put her red pack by her feet.

'So what happened? It wasn't . . . what was it you called it, turning a trick? . . . that wasn't the kind of thing Gordon the amateur pimp was arranging at all, was it?'

'No. I made that up.'

'So . . . what was the plan?'

'I was to lead Tombs on. Make him think, Christ, get in there, Toby, it's your birthday — then hold him at arm's length until the booze got to him and he flaked out. Which it did, and he did.' She shrugged. 'Then I just waited. Biting my nails. Soon as I heard a car toot its horn three times — round about eleven o'clock — I left the door ajar and ran down the fire escape.'

'But Gordon did set this up? And you don't know who for?'

She shook her head.

'And afterwards? You didn't see anybody? Didn't hide somewhere and wait to see who came up the stairs?'

She shook her head.

'I suppose what I mean is, you can't identify the killer?'

Again the shake. This time accompanied by a look of horror.

'God, no! Instructions were to listen for the signal, then bugger off sharpish.'

'All right.' I shrugged. 'That's it. I believe you.'

'Really?'

'Of course. You've told me the truth.'

'Right.' The speed of my acceptance had knocked her sideways. The white face had turned pink. Her blue eyes were moist. 'I . . . I really had no idea what was going on. I thought, I don't know, I suppose I thought someone wanted to talk to Tombs, like he owed money or something. Then, afterwards, I lied to you and Josh because, Christ, I was devastated when I heard what had happened. The poor man had been *stabbed*. So I figured if I stuck to a made-up story, if *nobody* knew the truth, then the police couldn't find out — '

'You did nothing wrong, Annabel. If you hadn't opened the door, the killer would have knocked. When Tombs didn't answer the knock, the killer would have forced his way in. Looked at that way, it was daft of them to involve you at all.'

'Yeah,' she said softly. 'I thought of that. Got a bit worried in case there was more to it. Something I wasn't seeing.'

'No. You're safe. Because I think it was the *killer* playing safe. I haven't worked out the details, but I think he must have waited to see you leave. When you came down the fire escape as planned, he knew the coast was clear.'

She nodded slowly. 'Right. And with that done and dusted and safely behind us, now it's down to business?'

'Definitely.'

'Brilliant.' She smiled happily. 'This, the photography bit, it's a dream come true. I won't, definitely *won't* let you down.'

'Going by the prints I saw on your walls, you're likely to show me up.'

'As if.'

I was talking and listening while delving into my tall cupboard. When I came away holding two Nikon D2Xs digital SLR bodies her eyes were wide again, this time with wonder.

'If you've been using a D50,' I said, placing the cameras on the desk, 'this one will be a doddle. It's got the same 3D-Color Matrix metering, same exposure modes but twice the number of pixels which gives excellent prints up to A3+ size.' I paused to let her take that in, then added, 'It's also got a top ISO of 3200.'

Her eyebrows shot up. 'Wow! I can shoot in low light without flash.'

'Mm. You might need that facility in church because of restrictions on the use of flash. And it'll be good for candid shots outside the bar, or wherever it is they're holding the late night shindig. But flash should be fine for the reception.'

'No problem. I've got a Nikon SB600 Speedlight.'

'Really?'

She glowed. 'I got it on eBay. Really, really cheap.'

'Right, well, I've got another for backup, so we're all set.'

I went back to the cupboard, hunted for a moment then took out a lens.

'This is a Sigma 17-70mm F2.8 macro zoom lens,' I said. 'You know the size of the sensor means the focal length of the lens is magnified?'

'Yeah. If it's like the D50, it's 1.5 times.'

197

'That's right. It does go up to two times in what's called highspeed crop mode, but that's only of interest to sports photographers, so forget it. The point I'm making is that the lens becomes, in effect, a 34-110mm, which gives you *just* enough room for the group shots at the wide-angle end, and at the long end reduces distortion and produces flattering portraits. Or am I teaching my grandmother?'

I don't know if she knew the old saying but I saw her smile as, head down, she played with the camera. She looked at me and pulled a face when she felt the weight of the body and lens, but when she saw the size of the monitor, switched on and began to run through the menus, she became totally absorbed.

I went round the desk, dipped into the drawer and came up with the A4 sheet I'd printed before she arrived. Most people, even if they've never held a camera, know what photographers do at weddings, so I'd kept everything simple. Common sense, really. The list began with bride getting out of car, bride on father's arm, bride walking down the aisle . . . you know the sort of thing. Anyway, I got that far, just glancing through the list, when I found myself wondering what kind of young woman I would see walking down the aisle on the arm of a known villain. How she would feel? How I would feel, knowing what I was investigating? Knowing that I had taken this assignment because I was looking on the bride's father as a possible suspect in a murder case?

And when at last I looked up, the paper limp in my hand and my mind miles away, Annabel Lee was watching me.

'You might be surprised.'

'Mm?'

'Ernie Gallagher. That's what you were thinking. About him, and Diane, his daughter.'

'Was I?'

'Yeah. I know I said he was a crook, but that's just what I've heard. Mostly about the past. So, you know, take no notice of what I said, just wait until you meet him.'

'This is my first wedding.' I smiled. 'Our first wedding. I think we've a right to be nervous.'

'You looked scared stiff.'

'Apprehensive. About the wedding, yes, but not about Gallagher. And I suppose I've been worrying all day about another matter. Something sparked by a man I met called Ryan Sharkey.'

Annabel rolled her eyes, yawned and stood up. She had her pack in one hand, the D2Xs in the other. She looked at me. I nodded. She put the camera into the pack as if it was made of thin glass, and slung the pack on her back with care.

'Ryan Sharkey's a Welsh poseur,' she said, on her way to the door.

I smiled. 'Absolutely.'

'But . . . very tasty.' She grinned. 'See you tomorrow?'

'I'll pick you up. Your place at ten thirty.'

'Brilliant.'

★   ★   ★

You've probably experienced one of those nights when you stretch your arms high to let a long soft nightie slide sensuously down your naked body, tumble into bed yawning your head off, turn on your side, snuggle into the pillow with one hand beneath it and curl up so that the hunk behind you can form the other half of a deliciously warm pair of spoons — only to toss and turn for hours as sleep hovers somewhere near the wardrobe like a tantalizing wraith, forever out of reach.

Well, on Thursday night that's exactly what happened, although I probably didn't help matters by phoning Gareth at his home on the outskirts of Chester before I followed Josh through to the bedroom. The plump solicitor was philosophical, but clearly not his normal chipper self.

I decided to cheer him up.

'I've been to see Ryan Sharkey,' I said. 'He, too, believes the card left on Farrell is pointing towards a Welsh solicitor as next to be murdered.'

'Yes, and at this very moment that solicitor is in a blue funk and writing his last will and testament which you and Joanna will witness — '

'Gareth!'

'Only joking. Well, half. Actually my will was signed and sealed ages ago and I'm in bed sipping Laphroaig on the rocks and reading Dale Carnegie's *How to Win Friends and Influence People.*'

I chuckled. 'And Ryan Sharkey is a gambler so he's probably in the back room at Jokers Wild making a book on your chances.'

'I think he's more than that. Mere gambler. An interesting character, our Ryan.'

He paused, and I knew he'd be remembering his reference to cross-dressing, and the very different reality that would have met my eyes at the Albert Dock.

With a slight tremor in his voice he said, 'Did he come up with anything useful — like, the name of the killer?'

'I wish. We more or less went over old

ground. But he did raise the possibility of there being two killers with different agendas. When you think about it, and given what we know, it's about the only way to explain the killing of Humphreys and Farrell.'

'Good point. I'll talk to my brother, see if the police are working along those lines.'

'Amongst other things. Have they spoken to you yet? They warned Humphreys when he was targeted, offered him protection. What about you?'

'Oh yes. Dancer came to the office this afternoon to give me the good news, but carefully avoided any mention of protection. I'm a defence lawyer, Penny, the nasty man in gown and wig who rips apart the evidence given by fine upstanding police officers and gets the accused acquitted.'

'Except,' I said, 'in the case of Jamie Lynch.'

'Yes, well, thank you, Penny Lane, and goodnight.'

Was I being tactless? Not really. Beating about the bush never really does any good, does it, and Gareth seemed to understand that because we spoke for a little while longer then closed the phone conversation with me sensing that he was a little more cheerful.

But when I did pad along the passage to join Josh in bed, that Thursday night really did turn out to be interminable.

I knew I was untroubled by personal problems, because in the first place I haven't got any and in the second place that's the way I work it: nothing of any consequence, financial or otherwise, is ever allowed to enter my mind during the hours of darkness — and particularly the wee small hours, in bed, after midnight — because time spent staring into space and worrying inevitably sees the cold dawn arrive with nothing changed except my appearance, which will have aged.

Yet sleep refused to come. It didn't take me long to realize that Ryan Sharkey's problem had become my problem, but because I had nothing more to go on than the tall gambler's preoccupation with disturbing thoughts as he gazed into his Sheridan's liqueur and the look in his eyes when I left him at the door, my brain was operating in a vacuum. Also, it was pretty obvious that I was scratching around looking for clues that would help me to solve multiple murders when the poor man I had walked away from at the Albert Dock could have been dwelling on nothing more than his next appointment with the dentist, or whether to fly to Europe with easyJet or Ryanair.

In the end, of course, what happened the next morning suggested that my concern had nothing to do with Ryan Sharkey but had been feminine intuition warning me that trouble was about to come a-knocking. And, strangely, even that intuition — if that's what it had been — turned out to be well wide of the mark.

Josh left for his morning swim at 7.30 and I was munching toast in a conservatory that was as sultry as a rain forest and looking with concern at the overcast skies when the doorbell rang.

Way too early for the postman, and anyway it didn't ring twice. No clink of bottles, so that ruled out the milkman. As I trotted to the door in bath-robe and fluffy slippers I thought it might be DI Dancer, but the shadow seen through the glass panels was much too bulky and when I opened the door I was confronted by a giant of a man in a broad-brimmed Aussie stockman's hat, plaid shirt and jeans, with gold gleaming at thick neck and wrists and a beard that immediately reminded me of Burl Ives.

'Hi,' he said, grinning. 'My name's Ernie Gallagher. Is the coffee on?'

17

Day Five — Friday 22 September

I left him in the kitchen sipping Carte Noire at the breakfast bar while I scooted into the bedroom and threw on jeans and a loose shirt. When I returned he'd switched on the strip light under the wall cupboards because the increasingly lowering skies were turning early Friday morning into a sort of yellow dusk. The effect was disturbing. Bright light was hitting him from an unusually low angle so that Burl Ives had become evil Eli Wallach from *The Good, the Bad and The Ugly*. Eyes that were hooded green slits glowed and danced with life. The heels of his booted feet were hooked on the stool's rail, and in the fading light and with the use of not too much imagination he might have been sitting in a smoky booth in a New York gin mill or on a high stool at a redneck joint in downtown Baton Rouge where topless girls danced listlessly on the scuffed bar top.

He wasn't. He was in my kitchen, Josh was not due back from the fitness centre for at least another hour, and this was a man I suspected of being a serial killer.

'You're wrong,' he said. 'About me.'

I ignored him, walked through to the conservatory for my cold coffee, came back and topped it up. Then I sat down on a stool a good way to his left, and frowned.

'Care to explain that remark?'

'Listen, the game I'm in — was in — missin' a trick can be fatal. So I've got fellers who keep me informed. I knew about you almost as soon as you dialled those three nines from the beach, and I guarantee I've been followin' your thinkin' ever since an' I know *exactly* where you're up to — and, like I said, you're wrong.'

He might have lived in Chester but his accent was pure Toxteth — if that's not an oxymoron.

'All I *know* about you,' I said, 'is that tomorrow morning I'm photographing your daughter's wedding.'

'Bollocks.' Then he cocked his head, mentally replaying my words, noting the emphasis. 'OK, so you don't *know*. But you've hit a brick wall and so you're beginnin' to *think* it's me behind Jamie Lynch's death in prison, Ffion Lynch's murder, and all the other killings — right?'

'Not yet I don't. I've kept an open mind.

But tomorrow I intend to kill two birds with one stone.'

'Yeah. Like I thought. Which is why I'm here. Saturday mornin' I want the air clear. My little girl's getting married, an' I don't want a wanabee private dick wanderin' round asking questions.'

'That was never my intention.'

'No? All right, how about takin' photographs of Diane, in *my* house, then losin' your way an' endin' up in *my* office? With a bloody big camera.'

'What a good idea,' I said, smiling. 'Do make sure you leave something out that's worth snapping.'

'I can think of one thing well worth it, and right now that's where I'm itchin' to put my hands,' he said, his gaze focusing at a point above my collar and below my chin.

'Oh, drink your coffee and shut up, you know this is all hogwash. I'll photograph the wedding and promise to respect your privacy; you'll go on being a villain — '

'Wrong.'

I cocked my head. 'Again?'

'Yeah, because you weren't listenin', were you? — which, for a PI, is not very clever. If you had been listenin' you'd have heard me say 'the game I *was* in'. I'm retired, sweetheart. To stop me from goin' brain dead

I play the stock market, shift my cash around, watch which way the pendulum's swingin' and live on great wads of interest. For leisure I've got a motor cruiser on the Dee at Chester, a boathouse called The Slippery Slope — to remind me not to go back to my old ways — where I keep canoes and kayaks for friends who feel energetic.'

'And you didn't order Jamie and Ffion and those other men killed in retaliation for the shooting of Nicky Nixon?'

'You're jokin'! Nicky was a hanger on, a useless scally not my long lost son. He dissed Jamie Lynch at a rave, and Jamie gettin' rid of him did me a big favour.'

'All right,' I said, 'so as someone who was in a game where it didn't pay to miss a trick, then who *did* murder . . . well, for starters, Jamie Lynch?'

'Think about it. Who did Jamie Lynch like to use as a nice soft punch-bag?'

'Ffion?' I frowned, then realized what he was getting at. 'Oh, come on,' I said softly. 'Are you telling me Terry Lynch had his younger brother murdered?'

'Why not? Ffion ended up as Terry's wife, and she would certainly have been pesterin' him to make Jamie pay for those beatings. And that, trust me, is a more likely scenario than me committin' genocide because Jamie

208

topped one of my lads.'

He sipped his coffee. I tried to picture Ffion in the bedroom with pink rollers in her hair, cream glistening on her face and a bottle of nail polish poised in her hands as she screamed at Terry to do something about Jamie — and it was all so, so plausible. So plausible I really couldn't imagine why I hadn't thought of it. Yet of course I had — or Gareth had — because suddenly I recalled his hinting as much when we talked in his office but somehow it had slipped away from me . . .

'An' then there's Ffion,' Ernie Gallagher said, watching me. 'She nipped off to the Caribbean and married Terry Lynch — and when that happened, who d'you think would've been pissed off?'

'Mick Doyle.'

'Right. And he was close enough to Lynch to've somehow wangled a key to the house. So it's pourin' with rain, right, Lynch is miles away at one of his clubs and Mick Doyle lets himself in when Ffion is tucked up in bed — '

'And then all your theories go pear shaped.'

Gallagher grinned. 'Yeah. Lynch had Jamie killed, Doyle slipped a knife into Ffion when she was asleep — so what's with the mysterious cards, the deaths that come after? Terry Lynch murderin' his kid brother still works, but if Doyle planted the first card, common sense says he planted the others. And went on to murder Humphreys, and Tombs, and Farrell. But why would he do that?'

'I've been through most of this. You're not very helpful, are you?'

'Christ, I didn't come here to do your job. But I have given you some fresh ideas — go on, admit it, Lynch and Doyle are brilliant suspects for two of the murders.' He flapped a hand. 'Anyway, I've said it, but so what? A bunch of villains're goin' round stickin' knives in each other — '

'Tombs was no villain.'

'Yeah, well, all I came here for was to put your mind at rest: *I'm* no killer. Christ, I'm not even a villain; I'm so sweet and cuddly I've got the enemy comin' to the wedding as an honoured guest.' He saw me struggling with that, and said, 'As in Ray Lynch.'

'Terry's brother?'

'Right.' He held a hand out, palm down, and rocked it. 'Not exactly all there, our Ray. You know, like, the lights're on, but there's nobody at home. Anyway, he's comin'. He likes drivin' — in more ways than one, 'cause he's always on the golf course — so I expect he'll come racin' up, tyres screamin' — '

'No Ryan Sharkey?'

Gallagher frowned. 'Why him?'

'Well, he is Ffion's brother, and that makes him Ray's brother-in-law — doesn't it?'

'Yeah, right. An' he hates Ray because he's Terry Lynch's brother; Terry because . . . well, because he's got him where he wants him and Sharkey would do just about anything to get out from under.'

'What does that mean?'

'Lynch has got his balls in a vice. My guess is Sharkey was caught doin' something wrong, a while ago, in Lynch's back room, an' if it's what I think it is and it ever got out . . . ' Gallagher shrugged.

'Mm.' For a moment I mulled over what I took to be a not very subtle hint of shady goings on at Lynch's poker tables, wondered what it gave me and could think only of more ramifications. Hating the Lynchs for whatever reason now gave *Ryan Sharkey* a possible motive for framing Jamie, arranging his murder, *and* for murdering Ffion. But, once again, that left the other unexplainable killings.

'The reason I mentioned the wedding,' I said, 'is because I was talking to Sharkey last night. He looked a bit . . . forlorn. Like there was something terribly wrong in his life and he could do with cheering up.'

I was digging, hoping that Ernie Gallagher

211

could enlighten me further on the problems
— real or imagined, past or present — facing
Ryan Sharkey, and help me get a good night's
sleep. But he was unforthcoming, uninter-
ested. He stood up, I joined him and thought
of mentioning, while on the subject of
relatives, that my assistant was Terry Lynch's
niece. I even had my mouth open to utter the
words when a key rattled in the lock and I
heard the front door open. Josh was back
from his swim, early.

When he walked in, tall and lean in his
track suit, Ernie Gallagher came up with
another surprise.

'Bloody hell, I knew the name but I didn't
connect it with *that* Josh Lane,' he said,
walking forward. 'Long time no see, Josh.'

Josh was clearly puzzled.

'This is Ernie Gallagher,' I said. 'Remember, I'm photographing his daughter's wedding
on Saturday morning?'

Josh took Gallagher's extended hand,
grasped it firmly.

'That's clear enough,' he said, looking into
Gallagher's eyes, 'but where and when did I
know you?'

'Way back,' Gallagher said. 'In the army,
when you were based in Germany. I was in
another squadron, I think we knew each other
by sight, but you were famous. Christ,

212

everyone knew Josh Lane, the corporal whose wife walked out on him when he was demoted, and thrown in Colchester for strikin' a superior officer.'

★ ★ ★

Josh quickly showered and dressed when Ernie Gallagher left, and when he came through looking pink and polished and ever so slightly embarrassed, I had his toast and coffee ready and we sat together at the breakfast bar.

'Did he deserve it? This superior officer?'

'Superior?' His grin was mocking. 'Definitely. In today's parlance, he dissed me.'

'Nothing much has changed.'

'Not likely to, is it? Boys being boys. I was captain of the cross country team and had an off day. We ran against a German team and I didn't finish in the top three. This pipsqueak of a subaltern was orderly officer and he and the orderly sergeant waltzed into the corporal's mess at the wrong time — '

'You were pie-eyed.'

Josh grinned. 'Wrong time, and with the duty sergeant looking anywhere but at me this damned junior officer opened his big mouth. He stood at the bar cackling about me running for Italy, wouldn't leave it alone,

213

and everyone in the army knew what that meant so I floored him.'

'And got what, six months in the glass house?'

'I think in the army they calculated it in days.'

'You never did tell me why Anne left you,' I said. 'I knew she did, that's not been a secret, but was it really because you got — '

'Reduced to the rank of sapper? Lord, no. That might have been the excuse she spread around, but trouble had been brewing for some time. You know the kind of thing. *'How can you say you truly love me if the army always comes first?' 'If you'd really wanted to you could easily have got off all those silly exercises playing soldiers in the woods.' 'I was so silly because Mummy did warn me . . .* ''

He bit savagely into his toast, his eyes registering an emotion somewhere between anger and — even after all this time — sheer disbelief.

I reached across and touched his knee.

'The story about decking an officer does explain a lot, though.'

He squinted at me over his coffee, and shook his head.

'Not really. That incident didn't shape me, Penny, I was already fully formed. It didn't

214

mould my character, it proved a point.'

'Which is?'

'I'm a kitten, always have been, but let someone cross that fine line that's a bit hazy even to me and I'm liable to snap.'

'With dire consequences, you being macho.'

'Definitely.'

'And that's another point you're still out there proving, aren't you? Daily at the pool. Wednesdays with the weights. And in a way I suppose your fictional private eye is you, exaggerated maybe, but — '

'Don't you believe it, kid,' Josh said, narrowing his eyes and twitching a Bogart upper lip. 'If there's anything of me walking those mean streets it's toned down to protect sensitive lady readers like your good self — '

'You're spitting crumbs.'

'Bacall would have sneered, then looked the other way. Anyway, you try eating toast while talking with a lisp.'

I chuckled, then left him sneakily sweeping the breakfast bar with his sleeve and hurried through the conservatory to close the patio doors as rain began spattering the glass. The skies weren't quite so yellow, but the low cloud was unbroken and I knew the rain was in for the day. All right, one day I didn't mind, but two would create major wedding-day problems and I wanted everything to run

215

smoothly for Annabel Lee.

That sounds like me being magnanimous, but actually the real reason was selfish: if everything went right for my talented assistant, then I'd be free to walk around with my camera as an expensive excuse for being nosy. Not, in all seriousness, that I expected to uncover any clues, expose any more suspects, or trip over any more dead bodies. People don't get murdered at weddings, I reasoned, leaving the patter of rain behind me as I walked back into the house.

But that, of course, was me once again being naïve, and a cockeyed optimist to boot.

18

With Josh safely tucked away in his office listening to a slow jazz CD as he worked on his novel, I busied myself in the kitchen while mentally tossing up whether to phone Gareth, or DI Dancer. In the end I did neither. Gareth I had spoken to last night, and as I'd been listening to Radio Merseyside off and on during the morning and no news is good news I had to believe he was still alive. Wow, is that mild little me talking? I can't *believe* how I'm changing. Anyway, Gareth was safe (fingers crossed); DI Dancer was unlikely to tell me how the investigation was going, and as I had got no concrete evidence to pass on to him there was little point in picking up the phone.

I had suspicions, of course, and I suppose suspicions can be called leads and be valuable to the police. But I was faced with the certainty that my suspicions about Lynch, Doyle, Gallagher and now Ryan Sharkey had been obvious to investigating officers from the start, and to tell Dancer that I was still poking my nose into a murder enquiry would see me splashing helplessly in hot water. That

I didn't want. Even though, if I tried to think, I felt swamped by suspects and bogged down in a mire of complications, I was still getting a big kick out of investigating a string of horrible murders.

Sounds awful, doesn't it? But it was true, and justified — to me at least — because I was confident that quite soon I would find the killer or killers. Or they would find me. Ugh!

Wary of falling between two stools, I tried to concentrate on one thing at a time and began by gathering together my equipment for the forthcoming wedding. I knew that many wedding photographers still back up their work with a film camera — taking every shot twice — but I didn't see the point. We — Annabel and I — would be toting two high-end digitals, we both had an Epson P-5000 80-Gigabyte portable storage device to back up the image files from camera memory cards, and downloading to my laptop would provide family and guests with instant feedback. Which means they could see the photographs almost as soon as they were taken, and I could begin taking orders for prints not long afterwards.

The packing was reduced, of course, because Annabel had taken one camera body and lens. Preparation came down to nothing more than loading everything into my medium-sized Crumpler camera bag — not forgetting the Nikon Speedlight flash, an extra 1 gigabyte memory card and a spare battery — and I was done.

Still determined not to think too deeply about Ryan Sharkey, once a suspect, then a deeply troubled man and now, after Gallagher's visit, back to being suspect again but with a very strong motive, I prepared lunch and called Josh out of his den. That light meal took up a pleasant hour, Josh returned to work and I settled on the settee in the living-room with a pile of *Professional Photographer* magazines in which I knew there were pages of high quality wedding photographs. Nothing like filching good ideas from the experts.

Not long after two I must have fallen asleep, sprawled in ungainly fashion on the cushions. Josh woke me at three with a juicy kiss on the lips followed by coffee and biscuits, and we sat and chatted until almost four. Actually, most of that was Josh talking through the current stage of *Dying to Know You*, a regular routine that always helps him to unravel complicated plot problems. After that, pleased that the day was almost over, I again ruthlessly pushed Ryan Sharkey out of my mind and concentrated on updating my website while Josh jumped in the Ka and drove into Heswall for necessary supplies: six bottles of wine, and a bottle of the Sheridan's liqueur I'd so much enjoyed at Ryan Sharkey's.

Damn. Him again. The lean mean gambler just *wouldn't* go away.

And this time, he'd returned to stay.

I had been staring at a monochrome portrait on the screen. The male figure's eyes had brooded on dark secrets, and suddenly I was back in the doorway of the Albert Dock flat looking up at Ryan Sharkey as I left and the message in his eyes came to me in a flash, hitting me so hard I jerked upright in front of the computer with pins and needles prickling my scalp. My stomach churned. Thoughts ran wild.

DI Dancer had mentioned Ffion Sharkey, *a pretty Welsh girl who came over the border and got in with the wrong crowd.* If Ryan Sharkey had a Welsh sister, wouldn't that make him Welsh too? Indeed, hadn't Annabel opined that Ryan Sharkey was *a Welsh poseur?* Then my son Adam informed me that although Ryan Sharkey didn't cross dress, he once went to a fancy dress ball dressed as Madonna — and for that I knew he must have worn a wig. Why am I rabbiting on about Welsh and wigs? Because, if you remember, the card left on Joey Farrell by his killer had pointed to someone Welsh who wore a wig as his next victim, and everyone had been assuming he meant Gareth Owen, the cute little bewigged solicitor.

But if I looked beyond Gareth, I was left with just one conclusion.

I stood up, literally shaking, appalled by my stupidity.

Ryan Sharkey wasn't a suspect, he was back where he had been when I watched him walk out of Jokers Wild. Ryan Sharkey, gambler and poseur, was soon about to die.

But not if I could help it.

19

'Call the police.'

'I've been told to butt out.'

'Wasn't there a suggestion — warning — to phone Dancer if something comes up?'

'Yes — but has it? This could be me making up improbable stories. Anyway, it was Gareth who told me about the latest card, he got it from Ffion and I'm not supposed to know about it.'

'All right, phone Sharkey.'

'I have. I told you. He's out — and there's no answering machine.'

It was seven o'clock, we were at the dinner table with table lights glowing yellow in three corners of the room and the rain a gentle patter heard through the open window. Josh had taken some time doing the essential shopping and I had paced the floor after leaving the office, trying to decide what to do. Now, with the late summer's evening strangely murky and muggy under heavy skies and my mind bogged down in a quagmire of imponderables, I was staring moodily into my Chilean Merlot and not doing very well — as Josh would have put it

— at extracting my digit.

'If you can't make up your mind,' Josh said at last, 'how about this? As you know, I've got a meeting at Liverpool Harriers on Mather Avenue at nine. I can stop off at the Albert Dock, and depending what the situation is, we then play it by ear.'

I brightened at once.

'You don't mind?'

'Well, I think you should phone the police, but . . . ' He shrugged.

'If Sharkey's not at home,' I said, 'I could go with you to the Harriers. If he is, I could stay and talk to him for a while and you could pick me up on the way back.'

'And if the police are there, at yet another crime scene — ' He held up his hands. 'Sorry. That really wasn't very funny.'

'I'll forgive you,' I said, 'if you can be ready in fifteen minutes.'

He was.

★   ★   ★

We parked some way away from Ryan Sharkey's flat in the Albert Dock's residential area and, knowing from my first visit roughly where the gambler's windows were located, I led Josh around to the river side of the building and peered high up into the gloom to the topmost of the stacked balconies. Sharkey's living-room light was on — I was almost certain.

'There,' I said, pointing, and Josh grunted.

'Means nothing. Do killers turn out the light?' He grinned at me. 'How's that for the title of a book?'

I punched him hard on the arm and, bathed in amber sodium lighting, we walked back through rain that had now turned to a fine drizzle. I was wearing a light blue waterproof jacket, Josh something similar in navy — I think they were both by North Face, something like that. When we had almost reached the heavy timber main door of the block a tall man stepped out of the shadows, coming away. My heart flipped.

'That's Terry Lynch,' I whispered, and grabbed Josh's arm.

Had I heard the door close? Could I be sure Lynch had been inside? Did he have a weapon tucked inside the short mac he was wearing — which would mean we were probably too late? Out of the corner of my eye I watched him walk past, with an involuntary shiver felt his gin-pale gaze wash over me like iced water as he hurried towards a silver car.

'Now what?' I said, once again dithering indecisively.

'Ring the bell.'

I did. Something clacked inside a little grille in the brickwork close to my ear. I realized it was a speaker. Then a familiar voice whispered to me.

'Yes, who is it?'

I closed my eyes, leaned into Josh's warmth and strength.

'Ryan, it's Penny. Are you all right?'

'Sure. Why not?'

'Let me in. We need to talk.'

I thought he wasn't going to; if he really was in danger, he would be expecting trickery. Then, after a moment, a buzzer sounded. I tentatively pushed the door and it clicked and swung open. I looked at Josh.

'OK?'

'I am. What about you?'

I worried my lower lip with my teeth, then nodded. 'You shouldn't be more than an hour and a half. Nothing can happen to me while Sharkey's there' — I shook my head impatiently at his raised eyebrows — 'but I've got my mobile and if I do need you . . . '

'That's me you hear breaking down the door.'

He smiled encouragement, leaned down and kissed my wet face — and then he was gone, walking towards the Range Rover with his head ducked against the fine rain.

I opened Sharkey's front door and pressed the button for the classy lift.

★ ★ ★

'What did he want?'

'What did *who* want?'

I took a deep breath of relief, let it out explosively.

'He didn't come in, did he? Josh and I must have disturbed him. He was going to ring the bell, *going* to wangle his way in under some pretext, but we arrived and he about turned and hurried away.' I smiled brightly. 'Gosh. We actually saved your life.'

He pursed his lips, rocked his head from side to side as if debating whether to call the men in white coats, then smiled.

'I'll pour the drinks, you sit down and get your mind in gear. When I come back you can tell me who didn't come in and how, by preventing him coming in, you saved my life. Fair enough?'

I nodded.

He moved to the cocktail cabinet and I swung one of the easy chairs to face the patio doors leading to the small balcony, sat down and looked at the distant lights of the Wirral fragmented into a million glittering shapes by the raindrops running down the glass. My

226

home was out there. Near enough to touch, impossible to reach. Was that the way it was to be with the villains I was hunting without much success? Were *they* close, closer than I could possibly imagine — unseen yet close enough to be dangerous? I thought of Josh's Range Rover, tyres hissing on the wet roads as it purred towards the Geoffrey Hughes Memorial Ground where the Harriers train; felt the first ache of loneliness, the sudden prickling of the skin at the realization that I was alone with a man I hardly knew and he was behind me and I could hear no sound.

Hastily I turned the chair with my feet. He had finished pouring while I was lost in thought. Two glasses of Sheridan's were held in hands that looked delicate enough for brain surgery but could probably split concrete blocks. Black over white. A sweet coffee and vanilla liqueur being served by Cary Grant with a hint of steel, a man who could effortlessly sweet-talk a nun into dropping her habit.

A man whose life I had saved.

'If Terry Lynch *didn't* come in,' I said, 'if he was about to ring your bell when we disturbed him — then you realize I'm right? We did actually save your life?'

He sat down opposite me, lit half by the table lamp, half by the weak daylight seeping through windows and patio doors.

'I'm grateful, but I don't think I'd go that far. You see, I'd worked out the details last time you were here, Penny. Poker players are people watchers. Like those clairvoyants who drop test questions into a crowd and watch for reactions. And we're great at working out puzzles, especially those that are classic misdirection.' He cocked his head. 'But I tip my hat to you. Not only did you sense that I was worried, but you worked out why.'

'Not until this afternoon, when a moody portrait on a computer monitor gave me the first intelligent thought of the day. Then I realized that a Welsh solicitor had been scared witless by a drawing that was pointing to a man who had once worn a Madonna wig.' I watched him sip his liqueur. 'I phoned earlier. You should get an answering machine.'

He shrugged. 'If people really need me they'll call again. Perhaps in person' — he raised his glass to me — 'even if it was a waste of time and effort.'

I pulled a face. 'I know that now. If I could see in your eyes that you were worried, then you already understood the card's message and it was pointless warning you. I suppose if Lynch had got in, you were ready for him — right?'

He nodded. 'Ready for *someone*. It's you

telling me it was Terry Lynch.'

'Because he was outside. He hurried away. I know just being here doesn't make him guilty of anything — '

'But until another reason pops up . . . '

I tasted the Sheridan's. 'So . . . what now? Are you going to the police with your suspicions?'

'*My* suspicions? Have I got any?' He raised an eyebrow, tipped his head to look at me in a dark up-and-under way that would have enticed Boadicea down from her chariot.

'Ours, then. Yours *and* mine. Because he came after *you* and *I* caught him in the act and that's not the end of it. Can't be.'

'I agree.'

'When I was here on Thursday you were building up a pretty good case against Terry Lynch. You could see why he might have murdered Ffion and Tombs, and might go after Gareth Owen.'

'You're right, I did. And those reasons still stand. But now it seems he's changed tack. Instead of going after Owen, he's after me.'

'Why?'

He shrugged.

'This morning,' I said, 'I had a visit from Ernie Gallagher.'

'Did you now,' Sharkey said softly.

'Yes. He mentioned that Ray Lynch was a

guest at his daughter's wedding — I'm doing the photography, that's why he came to see me — and for some reason I brought your name into it; I think I asked if you would be there. Anyway, Gallagher told me it was unlikely because you hate Lynch's guts. He said Lynch has some sort of hold on you. So I was working out what that meant — on the way here — and, whoops, suddenly you're a suspect again.'

'Now you *are* being silly. You think I'd murder my sister to get back at Terry Lynch?'

'I know, it's daft, isn't it?' I said, and shook my head in disgust. 'I thought of it, you arranging Jamie Lynch's imprisonment and death, then murdering Terry Lynch's wife — but then of course I remembered that Ffion was your sister, and I realized it was nonsense.'

'If you thought that, you really are naïve,' Sharkey said, himself changing tack. 'You're an old softie, Penny, and you're judging other people by your standards. If you're serious about this PI business you're going to have to understand that the really bad villains don't act or react in a normal or conventional manner. A cold-blooded villain would skin his grandmother alive if it paid him to do so. If I was one of those bad guys and killing my sister would benefit me in some massive way

— well, I'd have done it without a second thought.'

'And are you?'

'A bad guy?'

'Yes.'

He grinned, then drained his glass.

'You'll have to work that out for yourself. And you'd better do it pretty quickly, because in the interests of your PI career I'm going to ask *you* to do something unconventional — and if you agree, you're going to spend the rest of the evening with me in what could turn out to be a very tricky situation.' He gave me that up-and-under look again. 'Are you on?'

'Try me.'

So he did.

20

I phoned Josh at Liverpool Harriers to tell
him what I was doing and, of course, that
caused an argument when I walked out into
the rain with Sharkey because my considerate
husband had never left the Albert Dock. He'd
watched the door close behind me as I
entered Sharkey's flat, then walked towards
the Range Rover, climbed in and settled back
in his seat for the long wait. Not trusting the
tall gambler, he'd wanted to be within bugle
call if I sent for the cavalry. I loved him for his
concern, and for his instant and utterly
correct reaction to Terry Lynch's threatening
presence outside the flat and my determination to go ahead and talk to Sharkey, but it
did make things awkward, because Sharkey
wanted me to participate in something
unconventional and I knew if I told Josh the
truth he'd throw an arm lock on me and toss
me in the car.

In the end I simply said that Sharkey had
come up with an idea and I was going with
him to see if I could dig up some
information that would be useful to DI Billy
Dancer. Smooth! When we'd done, Sharkey

would drive me home. It wasn't total poppycock, because if I did unearth evidence that's exactly what it would do — help the police, I mean. It didn't entirely win Josh over because I'm sure he knew I was up to no good, but at least we parted on good terms and with the same arrangement in place that we'd agreed earlier: he was at last heading off to Liverpool Harriers, I had my mobile, and if I called he'd come running ready to break down the door. The trouble was, this time he didn't know where the door was, and neither did I.

You see, I had to make that story up about helping the police in their inquiries because poker player Ryan Sharkey was holding the cards with details of the night's mission very close to his chest.

I hadn't a clue where we were going.

For a while after I waved off Josh's Range Rover I lived with the absurd notion that Sharkey was taking me straight home. That was knocked on the head when we took the Queensway tunnel under the Mersey and instead of pointing the nose of his silver Lexus towards the Wirral coast when we emerged into the damp Birkenhead dusk he cut onto the New Chester Road and put his foot down.

Once, I did ask him where we were going.

233

He looked at me, grinned, and tapped the side of his nose with a forefinger. I glowered, then slumped down in the oh-so-comfortable seat to enjoy the ride. It was to last a little over half an hour, but for me, time flew. The light was fading fast, the rain was persistent, the flapping wipers were hypnotic and closing my eyes to blot out the dazzle of oncoming headlights led to the inevitable.

I fell asleep.

★　★　★

The car had stopped. Rain was drumming on the roof. Heavier drops showering from overhanging trees when the wind gusted landed like handfuls of tossed gravel. When I looked across, Sharkey was watching me, the planes of his thin face highlighted in the glow from the dash lights.

I groaned softly. 'Where are we?'

'There.'

'Ha bloody ha.'

I yawned, pushed myself up in the seat, looked out at a narrow road in a leafy suburb of somewhere — Chester, I supposed — with uneven pavements bordered by rustic stone walls and tall dark trees. We were parked midway between street lights. I could see the opening to a drive, wrought-iron gates gaping, engraved lettering on a wet slate plaque.

'Dunacre,' Sharkey said, watching me. 'We're outside Terry Lynch's house, and you're about to break in — well, sort of.'

I blinked. 'Oh no. Like John Wayne used to say, 'The hell I am'.'

'Go on, jump out,' he said, grinning. 'And put your hood up.'

I stepped out into the road, walked around the car and joined him on the pavement. The night was warm. Inside my hood the faint sound in my ears was like rain pattering on the roof of a tent.

'What's this for?' I said, touching my hood. 'Disguise?'

But he was already away, the collar of his black leather jacket turned up and rain glistening on his dark hair as he walked towards the open gates, feet splashing through puddles then crunching on gravel as he turned into a wide drive.

'Why is it?' I said, catching up, 'that the most expensive neighbourhoods have the most neglected roads?'

'Keep your mind on the job.'

'I am. And I'm an investigator not a burglar. I gather evidence, not other people's jewellery.'

'There you are, you see,' he said, and for the first time I detected a faint Welsh accent.

'What d'you mean? Evidence, clues? Is that why we're here?'

'You turned up at my place. Lynch was there, and we both believe he was out to commit murder. Mine. All right, we need to know more, and he'll be at one or other of his clubs until the early hours. There'll never be a better time to search his house.'

He had a long stride, and he was hurrying up the deeply shaded edge of the drive under the dripping trees. I was struggling to keep up.

I said, breathlessly, 'What if someone else is there?'

'His wife's dead, remember?'

'Yes, but he might have installed another . . . floozy.'

He chuckled. 'You've been mixing with the wrong kind of gumshoe, those terms went out in the forties. Anyway, forget that idea. I work for Lynch, so I know: he lives alone.'

We'd reached the house. The front door loomed large. I was about to break in, he'd said, and I almost patted my pockets looking for skeleton keys I didn't have. But they weren't needed. Sharkey walked straight up to the door, took a key from his pocket and let us in.

'Christ,' I said softly, 'where'd you get that?'

'Lynch leaves them lying around,' he said. 'Cobblers will cut one while you wait.'

'Another word from the past.'

'Or from the present but used in the wrong context,' he said, pushing the door.

He'd told me Lynch lived alone, presumably because that's what Lynch had told *him*, but how can one liar believe another? If that possibility was aired, would the answer be a rousing chorus of 'cobblers'? Stomach churning I followed him into a dark hall rich with the scent of potpourri, and closed the front door with a click so loud in the stillness I almost wet myself. I could hear the hum of a fridge or freezer, the ticking of a clock, the plink of a dripping tap. Doors opened to left and right. Stairs directly ahead climbed to an unseen landing.

Someone was breathing heavily.

'For Christ's sake,' Sharkey said, 'shut your mouth.'

I swallowed with an audible gulp.

'Where do we start?'

'His office. It's on the first floor.'

And he was off again. I followed, legs trembling. We climbed the wide carpeted stairs to where a small window with vertical blinds let in faint illumination from low

237

clouds reflecting city lights. Along the landing, that light gleamed on white doors and brass handles. Or were they gold plated? Solid? We passed the bathroom, which gave me the location of the dripping tap and reminded me that a loo was close by, should the need arise. I stifled a giggle, because the need had arisen as soon as we stepped inside Lynch's house. Please God, I thought, don't let anyone give me a fright.

Ahead of me, Sharkey turned into another room where a computer monitor shone eerily. He let me walk past him, then shut the door and switched on a desk lamp that bathed the room in dim green light.

'You've been here before,' I said.

He grunted.

The furniture was flat-pack from Staples, the swivel chair in front of the computer faux leather, the computer a dated desk-top on one of those work-station things. A four-drawer filing cabinet stood alongside a small bookcase. Another longer desk took up most of one wall and this one was of antique pine, the chair Sharkey now plonked himself down in upholstered in genuine hide with a smell strong enough to make a cowboy homesick.

'Start with the filing cabinet,' he said, busy at the big desk's drawers.

I tried. 'It's locked.'

Without looking up he tossed a bunch of keys in my direction. Marvelling, I jingled it until I found the right one, then opened the lock and slid out the top drawer. Suspension files. The other three drawers, when I slid them open one by one, held more of the same.

'Business accounts, stuff like that, mostly to do with his night clubs,' I said, riffling like mad. 'Any use?'

He didn't answer.

'Ryan?'

'What?' He looked across at me and shook his head. 'No. Forget those. Come and read this.'

He swivelled the chair and rocked backwards. The centre drawer of the desk's right pedestal was open. He had a torn envelope in one hand. The other was holding out a single sheet of white writing paper that took on a warm pastel shade in the green lighting.

It was a letter, addressed to Lynch.

Dear Terry

In case you've been wondering what your brother Jamie was doing playing Al Capone at the Valentine's Day Massacre, the answer is, he wasn't. Jamie did not fire the shot that killed Nicky Nixon, he was framed. Incriminating evidence was passed to the police surgeon working the case by a concerned member of the public. The surgeon's name is Sebastian Tombs, and I know after you've read this his days are numbered. The concerned member of the public may live a bit longer, because this young lady (yes, it was a woman) has recently wormed her way into a position of privilege that may yet guarantee her safety. Let's put it this way. Her life probably hangs on just how much you care for your beautiful, treacherous wife.

Yours feelingly

Another concerned member of the public

'Doyle told me about this,' I said softly. 'He said Lynch received an anonymous letter soon after he and Ffion got back from the Caribbean. Does the date on the envelope match that at the top of the letter?'

'Yes. It was sent exactly a week before Ffion was murdered.'

'Yes, but by whom?'

He scanned the page again. 'Not your average scally. Too clever by far. Almost official. Sounds almost like legal language, or police speak.' He grinned. 'How many coppers do I know who've got it in for Lynch and don't mind bending the rules?'

240

'So if this is genuine, it's damning. It's screaming to anyone who cares to listen that Terry Lynch murdered his wife.'

'Don't forget Tombs.'

'Here we go again,' I said. 'Two deaths explained — but we're still stuck with the others.'

'I did suggest two killers.'

'So we're halfway there.'

'We?'

'Well, we are upstairs in someone else's house, without his permission, rifling his desk. For the moment, doesn't that make us partners in crime?'

He grinned. 'Partners in the *investigation* of crime.'

'Got a nice ring to it,' I said thoughtfully. 'Lane and Sharkey, private investigators . . . '

'Sharkey and Lane works better.'

'Yes, but it's my business and the other way is alphabetical order and — '

He touched a forefinger to pursed lips. 'Put that on hold,' he said. 'I haven't quite finished.'

I watched him swivel back to the desk, realized he'd left me holding the letter and quickly picked up the envelope and stuffed that and the single sheet of paper into my pocket. Meanwhile he was taking me at my word and thoroughly searching Lynch's desk, dragging out drawers one by one, flicking quickly through the contents then moving on to the next.

'If you told me what you were looking for . . . '

He slammed the last drawer, turned away and sat back, lips pursed, eyes brooding.

'Something small, pack of cards size and shape, very ordinary, no cash value but irreplaceable — '

'Bedside table.'

He shot me a glance.

'That room was a crime scene.'

'But from your description this thing you're looking for wouldn't interest the police.'

'You're right.'

He swung his gangling form out of the chair and glided past me as silently as a ghost. I followed him out of the room and along the landing into the next, a master bedroom. A duvet was crumpled on the king-size bed. Radio alarms glowed on two bedside tables, their red numerals casting a faint lurid glow over the room. Either Sharkey knew something I didn't or he was taking a guess, for he was already on his knees opening the drawer in the glass-topped table on the right side of the bed. Then, as he rooted through the contents, I realized he could show me a thing or two about detecting: he had chosen that side because the way the duvet was crumpled it was clear that Lynch slept on the right side of the bed. On the other pillow, incongruous in the circumstances, there lay a neatly folded filmy nightdress.

As Sharkey rattled away in Lynch's drawers, I sat on the corner of the bed and thought back to what I had read; how a killer had slipped a knife between a sleeping woman's ribs, and walked out of the house into the rain.

That was Lynch, I thought. Her husband. A letter was delivered to him, and on the strength of its contents he murdered his wife. Yet at what cost? Each night he must lie here, imagining the warmth of her body next to his. Inhale the familiar perfume on her nightdress, lying so close to his face. Does he cry himself to sleep? Are his cheeks wet with tears — ?

'Got it!'

Sharkey was sitting back on his heels. He was holding what looked like a small box, turning it in his hands. As he twisted it I saw that one of the flat, oblong sides had a mottled red pattern enclosed in a thin black border. Then I realized that the pattern was on a card, glued to the flat surface of the box, and I knew what I was looking at.

'You said *like* a pack of cards,' I said. 'That *is* a pack of cards.'

'Yes. They're my cards.'

'Why would Lynch have them? What use are they to him? And why irreplaceable?'

He said nothing but stood up, slipped the cards into his pocket, came round the bed and stood close to me where I sat.

'My turn, isn't it?' I said. 'To work things out. So let's see what I can do. You didn't come here for evidence, or clues. The one reason, the *only* reason you came here, was for those cards. And what do we know about you and Lynch? One thing: according to Ernie Gallagher, Lynch has a hold on you that makes you dance to his tune. Gallagher said he thought that hold was linked to something that happened in the back room at Jokers Wild. I've been there. I saw you walk out of that room holding a couple of glasses. And behind you, men were playing cards.'

His smile was twisted in the gloom.

'They're marked cards, aren't they, Sharkey?'

'What if they are? I say they're my cards, and perhaps they are, but how can Lynch prove that? — and he would need, without any shadow of doubt — '

And then he broke off, because both of us heard the crunch of gravel as a car drew up outside, the slam of a door, the sound of footsteps approaching the house. A key turned in the lock. Then there was a breathless pause as we visualized the door opening. A switch clicked. And suddenly, under the bedroom door, a thin band of bright light was visible as someone began to climb the stairs.

21

I rushed into my office as soon as Sharkey dropped me off at home, photocopied the incriminating letter, and was waiting impatiently just inside the open front door when Josh pulled up in his Range Rover.

Without telling him too much I got him to drive me swiftly through the now much heavier rain to Hoylake Police Station. When I splashed across the car-park it was to find that DI Dancer was off duty. I handed the original letter — now in its envelope — to the desk sergeant and asked him to make sure it got to the detective inspector.

I made sure he signed for it, too, over a brief description: *anonymous letter sent to Terry Lynch shortly before the death of his wife. Recovered from his house.*

Then Josh drove me home. On the way I gave him a shortened version of everything that happened after I left the Albert Dock with Sharkey. He was attentive, but did little more than grunt. I knew he was looking at the evidence from a crime writer's angle. Exactly what I needed: someone to probe deeply, tear it apart and expose the flaws.

Back home and at last in out of the rain I had one final chore before I could relax. Still in my wet jacket, I went to my office and picked up the phone.

'Hi, Gareth?'

'I don't believe it,' the little solicitor said. 'It's close to midnight, I am once again lying in bed sipping Laphroaig on the rocks — '

'Top it up now, make it a large double. You're safe.'

'Well now! I'm out of the office all day tomorrow, so you're saying I don't have to keep looking over my shoulder for the bogeyman?'

'That's right. Unless, of course, you're going to be associating with baddies, as you sometimes do in your work.'

He chuckled. 'No, just . . . out and about, here and there.'

There was a silence and I heard liquid being sipped, which made me smile.

'This good news,' he said, 'does it mean you've caught the killer?'

'We're getting very close.'

'We?'

'Well, me. With some help. Anyway, to make everything clear, the card left on Farrell's body wasn't pointing to you, it was pointing to Ryan Sharkey. He's Welsh. He's famous for once wearing a Madonna wig.

And tonight we accidentally chased Terry Lynch away from Sharkey's flat in the Albert Dock when he was almost certainly up to no good. Lynch looked absolutely *furious*.'

'This was you and your helper doing the chasing?'

'No, this was Josh. Well, yes, Josh is a helper, of course, but — '

'Penny.'

'Yes?'

'You sound knackered. Thanks for the call, and the excellent news. Now go to bed.'

'With a double Laphroaig?'

'Whatever floats your boat.'

I chuckled, made a kissy noise and put down the phone. Then I obeyed orders. With Josh instead of expensive whisky.

22

Day Six — Saturday 23 September

The telephone rang before breakfast when I was using a sharp little kitchen knife to loosen juicy segments of grapefruit that kept spitting stinging snake venom in my eye. Josh was back from the pool and in the conservatory doing his morning stretching exercises. Rain was drumming on the glass roof.

It was Dancer. He didn't mince words.

'Where did you get that letter?'

'Why, is it a fake?'

'It's addressed to Lynch, at his address, the writer calls him Terry, it deals with issues important to an ongoing investigation — so, no, it looks like the genuine article, but that's not what I asked. Lynch has been pulled in. When I walk into that interview room I want to know what I'm doing. I do *not* want to be bush-whacked by a smart arse solicitor with more answers than I've got questions.'

'OK. It was found at Lynch's house, a big desk in his office, middle drawer, right-hand side.'

'You took it from there?'

'No.'

The hiss of his breathing intensified. I thought of a steam boiler, overheating, nearing bursting point.

'Help me out, Penny,' he said. 'You handed that letter in last night. How did vital evidence of that nature come to be in your possession?'

'You sound like PC Plod,' I said, ready to giggle, but instead screwing my eyes shut in anticipation of an explosion. 'Sorry, Billy,' I said, plastering on the remorse. 'Someone found it, and gave it to me.' I hesitated. 'A concerned member of the public.'

'Is that meant to be funny?' he said, in a strangled voice. 'Or by quoting those words are you saying the person who *wrote* this handed it to you?'

'God, no, where did that come from? The person I was with *found* that letter . . . ' And then my voice trailed off and I stood there with the phone in one hand and the curved little knife in the other and I let what Dancer had said sink in — about the person who wrote the letter handing it to me — and I began to feel sick.

'I don't know,' I said meekly. 'Please, don't ask any more questions, Billy. Talk to Lynch, see if he can explain — '

'No, let me explain. When Ffion Lynch's

body was found, all the main suspects were interviewed, all had alibis for the time of the murder, all were released without charge. Same goes for Humphreys, Tombs, and Farrell — we pulled in everyone connected in any way. So the bottom line is, stop wastin' your time, stop going over old ground — '

'Going over old ground produced that letter. Maybe you should try it some time — '

'Thanks for the advice.' Dancer cut me short, and the phone went down with a crash.

Josh was watching me, green army towel round his neck.

'Trouble?'

I stuck the knife in the grapefruit and pulled a face.

'Well, as I'm now telling the police how to do their job,' I said, 'that's like asking me do dogs have fleas.'

★　★　★

'So who was it who walked into Terry Lynch's house and almost caught two bungling burglars?'

'That was Ray. His not too bright brother.'

'He lives there?'

'Well, yes, I suppose. Sharkey thought Terry lived alone. Seems he was wrong. My guess is he was half right: Ray's move to Terry's house

251

was probably very recent. Anyway, he came upstairs, visited the bathroom, we heard the toilet flush. Sharkey opened the master bedroom door a crack — enough to sneak a look. He saw Ray walk into one of the other bedrooms. The door slammed, shoes clattered — we guessed Ray was getting undressed — and then a TV was switched on. He was obviously settled for the night. We sneaked out, and the rest you know.'

'Bits and pieces, yes. Like, Sharkey went there looking for a pack of cards that Lynch was holding as a threat. In the search, he came across a letter that you believe gives Lynch an excellent motive for murdering his wife and Sebastian Tombs.'

'His wife, definitely; according to the letter, she got Jamie Lynch convicted of murder. Whether Terry Lynch would bother going after the police surgeon . . . well, it's possible, but it's also possible that getting rid of the person who gave the damning evidence to the police would be enough. Either way, that still leaves us with several murders unsolved.'

'And more suspects for Ffion's murder than when you started. It began with Terry Lynch and Ernie Gallagher, because they were rivals and there'd been a gang killing. Mick Doyle appeared on the scene, and he was a suspect because at some time in the past he'd fancied Ffion, and she married Lynch. Then, on Thursday, Gallagher told you a tale about Ryan Sharkey that gives him a strong motive to hurt Terry Lynch — and murdering Ffion would certainly do that.' He rocked his head, thinking. 'And then there's Ray.'

'With a couple of screws loose, according to Gallagher.'

'So what? You don't need brains to murder someone and stick a credit card down her frilly nightie.'

'No, but you need a motive.'

'That's easy: Ray found out Ffion had framed his younger brother — and Ray is the oldest of the three.'

'Damn. You always know everything.'

'There're things I know that you don't know I know,' he said, grinning, 'and there're even things *I* don't know I know until I rake the glowing embers — '

'Dying embers,' I said, and stuck out the tip of my tongue.

Breakfast was just about finished, and we were sitting at the kitchen table drinking coffee. It was pushing towards eight, and I had to be at Annabel Lee's house by 10.30. Plenty of time . . . and I could see Josh's keen plotting mind working overtime as he finished nibbling a piece of toast.

253

'I heard you ask Dancer if the letter was a fake. What did he say?'

'Genuine, as far as he's concerned.' I watched his fingers steeple, touch his chin, and knew he was slipping into deep thinking mode. I added, 'If he's right, that letter was posted and arrived at Terry Lynch's house just days before his wife was murdered.'

'I'm not convinced,' Josh said. 'There're any number of ways a scam could be worked.'

I blinked. 'Really?'

'No question. Look, let's say the writer wanted it to look as if Lynch had received that letter, when actually he hadn't. All he'd have to do is post it, turn up in Lynch's drive early the next morning in green overalls and with dirty fingernails, and meet the postman. All postmen are in a hurry. He'd think this bloke was the gardener, and gratefully hand over the mail. Now the writer's got the letter back, neatly postmarked.'

'But he hasn't. It was in Lynch's drawer.'

'Was it?'

'Of course it was. Sharkey found it there, he held it up and *showed* it to me.'

Josh shook his head. 'It was night, there was probably a forty watt bulb in that green light. If you didn't actually watch him take it out of the drawer, it could have been in his pocket — couldn't it?'

'Well . . . yes. I was over by the filing cabinet, doing some rooting.' I thought for a moment then said, 'I didn't actually tell you, but when I was talking to Dancer on the phone he asked me if I was saying the person who *wrote* the letter handed it to me last night. I hadn't given him a name but, of course, the person who handed it to me was Sharkey. Is that what you think? Do you think *Sharkey* wrote the letter?'

'I'm bothered by the fact that he found it. And I don't understand why he waited until you came on the scene to go after the pack of cards Lynch was holding to his head like a loaded pistol.'

I frowned, trying to think like Josh. At once, I saw holes in one of his theories.

'If you're right and Sharkey did have the letter in his pocket and produced it in my presence, in Lynch's office, then Terry Lynch hasn't read it, hasn't even seen it. So why did he murder his wife?'

'He didn't,' Josh said. 'That was Ryan Sharkey.'

'Christ,' I said softly, mind whirling. 'That's why he waited to plant that letter until I came along. He needed a witness. If Sharkey murdered Ffion the letter was written by him to frame Lynch, but sending it wouldn't have worked. Lynch would have destroyed it, or taken it to the police.'

'Or actually done the deed: murdered his wife.'

'Which, if we're right, Sharkey didn't want to happen; he was saving that for himself.' I shook my head. 'I don't know about you,' I said, reaching for the coffee pot, 'but I'm getting dizzier by the minute.'

'Yes and, as usual, I've been thinking complicated when it's all very simple. If the writer wanted to hold on to the letter, but have it postmarked, he didn't have to go through that rigmarole of dressing up for the postman. Terry Lynch would take some of his personal mail into work, a lot of businessmen do. Sharkey works for him. All he had to do was pinch one of those letters a few days before he murdered Ffion, dump the contents but keep the envelope.'

'Right,' I said, thinking fast. 'Murdering Ffion would be the first half of his revenge, and with that done he could wait, bide his time — '

'He wouldn't even have to write the letter,' Josh said.

'No, you're absolutely right. He's murdered Ffion, he's got the envelope with the right date, he's carrying on as normal. Weeks stretch into months. Suddenly, there are dead bodies all over the place . . . ' I stopped, looked at Josh. 'So that means there *must* be two killers.'

'Not necessarily — but don't stop, keep going.'

'Right, dead bodies dotting the landscape and, out of the blue, I turn up on his doorstep, an eager little PI with notebook at the ready. I learn nothing at that first meeting, but as I'm leaving Sharkey makes sure I read something in his eyes, see how troubled he is — easy for him, he's a professional gambler and used to bluffing and misleading — and so he knows for sure I'll be back. Now, *now* — he writes the letter.'

'And the rest,' Josh said, 'is a piece of cake.'

'Damn,' I said, and flicked a frustrated look across the table. 'D'you realize I sort of like Ryan Sharkey? We were even arguing, in a light-hearted way, over what name to call ourselves when we formed a brilliant PI partnership.' I pulled a face. 'Well, there's not much point thinking about that if the man's a murderer.'

But Josh was off on another tack. He said, 'Of course, we could both be very cleverly plotting a scenario that's pure fiction. Look at it this way: Doyle told you about the letter, so either he heard about it from Lynch, or *he* sent it.' He shook his head with some irritation. 'So let's say Sharkey didn't write or send the letter, Doyle or someone *else* did, knowing exactly what effect it would have. It arrived. Lynch read of the treachery and murdered his wife. Last night Sharkey went along with you as a genuine helper, and really did come across that letter in the drawer. The deck of cards Lynch was holding over his head turned up as a bonus . . . ' He shook his head irritably. 'But it's nonsense. I don't really believe *any* of that.'

He was watching me as he spoke, looking into my eyes, watching for my predictable reaction.

'Different as chalk and cheese,' he said softly and with gentle concern. 'I believe very little without double checking, you believe almost everything because that's the way you're made. Trusting. An old softie. And that, when combined with a cavalier attitude, can be very, very dangerous.'

23

I slipped into a neat grey trouser suit which was dressy enough for a wedding but would give me freedom of movement, donned Hotter shoes with no heel that would keep me small but comfortable, gathered together my gear, kissed Josh and lugged everything — one medium-sized Lowepro camera back-pack with laptop compartment — out to the Ka knowing that my dear protective husband, while certainly beginning to repeat himself, was absolutely right. Danger was out there. The trouble was, I didn't know which way to look.

Josh had constructed an impressive argument that seemed to make Ryan Sharkey the prime suspect for Ffion Lynch's murder. Then he'd taken away the bottom brick and the whole pile had come tumbling down — and that was what was so confusing. As Josh had pointed out, cold facts could be intertwined with clever fiction until the fine twisted line between them blurred, and so it seemed to me that until I got the chance to talk to Ryan Sharkey — confront him, if you like, little old me and the lion's den — the safest thing to do was to ignore side tracks, take everything that had happened last night at face value and look at likely consequences.

Terry Lynch was about to have a potentially incriminating letter dangled in front of his eyes by DI Dancer. Big shock. As far as he knew, that letter was tucked away in a drawer in his home office. So, if the letter was in police hands, someone had been in his house — and Terry Lynch was no fool. The last time he'd seen me I'd been splashing through the rain towards Ryan Sharkey's front door. When, sooner or later, he discovered that a deck of marked cards belonging to Sharkey had also gone missing from his house, he'd make the connection and come looking for me. Or send one of his goons.

No sooner had the thought crossed my mind than a routine glance in the mirror as I took the turn off the A540 towards Parkgate revealed a green Mondeo that appeared out of nowhere to snuggle up to my rear bumper. Memory of another green Mondeo I had seen several times not long before I was roughly dragged into a Liverpool back entry welled like sickness in my throat. I felt an icy hand touch the nape of my neck, and gooseflesh prickled on my upper arms. One occupant, the driver. Sunglasses — under grey skies and pouring rain. I couldn't be certain, but as I cast another nervous glance at the mirror I thought I saw teeth flash in what could have been a grin, but was probably a snarl.

Once off the main through road, traffic was light. By the time I reached Boathouse Lane there was just the odd car leaving the coast for Birkenhead or Chester, and when I turned onto The Parade it was down to my Ka and the Mondeo.

Dilemma. I could be jumping at shadows, the man behind me could have been sneering at a speed camera — but if my instincts were spot on and he was dangerous, should I lead him to Annabel Lee? I was still undecided as I drew closer to the cottage without daring to take my foot off the accelerator, but the decision was abruptly plucked from my hands. With a roar that sounded like a badly holed exhaust the Mondeo pulled out, raced past me in a cloud of spray and was gone.

When Annabel came dashing out at my toot her blonde hair was snatched back in a tidy pony-tail and she was dressed in a trouser suit that was ideal for a photographer working on a summer wedding but made mine look like something stitched together from sack cloth. Her sparkling appearance even put the skies in a brighter mood, and by the time we were skirting Chester on the way

261

to Ernie Gallagher's house the rain had died away completely and I had reached another decision.

I wasn't to know it at the time, but it was a decision that would put at least one life in danger and the investigation on a roller-coaster ride to near disaster.

'Ernie Gallagher came to see me yesterday,' I said.

'You're kidding!'

'Mm. And he was surprisingly pleasant. The problem is, he was one step ahead of me.'

'Yeah, right. Like he knew you were going to use the camera as an excuse for snooping.'

'He politely called it photographing Diane, in *his* house, then losing my way and ending up in his office. Anyway, that's out. I'm not saying Gallagher's squeaky clean, but I'd be wasting my time going there. So I'm sending my assistant.'

'Thanks a bunch. And you want me to do your dirty work?'

I flashed her a smile. 'No. I want you to do what you're good at, Annabel. Take lots of candid shots, general chaos in the house with clothes and shoes and sweet-smelling carnations mixed up with ironing boards and glasses of Scotch or gin, charming pics of the flushed and flustered bride and bridesmaids as they get ready.'

Her camera bag was in her lap. She clutched it, and looked sideways at me with sparkling eyes.

'Brilliant. I'll also try for moody, subtle light and shade, and anything suitable I'll change to monochrome on the laptop . . . '

She broke off, staring with a frown at what lay ahead as we approached what I thought was Gallagher's road. If it was, we weren't going down it. A sign on a red and white barrier announced that the road was closed for essential repairs to water mains.

'Well, well,' I said, my thoughts at once making the nervous leap to villains and deviousness, my eyes trying in vain to probe the thick bushes blanketing lush sloping gardens. 'I suppose there's another way around for the wedding cars on their way out, but it looks like you walk the rest of the way.'

'No problem.' She had already clicked the door open as I pulled up, and was slipping out almost before I stopped. 'I'll see you at the church then?'

'Yes, I'm going to look around the churchyard — Josh would call it doing a recce — and see where we can take the formal photographs if the rain comes pouring down.' I looked across at her, a vision of sparkling youth, her bright blue eyes full of life as she stood with her hand on the open door. 'Take care, you hear me, Annabel? I don't want to lose my new assistant before she's started.' She stared at me as if I'd gone mad, and I sighed. 'Never mind. It's just . . . well, any problems and you've got my mobile number. Same if you can't get a lift to the church: call me and I'll pick you up.'

She gave me a grin and a careless wave, slammed the door and was off, her bag with its expensive contents slung casually over her shoulder.

I watched her go, looked with deep misgivings at the absence of tools or equipment anywhere near the barrier that announced urgent work, then drove on to the next genteel side road and quickly turned the Ka round. When I drove past Gallagher's road, slowly enough to draw an impatient honk from behind me, there was no sign of Annabel Lee.

I wouldn't see her again for another thirty-six hours.

24

The first thing that caught my eye when I drove onto the gravel car-park at the side of the Norman church on the outskirts of Chester was a green Ford Mondeo parked well back under the trees. It was close to the spiked iron railings enclosing the cemetery sprawling at the rear of the church, and tilted a little in the long grass. Empty — as far as I could see. Although there had been no rain for some time the skies were still grey and, as the day warmed up, a mist had risen from the wet ground to meet the light mist clinging to the branches of the crooked old hawthorn trees on either side of the lych-gate. As I climbed out of the Ka with my bag I thought that spooky was the term that might have described the scene but, after everything that had happened over the past week, the one that sprang to mind was sinister.

I cast one final glance at the lonely Mondeo, suppressed a shiver as I was hit by a sudden feeling of sadness, then began to do the job I was being paid for.

The vicar was a tiny, chubby Irishman with green eyes who was happy to show me the locations used regularly by professional wedding photographers, and when I'd taken note of those, we went into the church and discussed the photographs I would be allowed to take during the ceremony.

As expected there were rules governing the use of flash in church, on where I could stand, on when I could photograph the newly weds signing the register (has to be a blank page nowadays because of data protection, security or human rights — or all three), and the little Irishman in his cassock took me everywhere with my hand in his so that it felt as if I was taking Adam for a walk, five years old again but dressed in a frock.

By the time we had covered all the rules and regulations and pinned down every vantage point, cars were arriving and the church was already filling up. I went back outside, located the Best Man on the pavement outside the lych-gate, asked him to keep me posted as family and important friends arrived and enlisted his help for later when guests needed to be called in the right order for the formal and more relaxed group photographs.

Then I unzipped my bag, got out my Nikon and set to work.

The rain stayed away. Cloud lifted and

thinned. Sunlight was at first hazy, then much brighter as patches of blue sky shimmered through breaks in the thin cloud. A particularly bright shaft bathed the dark timber of the lych-gate in brilliant sunshine as the bride drew up in a white beribboned Mercedes with her father, Ernie Gallagher. I got a shot of them in the car, another posed outside it, and using rearrangement of the long white wedding gown as an excuse to get close, I managed to ask Gallagher the whereabouts of my assistant.

'He didn't turn up,' he said, out of the corner of his mouth.

'It was a she,' I hissed, stepping back with camera raised.

'Same answer.'

If I tell you that the wedding ceremony, the altar photographs, the signing of the register and even the start of the formal photographs which I was to take on wet grass under the trees all passed in a dream — I'm sure you'll understand. My mind locked when Gallagher told me Annabel Lee was missing. For the next hour or whatever it took I was squinting through my lens at guests in dark suits and expensive dresses glittering with jewellery and seeing the overlaid image of a blonde young girl with her throat cut. Or the same young girl merrily trotting down to the nearest pawnshop clutching my expensive Nikon camera.

I know at one point I was shocked by the sight of Terry Lynch and Ryan Sharkey sitting some way apart from each other at the back of the church — gatecrashers, I assumed — and I remember looking around at the time and wondering if Doyle was there and which of the male guests was Ray Lynch. But those were in the lucid moments. Mostly my mind was obsessed with disturbing images of a young girl who was either dead or a thief, but one way or another had gone missing, and it wasn't until the Best Man grabbed my arm, drew my attention to the men and women standing talking and staring in my direction with their heels slowly sinking into soggy grass and told me he was ready to get moving with the group photographs that I really came to my senses.

And almost at once, I wished I hadn't.

'Anyone seen Ray?' Ernie Gallagher shouted.

The consensus was no.

'Look for his car,' Gallagher said, and my skin went like ice. 'A green Mondeo with a dicky rear spring.'

I turned and ran.

Someone shouted, 'Where's she going?'

A woman squealed, 'Look, there's Ray's car, over there!'

They came running after me, but they didn't stand a hope in hell. In trousers and springy shoes nobody was going to catch me, and I went haring across the grass and between monumental gravestones and over the low stone wall and that brought me tumbling recklessly into the gravel car-park and from there it was a short, breathless sprint to the long wet grass where Ray Lynch had parked his green Mondeo.

Or somebody had.

A snatched glance inside the car told me it was indeed empty. But my legs were still moving and that sideways glance was my undoing. My foot skidded into a muddy hole, twisting my ankle. Momentum threw me sideways away from the Mondeo. As I began to fall my out-flung arm flapped against a soft, immovable object. I clutched with clawed fingers, hung on and heard something tear. When I tried to heave myself up, the pain in my ankle was like a hot knife. I bore my weight with my hand, twisted my head and found my face buried against the coarse cloth of a man's jacket. He was bent face down over the railings. Both arms were hanging loose, the fingertips touching a flat gravestone. I was tight up against him, breathing his stale sweat. I gagged, grabbed at the railings with my other hand and struggled to my feet. I had been hanging on to his jacket. My weight had jerked it across his shoulders, and the tearing sound had been me widening the rip through which one of the railing's rusty iron spikes protruded. Ray Lynch was impaled. The spike was slick with blood, and something like pink fish bait adhered stickily to its point — something that looked like a sliver of bloody tripe.

I reached over, touched the dark wet hair and tilted the hanging head so I could see the face. It was as white and shiny as a fish's belly. Eyes like dark wet stones shone through slitted lids. The mouth gaped, wedged wide by something lodged between partially false teeth.

I slid down the railings, sank to the ground and, uncontrollably but politely, I turned my head to the side and vomited on the wet grass.

★　★　★

I seemed to be spending my new life as a PI reeking like the floor of a city-centre pub on Saturday night.

DI Dancer's merry men had moved me well away from the body so they could string their crime-scene tape like wedding day satin and I was leaning back against the railings

270

with a throbbing ankle and a damp bottom from sitting in wet grass. I was sick and weak and sorry for myself, and my mind was tortured by the thought of Ray Lynch desperately clinging to life, hanging agonizingly from a rusty spike that had pierced his body, then having to put up with a crazy woman who threw herself at him and tried to climb up his back. Even now, knowing he had been long dead when I arrived, it was all too easy to imagine what my weight would have done to his bloody wound. I clenched my teeth as once again I got the dry heaves, then stood there quivering and racked by painful spasms as I tried to support myself as best I could with both hands braced on my knees.

My retching attracted the attention of the police surgeon who'd replaced poor Sebastian Tombs. A tall man in a grey suit with a carnation in the lapel, he glanced across from the corpse with a dark look that seemed to lay blame at my doorstep.

I know, I thought. Ray Lynch ruined your day, and if you'd been closer when I got a good look at his body I'd have ruined your smart grey suit. Somewhere ahead, I knew, there lay more bodies and the sour delights of the hat trick — but where, oh where, lay my Annabel Lee?

Tears blurred my vision. My lip trembled.

A man appeared at my shoulder and Billy Dancer's voice whispered condolences in my ear.

'What are you doin', Penny, makin' these murders up as you go along? What was it Churchill said, 'We'll fight them on the beaches, we'll fight them — ''

'Yes, yes, all right,' I said out of a throat raw enough for a costermonger. 'He followed me, you know. Ray Lynch.' I looked at the rumpled DI, a thin man wearing a fat man's suit. 'And I'm sure I saw that same car several times before I was attacked in Liverpool.'

'You saw him today?'

'Was this murder the same as the others?' I blurted. 'Did the killer first use a knife? Did the card I saw clenched between false teeth indicate — ?'

'Hang on. I asked you if you saw Ray today.'

'Not Ray, no. Not today nor any other day. But I did see the car more than once, and today the driver was wearing shades so it could have been — '

'Where?'

'In Parkgate. I was picking up my assistant; the Mondeo overtook me . . . '

He was looking around, no longer listening.

'Where is he, this assistant?'

'She. And she's gone missing; that's why

I'm telling you about the Mondeo being there when I was picking her up because — '

'Yeah, but the Mondeo's here and the driver's dead so what's that got to do with a bird goin' missing?'

I sagged. 'I don't know. I suppose I'm not thinking straight . . . '

'Anyway,' Dancer said, 'there's no law against an adult goin' missing.'

'Yes, but in the circumstances — '

'Go home, Penny — '

'I can't, I've got a job to finish, I . . . '

I took a deep breath, opened my mouth again to ask about the murder but Dancer was already walking back towards the crime scene. In a way, I was pleased he hadn't answered. I knew the card left on the body was likely to be the Visa lost by Terry Lynch, but if that was so then Terry Lynch seemed to be in the clear and I was looking at Ryan Sharkey as a possible killer. The thought filled me with sadness, but also seemed to take me by the scruff of the neck, straighten my posture and stiffen my resolve (Josh would love the mixed metaphors) and as I moved away across the wet grass with my mind elsewhere but my spirit once more indomitable, I thought I heard an authoritative voice ring out across the churchyard like a call to arms.

'Right then, if you're all done with eyeballing the crime scene I think we'd better get on with the group photographs.'

It was no fantasy. The voice was mine and, coming as it did in the presence of death, it just about stopped the church clock.

25

It didn't, of course — only the grim reaper
can do that, and he was worn out — but even
if time had stopped that wouldn't have been
good enough for me.

At eight that evening I was sitting on the
sagging loose-covered settee in the bar of the
Golden Fleece with lights twinkling on three
glasses of gin and tonic bright with juicy
yellow slices of lemon and trying desperately,
in my mind, to turn the clock back. I wanted
it to be late morning again, but this time
round I would go with my original plan and
drop Annabel Lee at the church before
driving to Ernie Gallagher's, stepping out of
the Ka at the end of the blocked road where
water mains were being repaired — and
taking my chance. Yet even that version of
events might have changed nothing. If it had
always been her intention, Annabel Lee
would have done a bunk no matter where I'd
dropped her. If she had fallen foul of villains,
the other horrific possibility I was trying to
put out of mind, well, for the moment the
odds for or against were being looked at by
the plump little solicitor, Gareth Owen.

Josh was deep in one of the easy chairs, lanky and relaxed in chinos and loose sweatshirt, sipping his drink and watching me with compassion. Gareth Owen's drink was on the table in front of his empty chair, the glass misty with condensation that was running down to turn the print on his cardboard coaster into a blood-red stain. The solicitor was over by the window searching for a signal on his mobile, and even as I glanced across he nodded and began talking into the phone.

'I can read his face,' I said stiffly. 'It's bad news.'

'Behind every cloud — '

'Christ,' I said, glaring at Josh, 'don't you start. If Annabel Lee's been taken, where's the silver lining?'

'For the first time in a week-old investigation,' he said, 'you'll have something to get your teeth into.'

'Explain.'

'The killer's rattled. He's done something out of character, probably been driven to it.'

'By me? By what Sharkey and I did last night?'

'Well, we don't yet know if Terry Lynch has been charged, or somehow wriggled his way out of Dancer's third degree — but no, I think you and Sharkey did no more than create a few disturbing ripples. Something else has happened, something *important* has come up. When it did, it shocked our killer, hit him so bloody hard he had to risk coming out into the open. Christ, Penny, he's turned to kidnapping and committed murder *at the scene of a wedding,* and if you can find out why — '

He broke off as Gareth made his way back to the table, tasted his gin, for an instant closed his eyes with pleasure. When he looked at me, his face was grim.

'I got through to a contact in the authority likely to be involved in that part of Chester. Your fears were justified: no repairs were scheduled in that area.'

'So the killer erected that barrier.'

'It looks that way. But if he did, what was his motive?'

I frowned. 'That's obvious: he wanted to get at Annabel Lee, so he made sure she faced a lonely walk from the end of the street.'

'No, you're not thinking this through. How could he know you were employing Annabel?'

'Well . . . Josh knew.' I glanced across and he shook his head emphatically: the leak hadn't come from him. 'But anyway, it was no secret. Annabel was chuffed with the job, and likely to tell anybody who cared to listen.'

'All right, suppose she did. The killer still didn't know what *she* was doing, because the original plan was for *you* to go to Gallagher's house, Annabel to the church — right?'

'Damn. Yes, it was.' I followed his train of thought, saw at once what he was getting at. 'If she'd told someone, let them know exactly how we were doing the wedding — who was going where, and so on — the killer must have been after me. He was expecting *me* to get out of the car.'

'Annabel,' Josh said, 'is Terry Lynch's niece. Telling *one* relative the good news about her job would be as good as telling *all* of them — '

'She must have told Ray,' I said, cutting him short. 'I remember, Annabel was friendly with Ray Lynch. She took a picture for him, framed it. I know he still hadn't paid her, and if she phoned him chasing her money she might have mentioned the job, the wedding . . .'

I trailed off as the doors opened and DI Dancer walked in followed by the redheaded detective sergeant, Hood. The DS looked across at us but went straight to the bar and climbed onto a stool. Dancer made a beeline for our little group.

'Apologies first of all, Penny,' he said, waving away Josh's offer of a drink and

278

nodding hello to Gareth. 'If I was abrupt at the crime scene, then I'm sorry, but what I said still stands: there's nothing we can do about looking for Annabel Lee until she's been missing much longer. Even then, without suspicion of wrongdoing . . . well, she's a big girl and more or less free to do what she likes.'

'Of course, and you've got your hands full already,' I said, nodding acceptance as he sank into the last of the armchairs and stretched his legs, his alpaca suit hanging like an ill-fitting shroud. 'But what about the death of Ray Lynch? Any . . . similarities with the others?'

He rolled his eyes, accepted the large Scotch brought to him by Hood, then took a hefty jolt and watched the DS return to the bar before answering.

'You know there was a calling card because you saw it. But what about the name?'

I shook my head.

'Well, as expected it was Terry Lynch — and I'm being nice and telling you only because I reckon you deserve it after what you've been through.'

'But the warning still stands?'

'Keep me informed? Absolutely — only more so.' He hesitated, eyes narrowing slightly as he chose his words like a man tiptoeing through a minefield. 'Although I can't do anything about the girl, that doesn't mean I don't have an opinion. If she has been abducted — and, off the record, I think it's possible, even likely — then that's all the more reason for you to stay well clear.'

Not taking his steady gaze off me, he jingled the ice in his glass.

'All the more reason, also,' he added, 'to pass on to the police any information that comes your way. Even,' he said, 'any wild ideas you consider and discard. I want anything and everything.'

'Yes, sir.'

He frowned, not liking the flippancy. 'Right, so what have you got.'

I donned a puzzled look. 'I'm not sure what you mean.'

'Come on, Penny. You've been workin' this for a week. Think. Think back, think forward — think today. Today Ray Lynch died. Before that you've been *talkin'* to Annabel Lee — yeah, we know you went to see her on Wednesday and she came to yours the next day — and she just happens to be Ray Lynch's niece. Now she's missing, with the possibility of foul play. So what's she said to you? Other than the relationship, what links those two?'

Feigning puzzlement, I looked at Josh. 'Has she said anything to you?'

He shook his head, lips pursed. 'I think I was in my office when she called to see you, wasn't I?'

I shrugged helplessly, and pulled a rueful face at Dancer.

'There you are then. If she's said nothing to Josh . . . '

'As far as I'm aware,' Gareth Owen said, 'the Lynch males prefer more earthy company.' He smiled brightly. 'Annabel's too . . . airy-fairy.'

'Yeah,' Dancer said under his breath, 'and I'm a monkey's uncle.'

He uncoiled from his seat, jabbed a finger at me and said, 'Keep your nose clean', then charged out of the door with DS Hood fast losing ground in his slipstream.

'Clever misdirection,' Gareth said, as the doors swung to behind them. 'No mention of anonymous letters, young girls taking snaps of a man who's just met a violent death. Trouble is, it didn't work — even *with* my contribution.'

'I know. He didn't believe me. The only reason he let it slide is because he doesn't believe I've an investigative bone in my body.'

'All you've got left after today is tired bones,' Josh said.

'Me too,' Gareth said, 'but for very different reasons.'

He didn't explain, and I couldn't be bothered asking. I watched him finish his drink, stand up and stretch.

'Right,' he said, 'everybody ready?'

'For the knacker's yard,' Josh said, following Gareth's lead and helping me with my chair. 'As far as I'm concerned, the night's over.'

I melted at the thought of a nightcap and warm bed, but knew in my heart that it wasn't to be. Even as we waved farewell to Gareth and I walked with Josh to the car, the night air warm and moist, the waters of the fountain like a shower of diamonds dancing on the surface of the floodlit pool, I was wondering how my husband, who was such a clever crime writer, so often managed to end up with his foot in his mouth.

26

The unease that had been tying my stomach in knots ever since Annabel Lee went missing somehow managed to transmit itself to Josh on the drive home. The man who had told Gareth he was ready for the knacker's yard became increasingly restless, sensed that sleep was slipping away, and when we walked into the house he saw me settled on the settee with a hot drink then went into his office to play literary cops and robbers.

I had changed my outfit after returning from the wedding and gone to the Golden Fleece in a loose orange smock worn over jeans and trainers and carrying one of those telescopic umbrellas that nearly shoot out of your hand when you press the button (secret weapon; make mental note). Instead of slipping into something more comfortable while Josh zapped the milk in the microwave I'd stayed as I was, minus trainers. Now, beset by an unreasonable but inescapable conviction that everything would shortly come to a head, I donned a pair of comfortable leather mules and wandered from living-room to kitchen to conservatory and patio to finish up in the fading light looking broodingly into my unfinished pond that, rather like me earlier that day, now had a rain-damp bottom.

Holding my mug in both hands, sipping milky coffee under the first glimmers of weak moonlight, I thought back to my remark about Dancer not following up on my obvious prevarication because, in his opinion, as a private investigator I'd make an excellent photographer.

As I gazed absently and unseeingly over my very own Death Valley (God, what a thought, given the circumstances), my mind wandered — as it does — and I found myself wondering if DI Dancer's disdain was founded on truth. *Was* I a useless PI? Were there, in fact, certain tasks at which men would always outperform women? Would a PI aptitude test — if one existed — have exposed me as too slow? Too soft? Too . . . timid? Would I always, in the end, turn to Josh or another male, closing my eyes and slipping into the background with a deep sigh of relief as . . .

As what?

My heartbeat quickened.

Soul searching done by anyone worth their salt always begins to raise personal hackles, and looking at possible inadequacies in my character had immediately sent my mind spinning off seeking someone even more inadequate. Or likely to delegate because the task they had set themselves was beyond them. Like . . . planting evidence to incriminate someone they hated.

My scalp prickled.

The letter Ryan Sharkey found in Terry Lynch's desk pointed an accusing finger at Ffion Lynch. Justifiably. If Jamie Lynch had knocked her about, she would want him out of the way for good. But what if Ffion couldn't go through with it? Or, what if she was perfectly capable of gathering and planting the evidence to put him away, but was too frightened of Terry Lynch to take the risk? What would she do? Well, exactly what anyone would do: she'd get someone else to do it for her (mental note; fish pond, suggest to Josh). And who would she turn to? Someone she knew would do her bidding. Someone she could bribe with a promise, someone she could twist around her little finger; someone susceptible to what spooks call a honey trap.

Mick Doyle.

I ran sloppily through into the kitchen, kicked the mules into the corner and, still in the dark, went to the sink and rinsed the mug and my suddenly dry mouth with ice-cold water. Stood there absently wiping dribbles from my chin and staring through the window across the moonlit garden.

Ffion Sharkey, as she was then, must have promised herself to Mick Doyle in return for that favour. Then, job done, evidence planted and Jamie Lynch heading for a life behind bars — she had coolly double-crossed Doyle by flying to the Caribbean and getting hitched to Terry Lynch.

If I was right, how would Doyle have reacted?

What I wanted to believe was that, blind with rage, he embarked on a vicious campaign of revenge. He arranged Jamie's death in prison, murdered Ffion, murdered Ray Lynch and was now going after Terry.

That's what I wanted to believe. But what I had to do now was go and confront Mick Doyle, I had to —

Whoa! Just hold on a minute.

I took a deep breath. Placed the mug on the draining board. Walked back through the shadowy conservatory, out onto the patio. Listened to the faint murmur of late evening traffic. Gazed at a moon floating like a pale Chinese lantern in clouds like thin smoke and thought of a room with red walls and dim lights where blue cigarette smoke hung in a diaphanous pall.

Jokers Wild.

That's where I would find him. Right now. And, as the saying goes, there's no time like the present. But — and it was a big, hefty 'but' packing a potentially lethal wallop — waltzing into a night club to ask a man like Mick Doyle if he's a serial killer could be *dangerous*. The idea was a good one, the right one — hell, if I was serious about this PI business it was the *only* one, but was it right for *me*? Was I up to it or, going back to my soul searching and contemplation of possible character inadequacies — did I need a man?

If I did, then there was one in the next room. Josh would —

No!

Josh would go with me, but I wouldn't let him. I wouldn't let him for the same reason, in spades and doubled, that it's wrong to have female soldiers fighting in front-line positions alongside male warriors. In any army. If a woman goes down, the male's concentration goes with her and the battle's lost. And Josh is not only much, much too close to me — hence the doubling — but he is also blissfully inclined to overestimate his abilities; my ex-soldier can run, but can he still fight?

I managed to chuckle in the growing darkness while chewing the inside of my cheek, indecision giving me the jitters.

Phone the police I thought, walking back into the house.

Phone DI Billy Dancer.

Better still, phone Ryan Sharkey.

★　★　★

Sharkey had blithely kept me in the dark when he ferried me across the Wirral to search Terry Lynch's house, so all I told him when he picked up the phone was that I had to go to Jokers Wild and didn't fancy a second mugging. I left a note for Josh under a bottle of Rioja on the coffee table, sneaked out, and less than an hour later I was parking the Ka as close as I could get it to Terry Lynch's night club.

Sharkey's Lexus was already there.

Removing the marked deck of cards from Lynch's house had lifted the threat of exposure and Sharkey had dumped the job at Jokers Wild and was no longer slave labour. I thought Terry Lynch would already have barred him, which would make his entry into the club difficult if not dangerous, but when I climbed those six steps and pushed my way in through the peeling door I found him leaning on the cloakroom counter talking to the man I had come to see. James Coburn meets Cary Grant. And little old me, of course, on

288

mission impossible.

It was Saturday night, the noise of talk and music was a pounding underfoot vibration felt through worn Victorian floorboards, and the glow of flashing lights visible around the edges of the inner door would have had the fire brigade reaching for their axes.

We exchanged greetings. Suspicion was strong. We stood as stiff as three wild dogs, all but circling, eyes meeting only to slide shiftily away. I clung to my bag, my only weapon a camera which last time had been nicked by the young girl watching me from behind the counter, and used against me. It wasn't courage that stopped me bolting for the street door, but fear of embarrassment; if I was destined to die, I didn't want it to be of shame.

'Going in?' Doyle said.

'It's you I want to talk to,' I said, 'and in there might not be the best place.'

He exchanged glances with Sharkey, shrugged, and gestured towards the stairs.

'The office is up there. Terry's taken a couple of days off, so let's go.'

He swung away from reception and started up. At Sharkey's nod and pearly smile I followed. He tucked in behind. It wasn't until I was halfway up and in darkness as deep as a coffin that I remembered there had been talk of two murderers and realized that if the killers were in cahoots and these were they, I was playing into their hot little hands.

It was cooler and quieter on the landing, and light from the street was filtering through dirty net curtains. Doyle led the way into an office as dusty as a cave, cleared two chairs by sweeping newspapers and polystyrene fast-food containers onto the floor — a couple of them half full — then sat behind the desk and switched on a banker's light. I gingerly took one of the chairs. Sharkey stood with his back to the wall. Better tactics than mine. But whose side was he on?

Doyle was watching me. He pointed towards a filter coffee machine and raised questioning eyebrows. I shook my head. He shrugged his shoulders and sat back in the swivel chair.

I cleared my throat.

'I have reason to believe,' I said, 'that you sent a letter to Terry Lynch.'

I think Ryan Sharkey quietly passed away; died, standing up. He stopped breathing, and his eyes went glassy. Mick Doyle just looked surprised.

'I work here. Terry an' me, we talk every day. Why the fuck would I write to him?'

'It was anonymous. You told him his wife had Jamie framed. I think you arranged that for her. Afterwards, she double-crossed you by marrying Terry Lynch. Then' — I looked at Sharkey, willing him to live — 'then the muck hit the spinning blades.'

'I bet it did,' Doyle said. 'If Lynch did get a letter like that he'd've murdered her — '

'No, you did that. Because of the double-cross. But first you had Jamie murdered in prison. Then — after murdering Ffion and with two boxes ticked — you went after Ray Lynch because he was family. You murdered him today, in a Chester church-yard. Three boxes ticked. And now you're going after Terry because he married the girl you — '

'Fancied? Is that it? Fancied *donkey's* years ago, yeah, but that was as far as it went and she never even *knew* about it — '

'Others did.'

'Yeah, well, it never happened — an' because of that, a non-event, I'm goin' round wipin' out the Lynchs?'

'Yes. I think so.'

'Who else have you told?'

'Just you. I wanted to confront you, watch your face . . . look into your eyes. If there was guilt there, then I'd go to the police — '

'Jesus H. Christ,' Doyle said. 'I really do not believe this — '

Then Sharkey woke up.

'I once tried to sell insurance,' he said dreamily. 'Cold calling, door to door. In Australia. I remember I was so bad trying to sell to a company director in a flash suit, made such a bloody fool of myself, the supervisor had to drag me out of the office. He was a Canadian, that supervisor, and so embarrassed he was slick with sweat.'

He pulled out a crisp white handkerchief, made a big show of mopping his brow, then pushed himself away from the wall.

'Time to leave the office, Penny. Time to go, while the going's still good.'

'I'm not finished,' I said weakly.

'You're right,' he said, 'you're not, but if you stay here one minute longer young Mick Doyle over there will make damn sure you are.'

27

The headlights latched onto me as I drove down Upper Duke Street, followed me when I turned into the city centre and were still just thirty yards from my rear bumper when I entered the Kingsway tunnel under the Mersey with nervous eyes flicking from road to mirror. But the rain had returned and it was like a wet night in Hong Kong with rainwater on the rear windscreen fragmenting following lights into a million shimmering stars. The vehicle behind me could have been a Mini Cooper or a double-decker bus, but in my fevered imagination it became a green Mondeo driven by a man with an iron spike through his back and I was petrified.

Josh, as crime writer, had frequently spoken to me about crime investigators using a motor vehicle to tail a suspect, and I knew that three operatives were a minimum requirement and other cars would be used as shields to avoid detection. My boy wasn't bothered with any of that. He was a cocky lone operative working a solo tail, and detection wasn't a problem because what he wanted to do was get close and frighten me to death.

I knew it wasn't Ryan Sharkey, because once he'd wrestled me out of Lynch's office he'd stayed behind in Jokers Wild's main room, probably looking for strong drink. If you wanted my opinion I'd have said Mick Doyle was on my tail, but chattering teeth would have made me difficult to understand, and if you'd wanted it confirmed in writing, well, maybe some other time when the hands had steadied.

By the time I reached Heswall I knew exactly what it was like to tow another vehicle ten miles along rain-swept roads at a steady fifty miles an hour. And when I turned into the bungalow's short drive and the following vehicle came in after me, clearly visible at last, I didn't know whether to laugh or cry.

As it happened, when Josh slammed the Range Rover's door and splashed alongside the Ka to help me out into the rain, I was crying. Softly, silently, from deep frustration, with my forehead resting on the steering wheel's rim. And much worse, of course. Because if it hadn't been raining as I stepped out of the Ka onto Josh's supporting arm I, like Ryan Sharkey's mythical Canadian supervisor, would have been slick with the cold sweat of haunting embarrassment.

28

Day Seven — Sunday 24 September

Soft lights, a soft settee, soft words to soothe my soul and hard liquor to bolster a sagging ego. A clock sonorously chiming the midnight hour. Distant rain dancing on a thin glass roof.

'I was listening on the extension when you phoned Sharkey,' Josh said. 'There was no way I could allow you to go alone.'

'You might have warned me. Before or after. Where were you when I came out of the night club?'

'Parked fifty yards back on the other side of the road. I flashed once, but that's how you went: in a flash.'

'Tail between my legs.'

'Why?'

So I told him. And, like Doyle, he couldn't believe it.

'Not the theory,' he said, 'which is as good as any and better than most, but that you'd actually walk in there with your accusations.'

'Boldly into the lion's den, and I emerged unscathed.'

'But cut down to size.'

'Yes, all right, rub it in,' I said, wrinkling my nose at him, 'but I still think I'm right.'

'So do I. Sort of.'

'You do?' I watched his thoughtful nod and said, 'Now *that* deserves a drink.'

'But not too strong,' Josh said, 'in case there's more driving to do.'

I thought about that while at the cabinet splashing Canada Dry into crystal glasses lightly dampened with Scotch, and felt a surge of excitement strong enough to banish shame. Tears were forgotten, a smile wouldn't stop twitching, and when I handed Josh his drink I planted a kiss on his forehead for, well, for being there.

'Go on,' I said, sitting down. 'Save the bit about driving until later, but tell me again why I'm so clever.'

'Because, of the known suspects, Doyle was the one double-crossed by Ffion.'

'Exactly. That's the way I saw it when doing some hard thinking out by our dust bowl earlier this evening. Doyle planted the evidence for Ffion, she gave him two fingers and flew off to marry Terry Lynch. So Doyle got rid of young Jamie to get back at Terry who'd taken his girl, murdered Ffion for dumping her, Ray was family so he had to go and, according to the latest Visa, Terry's next.'

'So far so good — but what about Humphreys, Tombs and Farrell?'

'I don't know about Humphreys and Farrell but, as police surgeon, Tombs was instrumental in putting Jamie Lynch inside — '

'Which is what Ffion *wanted*, and what Doyle helped her to do. So if Doyle's the killer — why would he kill Tombs?'

I sipped my dry ginger, sucked my lips in contemplation, then shook my head.

'The glint in your eye tells me you've got a brilliant suggestion. Come on, out with it.'

'Suppose you're — we're — wrong?'

'As opposed to right — which we were ten seconds ago?'

'Mm. I was thinking earlier about *Dying to Know You*. Just the title, not the book, and how you've always been intrigued by possible meanings.'

'So I'm still right, but without realizing it?'

'Right, but wrong. As in wrong man for the murders. Yes, Doyle looks good for this in every way — but what if he's innocent in one way, but as guilty as hell in another? And if — clutching at straws — we wanted to use the book title to explain the real killer's motive, it might be interpreted as, 'people are dying because I want to know you — want to know or *find* you — and they'll keep dying until I do'.'

'Bit complicated. Whose looking, and for whom?'

'If Doyle fancied Ffion years ago and was well over it, as he told you, there was no way Ffion could tempt him into planting evidence. So I think we've got that wrong; I don't think she even tried. Look, suppose all Doyle's feelings came roaring back when Ffion married Terry Lynch. He dreams up this story of planted evidence, composes a letter and sends it to Lynch *knowing exactly what will happen.*'

'Hang on. You mean it was all made up? No evidence was ever planted?'

'Right. Which is what I mean by innocent in one way, but guilty as hell. The letter arrives, Lynch reads it, goes berserk and murders his wife. And if, as seems likely, he knew damn well Ffion couldn't have framed Jamie on her own, wouldn't he then go looking for the man who helped her?'

'But nobody *did* help her. You just said it was all made up.'

'Terry Lynch didn't know that.'

My head was whirling.

'So if there was a helper — even if there really *wasn't* a helper — why all the other murders?'

'Because Lynch was hunting. Pouncing on suspects. Threatening them, torturing them

298

— then murdering them when he realized they were innocent and wouldn't, or couldn't, give him the identity of the man he was hunting.'

'Christ,' I said softly. 'If you're right, those poor men couldn't give him the name of the man who planted the evidence, because that man doesn't exist.'

'Exactly,' Josh said.

He knocked back his stiff drink, put the glass on the table and sat back, fingers steepled at his chin as he nodded slowly in thought. I clinked my empty glass against his on the table and stood up, walked restlessly to the window.

It was a good theory, yet I still liked the idea of planted evidence, someone helping Ffion to do it, the letter sent to Lynch truthful but intended to hurt, not drive a man to murder. The trouble was, if I was wrong about Doyle, there was only one clear favourite for the man who had helped Ffion with incriminating evidence — and to enlist his help she wouldn't have needed high heels, perfume and fluttering eyelashes.

'Ryan Sharkey,' Josh said, reading my face as I turned away from the rain-spattered glass. 'She was his sister. He'd do anything to help her. And if he did — and now we're back again with the letter genuine, and telling the truth — then he's the man Lynch is looking for. Which means you were right when you said that crude card left on Farrell's body pointed to Sharkey, not Gareth.'

'Yes, but we're getting bogged down again,' I said. 'Suddenly Terry Lynch is the man, but if he is, and he murdered Ffion and the others, how do we explain Ray's death? Why him, when the card was pointing to Sharkey?'

'Two killers out there? Didn't you discuss that possibility — with Sharkey, of all people?'

'Yes, I did. But that was before Ray's death and Annabel's . . . disappearance.' I hesitated, shaking my head in disbelief. 'You know, I can't believe I haven't tried to phone her. It's been, what, twelve hours now, there could be two killers out there — '

'You've been busy,' Josh said, cutting me short. 'I tried her mobile, several times. It's switched off.'

I took a deep breath. 'Silly me, where *would* I be without you?'

'Works both ways. When one falters, the other steps in. Like now. If Annabel Lee has been kidnapped, and there is a link to Ray's murder — then you already know where to start looking for clues, for something to go on.'

'In a photograph taken by Annabel and

sold to Ray Lynch,' I said. 'Surely the only possible link. And don't tell me I just came up with that, because I didn't. You were hinting at it at least half an hour ago when you spoke of more driving.'

'Doesn't matter who thought of it, now's the time to take a look at that picture. Get your burglar togs on, Penny Lane, we're going housebreaking.'

29

Annabel Lee's tiny walled garden was reached by a rutted grassy right-of-way that ran behind the small terrace of white cottages. Josh parked the Range Rover in the narrow side road that ran uphill into the trees, tucked it hard up against one of the white stone walls and slid across to the passenger side to tumble out after me. The rain was steady, painting a halo around the street lights, keeping the citizens of Parkgate snug indoors. In bed, too, most of them, because we were on the prowl at a good hour after midnight.

'How high's this wall of hers?'

'Three feet. No problem for us athletes. Anyway, there's a gate.'

'Hope she oils the hinges.'

Soft whispers. Talking for company and comfort. Scared of the dark, and of stupidity. Rain dripping down my neck. Wondering what the hell I'd got us into.

I was ahead of him, splashing down the centre of the right-of-way to avoid the trailing branches of rowan and willows, counting the back gates. Annabel's was the third house of five — but even so I lost count. Nerves like an over-wound clock. I stopped, confused. Josh bumped into me and trod on my heel. Hissed an apology as I bit my lip.

'I think this is it.'

'Think?' The lonely street light was glinting on his wet hair. 'I don't want to break into the local bobby's house.'

'There's no such thing anymore. Local or otherwise.'

He chuckled, eased me out of the way and tried the gate. The iron latch clicked. Six short strides took him across wet crazy paving to the back door. As he touched the brass knob he grunted in surprise.

'It's open.' He was bent over, looking closer as the door's hinges creaked to his touch. 'A glass panel's been smashed.'

He straightened, looked down at his feet and kicked away a heavy stone, clogged with wet soil.

As it rolled into reeds on the edge of a tiny pond filled with water on which pink lilies floated I thought wildly of the fingerprints being destroyed. My heart was hammering. I could feel cruel eyes boring into me from every shadow. But what had I expected? When Josh is writing his crime novels he has a notice over his desk reminding him always to consider what the bad guys are doing. Well, now we knew: they were beating us to the punch. Still by the gate, I looked up at the bedroom window. There was no light — no sound, no movement. I shook my head, walked quickly up the path.

'In.'

'What?'

'Go *in*.'

I pushed him in the back and he stumbled forward and bumped the door with his knee. It swung open, banged against the side of a cupboard. A fragment of glass fell with a tinkle. More glass crunched as Josh stepped onto a quarry-tiled floor.

I followed him into gloom and stale cooking smells, caught another spicy scent and saw woody geraniums wilting in pots on the window sill.

'Spare bedroom, that's where she works,' I said softly, as Josh stopped by the pine table where a familiar cafetière stood under the colourful knitted tea cosy. I blinked, felt a lump in my throat and realized the perfume Annabel used was there in the room like a fading memory . . .

'There's no one here,' I said. 'We can stop creeping.'

'And whispering,' Josh said in his normal voice. 'Come on, let's look at this computer.'

I thumped ahead of him up narrow

carpeted stairs, our waterproofs rustling wetly. The landing was just a square with a door on either side. The bathroom, I knew, would be downstairs, and guessing Annabel would sleep at the front of the house I turned right through the open door and found myself in a back office where the ceiling sloped towards a small window. Open curtains were letting in weak lamplight from the nearby side street. I crossed the room, drew them closed. Behind me Josh clicked a switch, and a desk lamp shone brightly on the total destruction of our hopes.

'Oh, Christ, no!'

The man who had broken a glass panel in the back door to gain entry had obviously had two rocks and found a screwdriver — or come prepared. He'd left the 17″ flat panel monitor intact on the desk, but removed the metal outer case from the computer tower standing on the floor and smashed the hard drive and all the memory.

Josh was picking through the ruins. He looked at me, eyebrows raised.

'Only hope is a print, isn't it? Did she show you one?'

I shook my head. 'No, but she's got a fair old gallery down there. Wait here, I'll have a quick look.'

I ran downstairs, used my tiny torch

instead of risking the living-room's main light and quickly scanned the prints displayed on the walls. Looking for . . . what? What had Ray Lynch wanted? Something abstract? A straightforward portrait? I'd noticed several of those on my previous visit, now I had to grit my teeth and recall the dead white face I had gazed at in horror behind the Chester churchyard. A waste of time, because all it did was make me feel sick. Ray wasn't there.

Back upstairs, breathless and queasy, I was struck by an idea. When I looked for Josh, he was not in the office. I crossed the tiny landing, found him tall and dark in the perfumed bedroom, the beam of his torch as narrow as a laser.

'Annabel would have had the Epson P-5000 with her for the wedding, but she told me she also backs up onto those flash memory stick things we use,' I said. 'They're small capacity, and small in size, so she probably uses them to hold recent work and I know she'll always carry one with her. If we can find the other one — '

'It was there, in the bedside table,' Josh said, and turned the beam on his right hand. He was holding a black object, three inches by half an inch, with a blue logo in the shape of an arrow.

'*Disgo* flash memory,' I said. 'One mega-byte. You, Josh, are my favourite, resident genius.' I let him come to me, stood on tiptoe to give him a warm, breathy kiss and said, 'Right, let's get out of here, fast, and see what's on that thing.'

★ ★ ★

The morning was bright, the sunshine hazy, the grass on fairways and greens glistening with dew. The man caught by Annabel's camera had just driven from the tee and was arched at the top of his swing, club held high, metal shaft gleaming, his head fixed as his eyes followed an unseen ball. In the background, five men were on the previous green. One was putting, the other four waiting.

'Something's wrong,' Josh said.

I was sitting in front of my laptop, frowning.

I said, 'I know. If three men are playing, you know two have invited a lone golfer to join them. Four's straightforward: a foursome or four ball. But five . . . ?'

I listened to him breathing; heard his tiny grunt of satisfaction.

'Ah ha, now who's the photography guru? Look closer, Pen. Two of them aren't on that green, are they?'

'Damn and double damn,' I said. 'Annabel was using a long lens. Those two men in the middle are much further away — probably as far as fifty yards, but the foreshortening effect of the long lens has brought them closer. I *thought* they looked smaller.'

'They're not on the golf course, either,' Josh said, 'they're on the beach.'

Quickly, I zoomed in. The memory stick was plugged into my laptop's USB 2 port and I was working straight from that using Picasa2 software and viewing at about 45%. When I zoomed to 100% I could clearly see the strands of wire in the fence marking the edge of the course, the two men frozen as they walked along the sand on the other side of it — on the taller of those two men the white track suit, wrap-around shades and bleached denim baseball cap I had last seen in the Hoylake Police Station car-park and The Thirsty Goose café.

'That's Terry Lynch,' I said, my voice strained. 'The other man's Ronnie Humphreys. I remember seeing two men ahead of me that day, on the beach. Then suddenly there was just the one. And then . . . '

My face felt tight. I clicked back to Picasa's library view which showed thumbnails of the pictures in each dated folder. The date on the folder containing Ray's photograph was right.

I looked at Josh, my heart thumping. Then I right clicked on the thumbnail, left clicked on properties. On the screen a panel popped up.

```
DSC_0019.JPG
Camera Make: Nikon Corporation
Camera Model: Nikon D50
Camera Date: 2006:09:18 09.30.25
Resolution: 3008 × 2000
Focal Length: 200.0 mm
```

'Funny old date,' Josh said.

'Backwards, that's all, then the time. The beauty of digital. And I was right about the lens. That 200 mm jumps to 300 mm with the Nikon sensor.' I smiled absently, then realized what I was looking at; what I'd know, in my heart, I *must* be looking at. 'That was last Monday, Josh, 18 September. At 9.30 and 25 seconds, to be absolutely precise. Not that I need to be. I was in The Thirsty Goose. Joanna had just gone to work.' I swallowed. 'These have to be the two men I saw walking along the beach far ahead of me. Then there was just the one. A few minutes later, I stumbled on Ronnie Humphreys' body. It was still warm.'

Josh drew a deep breath.

He said, 'This photograph puts Lynch right there, at the scene of the crime. This information's more than useful, it's crucial. Phone Dancer.'

And then my mobile trilled, a Vivaldi ring-tone loop gaily inviting me to a night of horror.

★ ★ ★

'Get hold of Ryan Sharkey.'

No greeting. Just the blunt order, delivered in a broad Liverpool accent.

'Who is this?'

'Shut up. Just get hold of Sharkey, soon's I put the phone down. Got it? Bring him to a boathouse called the Slippery Slope — '

'*Gallagher*? Is that *you*?'

'I *said*, don't *talk*. The Slippery Slope, right? — you know where that is?'

'Of course I do, you told me it was on the Dee, in Chester — '

'Are you sure that was really me, darlin'?'

I grabbed Josh's hand and squeezed as the caller's harsh chuckle made my heart lurch. Tears shimmered. The screen in front of me blurred and hysteria bubbled. Ray Lynch and the five golfers, I thought, I've been looking at stills of the new boy band and now I'm going boating in the rain . . .

'So that's where you bring Sharkey, OK? Drive down Souters Lane. Get out of the car and walk upstream. Half a mile. There'll be a light — '

'Is Annabel Lee there? She *did* reach your house, didn't she? You *bastard*, you — '

'An' another thing. No police, don't even *think* about it. Right? Just you and Sharkey, holdin' hands, a stroll in the moonlight.'

'It's pouring with bloody *rain*,' I said, almost spitting the words. 'And why d'you need me? Why the hell should I — ?'

'Should I tell her, then?'

'What?'

'Annabel. She's here now. In the dark. Cold. By the water. Should I tell her you're not bothered? Don't care what happens to her?'

'No,' I said quickly. 'Please. Tell her it's OK, I'll be there, I'll — '

The phone clicked in my ear.

I closed my eyes, heart thumping, hands like ice.

Josh was still holding my hand. His other hand came up, warm and hard, and squeezed my shoulder.

'I heard most of that. So *now* we call the police — '

'Wait.'

He sighed and drifted away, and I knew

311

he'd return with something tawny and strong in crystal glasses. I leaned forward, elbows on the desk, head in my hands, fingers like claws in my hair — mind in turmoil. We'd broken into a cottage and nailed a killer, and one phone call had sent certainty whirling into chaos. But I was gazing at a photograph incriminating Terry Lynch, so why was rival gang boss Ernie Gallagher holding Annabel Lee in a riverside prison? Was it because Annabel carried flash memory in her handbag, and had been caught? Were we witnessing opportunism, one gang boss seizing the chance to blackmail another when a wedding photographer turned up at his house and a red hot digital file fell into his hands?

But if that were true, surely I would be taking Terry Lynch to the boathouse, not Ryan Sharkey.

'Unless,' I said, 'Ryan Sharkey's involved with the other side and Gallagher's calling for his lieutenant.'

A cold glass touched the back of my hand, and I started.

'If he was,' Josh said, 'there'd be no need for you.'

'There's no need anyway. Why the hell *is* he asking me to bring Sharkey? His mobile's working, why doesn't *he* call Sharkey?'

'Doesn't matter anyway, because what you're going to do is ignore the request and inform the police that Annabel Lee is being held against her will in a boathouse on the River Dee — '

'Nope, can't do it. That young girl's in danger because she came to work for me.'

'No, she's in danger because before she met you she took a photograph of Ray Lynch that incriminates his brother.'

'Yes, all right, but now I *have* taken her on I feel responsible. That means I have got a moral obligation to do something.'

'Then do something: call the police.'

'No. Gallagher warned me.'

'Maybe. But what you're about to do is the equivalent of sticking your finger in the fire at someone's say so. And if you're going to do that then *I* have a moral obligation — '

'What? To go with me to the boathouse? No. You'll do something — '

'Stupid?'

'Heroic.'

'And this is not? This daring deed my lovable old softie is seriously contemplating, this is *not* heroic?'

I giggled into my glass, the sound so weird it terrified me. 'You know that old saying, a man's got to do what a man's got to do . . . you know that one?'

'It's nonsense.'

'*Sexist* nonsense. This is something I've got to do, and I'm a woman.'

I'd swivelled the chair away from the desk. Josh was sitting on the shredder, elbows on knees, whisky glass held in the tips of his fingers. His lips were pursed.

'You know, I don't think it is Gallagher in that boathouse,' he said. 'I think that call came from Terry Lynch.'

'I thought about that. They all sound the same, these scousers. But Lynch is the obvious one, because the photograph is his concern. Yet it's still academic, isn't it? Because I've still got to go, no matter who's doing the calling — and I *still* don't know why I'm needed.'

'If it is Lynch, that's obvious: you walked into his life and things have gone pear shaped. He's going to make you pay.'

'Then why Sharkey?'

'Well, he's pretty sure Sharkey broke into his house, because that deck of marked cards was taken. But I don't think that's the reason. Sharkey must be the man he's been hunting. Sharkey sent that letter, murdered Ffion, murdered Ray Lynch.'

'And arranged Jamie's death. OK, so why Gallagher's boathouse?'

'If the bodies are found in the boathouse,

guess who gets pulled in by the police?'

'Gallagher,' I said, nodding. Then I shot him a glance. 'What bodies?'

'Annabel's, Sharkey's — and yours.'

I shivered. 'What time is it?'

'Time to go — if you're going.'

'And you?'

He shrugged. 'Someone famous once said that, ultimately, every one of us is alone. If that's true, then nobody has the right to control another person; I have no right to stand in your way. But if you do go your way, then I'll go mine — and right now the only course I can see open to me is to be there with you and charge in with guns blazing.'

'I've said no, and I mean it. You're almost sixty. You haven't got a gun to blaze.'

He grinned.

'But if you do happen to be nearby — '

'Happen?'

'Well, who knows where chance will take you on a rainy night?'

'Indeed,' he said.

And as he eased himself off the shredder and took away the empty glasses, I picked up the phone and called the man I was now convinced was a murderer.

30

Ryan Sharkey's silver Lexus was parked with its nose to the river when I coasted down Souters Lane. The gambler was sheltering under a tree, tall, slim and knobbly in track suit and trainers. A woolly hat was pulled down over his dark hair, the track suit hood pulled over the hat creating a brooding, sinister image.

There was no sign of Josh's Range Rover.

I pulled in alongside the Lexus, climbed out and slammed the Ka's door.

Sharkey's teeth gleamed.

'Nice night for it.'

'You choose them well. It was weather just like this when we broke into Lynch's house.'

'This time it's his choice. Any idea why?'

'Pay-back time. He's called you here, so you must be the man he's been hunting. You sent that letter. Murdered his wife and brother.'

'Rubbish.'

He moved out from under the trees and set off walking upstream at a fast pace. I jogged to catch up, then settled alongside him without matching his stride. The rain was a steady drizzle, the river a broad flat ribbon reflecting street lights. Moored boats rocked gently, rope creaking. Our footsteps crunched. The air was dank with rain and river.

We passed several boathouses. Some I knew from previous visits to Chester belonged to rowing clubs whose teams trained regularly. But all of those were in darkness and I was looking for the gleam of light from a smaller building owned by a man whose wealth came from crime and whose premises were being used for the same purpose by a man with blood on his hands.

'There,' Sharkey said.

We stopped walking, slipped into the shadow of more trees. Our breathing was the only whisper of sound. Then my heart started thumping.

The hurricane lamp glowed in a window cut into a black timber wall, the wall not quite reaching the bank of the Dee, a concrete boat slip sticking like a lolling grey tongue from an opening in the building's front elevation with its tip tasting the river. A sleek white motor launch was moored a short way along the river-bank from the tongue of concrete.

'Why did you come?' I said.

His eyes gleamed in the dark. 'I was summoned by a lady with great powers of

317

persuasion. She phoned me, told me a story about a photograph and a young girl. How the photograph as good as names a killer, and how the killer got to know about it — '

'Really?' I laughed in disbelief. 'I don't think so. I think it's because, after the others, after Jamie, Ffion and Ray, Terry Lynch comes next. You announced it, using the credit card you must have stolen from Lynch's office and stuffed in poor Ray Lynch's dead mouth after you'd impaled him on churchyard railings.'

'To believe I'm capable of that,' Sharkey said, 'you'd have to be a fool — and I don't think you are.'

'So why *are* you here?'

'Because of the girl.' He smiled. 'And because it had to come to this. Yes, Terry Lynch believes I am that man. But he's wrong, and I've come to put him right.'

'So we're back to Doyle.' I searched the shadowy planes of his face. 'Yet when I confronted him in Jokers Wild you told a cute little story, made me out to be something you now say I'm not: a fool. Which is right?'

'Made yourself *look* foolish — that was the point I was making, and it's not quite the same thing. Accused, Doyle was bound to deny everything. You were wasting your time then, and we're wasting it now with idle chatter.'

'I know,' I said. 'But I . . . oh God, Sharkey, I don't know what to do because I came here convinced it was you and now it's Doyle again but it's you saying you're innocent and it's all happening too fast and, Christ, I don't know if I can *trust* you.'

'If we're going to be partners,' he said, 'then now's the time to show my mettle.'

He touched a cool finger to my lips and his strong hand grasped my arm just above the elbow. There was a rotting tongue-and-groove door under the lamp-lit window. He moved me towards it across earth made slick by the rain. Against the black wall we stopped to listen. There was nothing to be heard.

'If Lynch sent for us,' Sharkey said, 'why the hell are we acting like timid gatecrashers?'

And with that he grasped the tarnished brass knob and wrenched the door open.

$\star$ $\star$ $\star$

The tin hurricane lamp hanging in the window was the twin of another suspended from a solid cross beam by a long piece of nylon rope. This one had a conical tin reflector that directed the flickering light downwards. Beneath the lamp Annabel Lee sat cross-legged on the dirt floor, dark shadows cast by the flame moving like shifting stains under her eyebrows, her chin. A strip of dirty sacking was tied across her mouth as a gag. Her hands were red and swollen, lashed in front of her with thin twine that was cutting into her wrists.

At the sound of the door crashing open her head snapped round. She caught sight of us. Her blue eyes flared wide — flicked frantically left, left, and left again like an uncontrollable tick as she drummed her heels and behind the gag grunted and whimpered a desperate warning.

I followed Annabel's tormented gaze.

It was a typically littered boathouse, damp and dark with high, cobwebbed rafters and, scattered about the floor, dirty wooden boxes and crates I guessed had contained life jackets and outboard motors and other bits of boating paraphernalia. They were up against the timber walls, and along the edges of the central concrete slip that sloped down to the unseen river.

Terry Lynch was sitting on an oil drum alongside a stack of red, yellow and blue kayaks. Another closed door was behind him leading, I supposed, to a storeroom or office. On the other side of that, a stack of fibreglass canoes and an open-topped crate out of which jutted the shafts of wooden paddles worn smooth by use.

Lynch was as I knew him: shell suit, trainers, baseball cap — no shades this time, and there was another difference. In his right hand he casually held a blued-metal pistol. It rested flat on his right knee. It was pointing at Annabel Lee.

'Just in case either of you gets big ideas,' he said softly. Then he looked at Sharkey and grinned. 'You must've had a death wish from the start. Comin' here proves it.'

'Don't talk crap,' Sharkey said. He moved down the slip until the boathouse floor was level with the back of his knees, and sat down facing Lynch. 'Whoever gave you my name when you held a knife to his throat was lying to save his skin. I'm not your man.'

'No? It was Farrell who talked. It didn't save his skin, and talk won't save yours.'

His eyes flicked to me. The hand holding the gun lifted. I'd moved while they were talking. Now I was down on one knee alongside the bound and struggling young woman, my body between her and the pistol. My skin was prickling, one eye on Lynch, the other on what I was doing. God, what did it feel like, I wondered, a bullet in the back? I grasped Annabel's shoulder, pulled her against me, felt her go limp as she quietly sobbed. Then, as Lynch grinned, lifted the pistol and mimed placing a bullet in my head, I reached up and with straining fingers picked at the knot until it came undone and gently removed the filthy sacking from her mouth.

'Shit, shit, shit,' she whispered through dry, cracked lips, and pressed her face hard into my shoulder. I stroked her damp, matted hair. But in attending to Annabel Lee I'd missed something. Sharkey had asked a question. Lynch was staring at him in amazement.

'She was your *sister*. *That's* why you helped her.'

'Not enough. I'm a gambler, not a villain.'

'Bollocks, deep down we're all villains.'

'All right. So how did I help Ffion? What exactly did I do?'

'Planted evidence. Got Jamie sent down. Arranged his murder.'

'Why?'

'Jesus, you know why. He used his fists on your sister, again an' again, beat her black an' blue.'

'Fine. You're making sense. So far. But now we come to the letter.'

Lynch sneered.

'Yes, brazen it out,' Sharkey said, 'that's all you *can* do — because now you're lost. I don't know about you, but I can't think of one sane reason why I'd send you an anonymous letter betraying my own sister.'

There was a sudden silence. I spoke up, filling it with logic and an explanation that defied contradiction.

'Mick Doyle had a reason,' I said. 'He'd always fancied Ffion, and she offered him a deal: help me and I'll dump Terry, go with you.'

'No,' Lynch said. 'She wouldn't *do* that — '

'She never intended to see it through. But the point is she told Doyle she would, and so he did what she wanted — and then she double-crossed him and married you. When Doyle realized what she'd done, he was consumed by the desire for revenge. He arranged Jamie's murder. Then he worked on the idea of an anonymous letter, perhaps got someone to write it for him, someone with education who could put all the big words together and make sense — and when he sent it he was probably hoping you'd kick Ffion out into the street. You didn't, so he murdered her, then went after Ray. And you're next.'

Lynch was wavering. Sweat glistened on his face. His eyes were jumping, never settling. On the pistol's butt his knuckles were white and shiny and, as I comforted Annabel Lee and watched him fall apart, I could sense his mind racing: he was dithering helplessly, caught between truth and lies — and the gut feeling, the street instinct that helped him survive, was telling him he'd cocked up. He was realizing that Sharkey *must* be telling the truth: the tall gambler would never have betrayed his own sister. That Farrell, under extreme duress in a filthy back entry, would have lied for his life; with a sharp blade at his throat he would have told Lynch anything, given him the first name that popped into his head — something Lynch must surely have expected. And he would be casting his mind back over the years, remembering the hot glances exchanged by Mick Doyle and the young Ffion Sharkey that only a blind man could have missed — then reaching an appalling conclusion. He had used a knife to murder Humphreys, Tombs and Farrell, and when the last man died he believed he had the name he sought but the facts didn't add up: he'd arranged a showdown with the wrong man and, as if that wasn't enough, he found himself in a situation comparable to that of a hunter who's grabbed a huge alligator by its lashing tail and doesn't know how to let go.

'Maybe,' he said, but his eyes were on Annabel Lee, not Sharkey. 'Maybe you're right, an' I'm wrong,' he said, 'but if you are, that's easy fixed. Doyle's no problem.'

'What about your brother?' I said. 'Ray's dead; you don't seem concerned.'

'He was a big boy; he didn't need me to hold his hand.'

'Did you kill him?'

'Don't be bloody ridiculous — '

'But you saw the picture.'

He knew it was a statement, not a question; knew I too had seen it, and if I'd seen it . . .

'So now we get down to it,' Lynch said, his voice suddenly weary. 'Down to my favourite niece who went out happy snappin' and ended up with digital files and a piece of paper that could destroy her uncle. Only, yeah, Ray stuck that golfin' photo on the wall an', yeah, I saw it in time — so Annabel's here an' her computer's trashed and all the files destroyed — '

'No,' I cut in. 'Not all of them.'

Lynch shrugged. 'That's why I'm playin' safe. That's why I sent for you, that's why you're here — '

'My husband knows about the photograph. He's seen it. As far as I know he's taken a copy to Dancer — '

'Yeah,' Lynch cut in, grinning crazily, 'an' that's the cavalry I hear comin' over the hill — '

He broke off as the door behind him burst open with a splintering crash. A man exploded through. He stopped the door with his foot as it hit the wall and bounced back, held it with one hand then slammed it shut. His eyes swept left and right, taking in the situation. Lynch turned like a cat, swinging the pistol. The newcomer crouched, twisted, grabbed a paddle from an open-topped crate. Legs braced, he swung it like a flail in a high overhead arc. The edge of the flat blade cracked down on Lynch's wrist. Bones snapped. The pistol clattered to the ground. Lynch dropped to his knees, clutching his arm and groaning.

'Oops,' the man by the door said, tossing the paddle aside and stepping forward to scoop up the pistol. 'I think Terry's hurt his arm.'

When he straightened with the gun in his hand and moved into the pool of lamplight I saw him clearly for the first time, and my body went weak with relief.

It was Gareth Owen.

31

Terry Lynch was a limp figure, down on his knees, white-faced and drenched in sweat. Gareth Owen was prowling, gun dangling in his hand, his dark eyes watchful.

Sharkey took in the situation with one swift, sweeping glance, saw that the danger was over and stood up. He walked up the slip and came straight to Annabel Lee and, as I stepped aside, took a Swiss Army knife from his pocket and cut the cord binding her wrists. Then he helped her to her feet. She sagged against him, held in the crook of his strong right arm. He looked at me over her blonde head, and winked.

Tension was draining away from me so fast it was like an electric buzz and I couldn't stop grinning.

'I don't know how you did it,' I said to the plump little solicitor, 'but it was timed and executed to perfection. Maybe we should swap roles.'

'Yeah, I can just see you in one of those legal wigs,' he said, rolling his eyes. 'Actually, it was easy. Josh was on his way, but he had a front wheel puncture that pulled him onto ground so soft he couldn't use a jack to change the wheel. He knew I lived just outside Chester, so he phoned me. Probably thought I could get here faster than the cops.'

'And you did. But now it's over, so if you can get a signal on your mobile you'd better phone them.'

'Er . . . no.'

'Well, one of us'll have to — '

'No.'

That stopped me dead. 'Pardon?'

'That's not why I came.'

Suddenly the silence was like a dead weight pressing on my head. My temples were throbbing. Annabel Lee seemed to have stopped breathing. Sharkey didn't exist.

'Then why did you come?'

'I lost him.' He jerked a thumb at Lynch. 'For a full day. Then Josh phoned, caught me in bed lapping up the old Laphroaig. And bingo, back on track.'

'*You* lost Lynch?'

'Yeah.' He tapped his chest proudly with the pistol's muzzle. 'Me. Not Sharkey. Not Doyle. Because I knew Ffion before the lot of them, knew her, wanted her — *had* her, for a while, way back when to her Liverpool was just a name on the map.'

'Jesus Christ,' I whispered. 'You told me you came from the same village and I wasn't even listening — '

'Came from, in time caught up with her, and suddenly I had a chance again because she wanted something done and from her I was always open to offers.'

'You planted the evidence?'

'She asked me to. Made the warm promises. And when Jamie was convicted I told her I'd done it when actually there'd never been any need to do that. He was guilty, the eye-witnesses had come forward and all I had to do was tell her what she wanted to hear then sit back and claim my reward.'

'But instead she married Lynch.'

'Double-crossed me.'

'And you murdered her.'

'No.' His eyes were cold. 'I sent the letter — '

'Sharkey almost got there,' I said. 'We were in Lynch's house and he read it, said it was too clever for your average scally, the language almost legal in tone . . . '

But Gareth wasn't listening.

'I sent the letter,' he said, 'but it was Lynch who used his key to let himself into his own house. He murdered his treacherous wife. Then he came looking for the man who'd helped her plant the evidence, but because no evidence had been planted, none of the men he questioned knew what he was talking about.'

The man down on his knees clutching a shattered arm straightened slowly, then gasped in agony and rocked back to sit on his heels.

'I murdered her, I murdered them, and I'd've murdered *you*,' he said, 'for what you did — '

'You were killing your own men in vain attempts to find me,' Gareth said, 'when all I'd done was send you a letter telling the truth about your wife. I would have left it at that if you'd kicked her out — Christ, if you'd done that you'd've been happy and she'd have come to me, begging forgiveness. Instead, you stabbed her to death. So I went after you, all three stupid Lynch brothers, taking you one by one. First Jamie — easy to arrange, for a regular prison visitor like me. Then Ray.' He grinned and waggled the gun. 'And now you.'

Out of the corner of my eye I caught movement as Sharkey whispered to Annabel Lee then stepped away from her. He moved slowly, inching his way around the top of the launching slip until he was on the opposite side to the two men. Then he began to work his way along its edge.

On the other side of the slip, Owen's head

was turned away. He hadn't seen Sharkey.

Lynch had regained his feet. He was backing away from Owen, nursing his broken arm. Each slow step was agony. He was working his way along the crates, dragging himself towards the front of the boathouse. His narrowed eyes were fixed on the gun.

The boathouse floor was level, but the concrete slip sloped steeply down to reach the river through a large rectangular opening in the lower half of the front wall. With each backward step taken by Lynch the drop from floor to slip became greater — and Owen was following him.

I tore my gaze from Owen, turned to Sharkey and mimed 'Do something, *do* something,' and saw him nod without looking at me, and frantically flap his hand.

Keep away. Stay back.

'Gareth,' he said quietly, 'put down the gun.'

Gareth looked at him, and smiled. Then he turned back to Lynch and lifted the pistol.

'No!' Sharkey cried. 'Don't be a bloody fool, don't — '

And suddenly everything was happening in slow motion. Owen lifted the pistol, clamped it in his two hands, extended his arms. Lynch backed away, cowering; half turned and tucked his chin into his shoulder like a boxer

331

trying to ward off the bullet.

Then Sharkey sprang. One hand dropped to a low crate. He vaulted down onto the wet slip. I saw him land on his feet, his head snap towards the river — and then he froze.

Gareth Owen shot Terry Lynch.

There was a brilliant flash, followed by a faint crack. The bullet hit Lynch in the forehead. The smack of lead on bone was louder than the pistol's puny report. Lynch looked shocked. His eyes widened. Then he crumpled and went down in a heap.

As he hit the ground, the door between kayaks and canoes again burst open with an explosive crash. Josh leaped through, roared, 'Drop it, Lynch, drop that gun, don't — ' then saw Lynch on the ground and Gareth Owen holding the gun and broke off with the look on his face of a teacher who's screamed for the class to shut up just as silence falls.

Owen spun towards him. The pistol moved in a glittering arc.

I screamed, 'Josh, get back, he'll kill you.'

Owen was still turning, off balance. His foot skidded on the edge of damp, crumbling concrete. He jerked, cried out. The piercing scream faded and died in the dark, damp timber. Twisting, face contorted, Owen went backwards over the edge of the slip. He fell, arms flapping, into the arms of the police.

Slick, black and ugly, they came charging up from the river, yelling as only the police can.

Josh was standing with his mouth open. Sharkey was back against the wall of the slip, watching four armed police officers in riot gear kneel on Owen as a fifth clicked on the handcuffs.

I looked across at Annabel.

'Got your camera?'

She shook her head.

'No,' I said. 'Neither have I.'

Epilogue

'You saw them, didn't you? The police. That was why you stopped.'

'They were there, like shiny seals, waiting on the edge of the river,' Sharkey said. 'They waved me back and I thought, all those weapons, Christ, they've got *serious* fire-power, this is where discretion takes over from valour.'

We were in the bungalow, perched on stools in the kitchen, sipping sweet black coffee and listening to the rain dancing on the conservatory. The lights were out. The only illumination was leaking in through the streaming windows, a mixture of diffused amber street lighting and a distant grey dawn. Cosy. Sleep inducing. I yawned against my mug, almost spilled coffee down my front.

Josh's Range Rover had been hauled out of the ditch by the AA and, wheel swiftly changed, he'd broken the speed limit on the way to the boathouse. He'd phoned the police on the way, again breaking the law, but his wonderful diversion when he burst in through the door had been done without their knowledge, an instinctive reaction from a man used to extracting fictional heroes from impossible situations.

It worked for them, and it worked for us.

When the fur had stopped flying we were questioned by the police then given a lift in their high speed launch back to the cars. We drove away from the river in a sedate civilian convoy, Annabel with me in my red Ka, the Ka sandwiched between Lexus and Range Rover. We took Annabel to Chester A & E: she was examined, had her wrists bandaged, was pronounced fit, and was now tucked up in our spare bedroom wearing my winter pyjamas. Now we, the three stooges — I giggled, drawing a strange look from Sharkey and almost causing another accident — were . . . well . . . winding down, I suppose. Without too much satisfaction. For me, there was aching sadness, a dull feeling of being let down by a trusted friend. And I wasn't exactly proud of our achievements. A man had died, and the police had done the mopping up.

I yawned again, this time with more care. Josh was wide-eyed, but it was the thousand-yard stare: coffee mug forgotten in his hands, his mind was floating somewhere in a dark boathouse, absorbing and memorizing every tiny detail of his very first crime scene. No, of course not, it was his second: he'd been with

Annabel Lee in the B & B where Sebastian Tombs had died.

I liked the sound of that: *With Annabel Lee in the B & B where Sebastian Tombs had died.* Poetry, sort of. Mental reminder: tell Josh.

'We did well,' Sharkey said, stepping away from his stool.

'Depends on your standards.'

'Right result, though.'

'Reached despite, not because of.'

Josh came back to earth, smiling fondly. 'Ignore her, Sharkey, she's too damn tired to think straight or make sense.'

'Ha bloody ha,' I said, 'listen who's talking. Anyway, I'm willing to admit my limitations: I was invited to a party by a killer, and almost got trampled by the crowd.'

'So that's something else you should admit,' Sharkey said. 'You need a partner.'

'She needed Gareth Owen to feed her crumbs of insider information about current, unsolved crimes,' Josh said. 'With him serving life, she's a PI with nothing to investigate.'

'Unless I stumble over another body,' I said. 'But Gareth won't be sorely missed. Except by Joanna, poor girl, but I don't think they ever got all that close and she's nearly qualified so she'll continue the practice — and I'll have another contact. And there's

336

always Gareth's brother. My very own policeman, soon to retire, and sure to be at my beck and call.'

'That's all right then,' Sharkey said. 'The time will come, and when it does you know I'm just a phone call away.'

'Albert Dock.'

He grinned. 'Penthouse suite, excellent view, Sheridan's coffee layered liqueur . . . '

He spread his hands eloquently; again there came that mischievous wink. We exchanged high fives much to Josh's grey-eyed, twinkling amusement, and Sharkey headed out. By the time the door closed behind him and the Lexus kicked into life, Josh was already opening his — to the office. Too late for typing, I'd have said, but he has one of those micro-cassette recorders and I could hear him talking into it as I trudged leadenly along the hall to the bedroom and threw myself on the billowy duvet. His voice was still with me and I was still smiling as, fully clothed, I drifted towards a dreamless sleep.

Dying to Know You indeed I thought as I wallowed. Forget it, Josh, the story's over and we won.

We do hope that you have enjoyed reading this large print book.

Did you know that all of our titles are available for purchase?

We publish a wide range of high quality large print books including:
Romances, Mysteries, Classics
General Fiction
Non Fiction and Westerns

Special interest titles available in large print are:
The Little Oxford Dictionary
Music Book
Song Book
Hymn Book
Service Book

Also available from us courtesy of Oxford University Press:
Young Readers' Dictionary
(large print edition)
Young Readers' Thesaurus
(large print edition)

For further information or a free brochure, please contact us at:
Ulverscroft Large Print Books Ltd.,
The Green, Bradgate Road, Anstey,
Leicester, LE7 7FU, England.
Tel: (00 44) 0116 236 4325
Fax: (00 44) 0116 234 0205

Other titles published by
The House of Ulverscroft:

DEATHLY SUSPENSE

John Paxton Sheriff

When the police break into Joe Creeney's Liverpool home, his dead wife is hanging by a rope from the banisters, Joe is walking away holding the ladder and there is nobody else in the house. Yet Joe's sister, Caroline Spackman, is convinced her brother is innocent, so amateur PI Jack Scott is called in by solicitor Stephanie Grey. Now Scott, following a trail of violence and lies from a murder for which Creeney had been previously convicted, must also examine links to a woman's death in North Wales . . . and watch as more bloody killings lead him to a shocking denouement.

THE CLUTCHES OF DEATH

John Paxton Sheriff

When photographer Frank Danson took his wife Jenny to the theatre, they had two beautiful baby boys at home. But when they returned the boys had gone — presumably kidnapped. The loss was too great for Jenny to bear and Frank was left alone to grieve for his family. Then, twenty years later, the memories come screaming back. Who is sending him photographs hinting at unimaginable horrors, and taunting notes in blood? As the killings begin, amateur private eye Jack Scott must solve a mystery once buried in the past but now disinterred to make Frank's life a waking nightmare.

A CONFUSION OF MURDERS

John Paxton Sheriff

A possible murder and a man's sinister disappearance fascinate amateur private eye Jack Scott. In North Wales, Gwynfryn Pritchard's wife died face down in a stream. One year earlier, Gerry Gault had killed a girl during his knife-throwing act and disappeared that same night . . . Scott's investigation uncovers a paternity feud and a cryptic note. He is led to a retirement home where a gangster resides and it takes a brush with death, more corpses and a horrifying discovery before Scott can unravel a confusion of murders.

CHEATED HEARTS

Jane McLoughlin

Lucy Drake and Sue Stockland know nothing of each other's existence, yet both are in love with Paul Meyer. However, when Paul is found dead from a heroin overdose in a Soho alley, his connections to gang boss Big Saul Kramer cause Police Inspector Guy Dugdale to suspect murder. Lucy and Sue find out about their lover's double life and both tell Dugdale that the other is Paul's killer — then find themselves romantically drawn to the policeman. But Paul's estranged wife Vita Virgo has a motive for murder . . . Can it all be disentangled before there is further violence . . . ?